HER DIONYSUS

Isabella Presley

 FriesenPress

One Printers Way
Altona, MB R0G 0B0
Canada

www.friesenpress.com

ISBN
978-1-03830-808-5 (Hardcover)
978-1-03830-807-8 (Paperback)
978-1-03830-809-2 (eBook)

1. FICTION, ROMANCE, GOTHIC

Distributed to the trade by The Ingram Book Company

For Izar Beauvoit,
I honor you with love and passion.

1 Corinthians 13:4

Love is patient, love is kind. It does not envy, it does not boast, it is not proud. It does not dishonor others, it is not self-seeking, it is not easily angered, it keeps no records of wrongs. Love does not delight in evil but rejoices in the truth. It always protects, always trusts, always hopes, always perseveres."

New Orleans, 2021

I

I had always known I was a witch from the time I was a little girl but was often suppressed by my overly cautious parents. I wasn't able to figure out the history of my family, though I felt a pull to New Orleans unlike any other place in the world. Which is why I decided to move to New Orleans from New York City. Though I have always loved the flashy lights, the New Yorker attitude, and the whole city experience, I knew I had to leave. My intuition told me it was time to cut ties and move somewhere new. As a child, I always felt like I knew more than I should. I had prophetic dreams that would often come true – when I tried to explain this to friends or family, they would say it was just a dream or that I made it up. My family didn't understand the fact that I had special gifts. Witchcraft wasn't something that was taken seriously in my household and often I was told I was crazy – crazy till I'm correct. Now at the age of 29, I intend on using my gifts and all these changes are due to my intuition and to my best friend Ru (short for Rouge), she has always been there for me in my time of need, and in my time of celebration. She told me that I needed a fresh start in a new city, let go of old habits, old connections that didn't serve me, and move on with my life. I always felt that I could trust my intuition to lead the way, and my best friend who never steered me wrong.

I created my own tarot business and found what better place to end up than New Orleans, it already had a huge occult culture, from witchcraft, to voodoo, ghosts and vampires. It also had rich history with the English, Creole, and French cultures. I loved history as much as I loved witchcraft. It was something I often wanted to immerse myself in, I wanted to connect with where I came from. Something in me told me New Orleans was the place to go.

Now that I had a place to call my own, I could be my most weird and authentic self and it allowed me to work on my witchcraft without worrying what someone else thought. Most importantly, it got me away from toxic people. Which included my dysfunctional family. I was the odd one out, the weird gothic witch girl who didn't fit in anywhere. At least that's how I felt. Until now.

I found myself an apartment in the Old French Quarter, where I was inspired by the architecture and vampire lore. As soon as I saw the ad online, I felt like I could truly be at home there. Within days I was packed up and ready to go and now here I was in front of the old 17th century home that had many apartments configured inside, with a long narrow walk-up to my humble abode. The stone and marble finishings looked like icing on a cake. It reminded me of the Renaissance period and my soul screamed with joy knowing I was following my truth and my own personal history.

My eyes caught the old windows that slid up and down and I knew it would be a perfect place to set up my twinkle lights, the ledge of the window would be used for my crystal collection. I noticed as I moved into the new space that the moonlight came through my window at the perfect angle, a perfect spot to charge my crystals. In witchcraft it is believed that crystals absorb negative energies throughout the lunar cycles and under a full moon it was best to put them out under the moonlight to cleanse and charge them up for the next cycle to be used in spells, meditations or to just simply protect one's space.

I carried my final box up the marble staircase into the apartment and onto my bed. My apartment was already furnished, I just needed my personal items and of course my book collection which definitely had some spell books to go along with it. Walking into the bathroom to wash my hands, I noticed how intricate and old fashioned the pedestal sink and toilet was. The claw tub was my favorite. I always wanted one. *I'm definitely taking a bath in that!*

My green eyes looked back at me in the mirror to see my reflection, my eyes morphing into a deeper green hue the longer I stared. My long auburn hair was a sweaty mess from moving everything in. *Yes, a bath is in order tonight.*

The bedroom had a large Victorian style bed of black iron, and dark red sheets. Though, I also had a deep purple set of sheets. A psychic witch loves a dark purple color because it connects us with our third eye, the psychic eye. I always felt connected to those two colors in particular: red for passion, love, and desire, and purple for psychic ability and calmness.

As I unpacked the petite space and got my clothes into the walk-in closet (which by the way was a bonus) I got myself ready for the bath. I headed to the bathroom with my fresh towels and pajamas. As the hot water began to fill the tub, I put my rose and vanilla body wash along with my toiletries onto the ledge and undressed myself to get into the inviting solitude.

A sigh of relief escaped me. It was so nice to be in my own space, with my own thoughts and to be able to breathe, to *actually* relax, with nobody to tell me what to do, or to fight with. It was me, myself, and I.

After my bath, now in comfortable clothing, I looked around my new bedroom and decided to grab my tarot deck. I might as well check in with Spirit about what was to come for me in this new chapter of my life. What happened next, I *never* would have seen coming . . . ironic for a psychic.

Sitting down on the bed with the cards, breathing deep with my eyes closed, tuning into my intuition I asked my internal question and shuffled the cards. I placed them in the order that I felt was right and looked at the three cards splayed on the bed.

The Sun. The Lovers. The Knight of Cups.

Eyes wide in shock and mixed with happiness I smiled. Something very positive was going to come and it was in the form of a lover. The Sun was a sign of positivity. The Lovers was about soulmates, and The Knight of Cups represented a love offering, someone who would come in very confident, self-assured, and wanting romance. This I *wasn't* expecting.

After about a week of settling in, setting up my internet and finding the nearest cafe, I decided to get my witchcraft and tarot shop up and running. I needed to register in the state of Louisiana, and I figured I'd do it with a good cup of coffee. Luckily the barista job I held in NYC helped me save up to afford the life I was building here. Everyone back home knew I was a coffee addict and I swear it's more coffee than blood in these veins. The rustic and cute cafe had an elegant yet hipster vibe, the leather couch was comfortable to sit on and the cherry wood smelled heavenly, besides the coffee in my cup. The cafe was situated between Canal Street and Basin Street, not far from my apartment.

Logging onto my laptop, I found my old writer's community where I would blog about my day and meet like-minded occult fans. I had used it back in NYC to meet others like me, but when you had overprotective and hovering parents it was harder to meet people. I realized that this would be a good spot to market my business and find others in the area to relate to. My biggest interest besides witchcraft and history was writing. And since I was starting my new life, I wanted to find my soul family; people I felt myself with, people who wouldn't judge me.

As I scrolled through the blog site, I found someone that I didn't expect to see on here – a rock singer. He had an intense presence, a gothic vampire style. He blogged about his travels and on-the-road photography. I could see how magnetic he was, happy to be in his element, but I could tell he also liked to be a lone rider. Literally! This man owned a Harley Davidson. I couldn't help but giggle and smile watching this unknown man. He was more beautiful than anyone I had ever seen in my life.

He had soft blond hair that just touched his shoulders. The way the front curled and framed his face gave him a youthful look. His eyes were as blue as the ocean and grey as a cloudy autumn day. His mouth full, tempting and often adorned with a smirk. His nose was slender and long. He had the smile of an angel, but the demeanor of a devil. Some of his photos were very sensual and seductive. Him in leather pants, crosses, and the odd photo of him with a red velvet coat. I blushed looking at him, his mischievous nature felt like he was daring me to stare just a little longer.

I cleared my throat, blushing furiously, my heart beat wildly. "Who are you?" I asked aloud. Really. Who was he?? Where had he been all my life? I felt that his magnetizing energy was so strong, I *had* to get to know him. With my previous relationship in New York, things were so complicated and messy. We had been friends first turned into lovers, but there was always a back-and-forth energy, I wanted more, and they wanted less. My ex would often lie to me about where they had been, or who they were hanging out with, and I got tired of the lies. This was the other reason I had left New York; it wasn't just family issues that brought me to my decision. As I continued to scroll through this mystery man's bio page, I found out his band's name was The Devil and Desire. He was 39 years of age and was from Paris. PARIS! My heart leapt at this new information.

I always wanted to find someone from Europe, and to travel to Paris but I never did end up making it due to life's circumstances. Was he the key to my new start? Was he the one I was waiting for, the one from my tarot reading last week? It certainly felt like it. A rush of questions invaded my mind. So many of my friends and family didn't believe in soulmates but I always did. The energy I felt from him coming through the page was palpable. Undeniably present and pulling me towards him. I looked up at the ceiling praying out loud to Spirit. "Is this him? Is he it?" I looked back to the screen and clicked on the little Message icon. I took a deep breath, "Here it goes."

> Hi,
>
> I was just scrolling through the blog site to find fellow writers to be friends with. I just moved so I am looking for new friends, especially those with the same interests. I have to say, your blog interested me right away. If you're interested in talking, I'd love to hear from you!
>
> I hope you have a great day,
> Amelie :)

I hit the 'send' button and blew out a huge breath of air. *Did I really just reach out to a rock star???* Yes, I did. I then went to unpack more, I needed to reorganize my apartment, and maybe in that time I'd hear back. I did hope he would reach out.

For a couple of hours I dusted, cleaned, organized dishes and now finally I was in the shower. The hot water felt so good on my skin, warm and inviting. The muscles in my back and neck relaxed, as images of the unknown rock star flooded my mind. I bit my lip thinking of him. He didn't even know me and yet I was thinking of him in the most vulnerable and intimate way. I shook my head of the thoughts before finishing my shower.

Grabbing a fluffy purple towel, I started to dry my skin and eventually wrap my hair in the towel, before changing into my pajama shorts and t-shirt. I then heard my phone notifications go off to alert me that I got a message. I saw that it was my best friend Ru. She wanted to make sure I was safe and getting settled in.

I smiled, messaged her that I was okay and yes indeed settling in. *Do I tell her about the man? No, not yet.* For once in my life, I wanted something for myself. A secret nobody needed to know about. I was tired of telling everybody everything and it was a habit I often did back home in New York. I felt like I had to, or that everyone was worthy of my sacred information. Growing up I had people pleasing tendencies where I felt that everyone in my life deserved to know everything – or when my parents would ask me things, I felt like I couldn't keep things to myself for they would just keep butting into my personal life. Now I have decided to keep this to myself. For now. Once I knew more, I would tell Ru everything.

I picked up my dirty clothes and put them in the laundry basket before sitting on my queen-sized bed. The soft purple sheets underneath my skin were silky-smooth and immediately my muscles relaxed into the weight of my bed. Looking through my emails on my computer, I got a message in my blog's inbox. My eyes widened as a gasp left my lips.

OH MY GOD!! IT'S HIM!

He actually responded!? I was so blown away. I eagerly checked and read his message.

Bonsoir Amelie,

It is lovely to meet you and thank you for your kind words. Yes, when I'm not busy with music and life I come on here to get a break. I like to share my travels and other experiences with others. I do enjoy writing also, not just song writing ;) My name is Lyon Beauchene. I am not on stage for a little while, so I'll have some down time to talk. I'd love to get to know you too. Where did you move to? I'm from Paris, though I wasn't born there. I live here for work. Maybe one day I shall meet you on one of my travel trips haha!

I do hope you're having a wonderful night and I hope to hear from you as well.

Bonne soirée (Have a good night) ;)

Lyon xx

My heart pounded like it would beat out of my chest, I could feel the blood rise to my cheeks as I blushed. I grinned excitedly, his energy was the exact same as the first day I saw his profile which pulled me in, the attraction was next level. I knew that I wanted to talk to him every day if I could. My intuition told me he was the one – the one I'd been searching for my whole life. I guess that was an answer to my question from Spirit earlier. A witch's best gift is her intuition and energy doesn't lie. Even if this was something that happened at lightning speed, it didn't matter in the case of soulmates. These types of relationships often happened quickly, and I didn't care what other people thought. This was my life, and I was going to embrace it. There was no way he would leave my life now. I felt we were soul bonded from here on out. I sent him a quick message again before drifting off to sleep with thoughts of him.

The days following our initial meeting were busy with both of us either working, or he was taking downtime to talk to me between songwriting. The six-hour time difference was difficult, but we still managed to talk every day through the blog, multiple times a day. I even had my blog app set up on my phone just so we could continue to DM each other. We got to know our favorite bands, colors, tastes etc. We both were gothic, and into the same things. I told him my favorite food, and of course my coffee addiction. He would tease and called coffee '*my other lover*' and he would always send a wink or kissy emoji.

We flirted recklessly and supported each other throughout the day or night depending on his schedule. I knew he was stressed with work. He told me he was itching to travel somewhere new. I definitely wanted him here, even if we only knew each other for a week which felt like forever. They say time has no meaning for people in love. I heard my Spirit Guides telling me to trust Lyon, that he was who he said he was. He wasn't lying. I needed that confirmation as I didn't trust easily due to my past. Spirit always gave me the truth, even when it hurt. Though I didn't think it was right for me to ask Lyon to drop everything in France and come to New Orleans. Although he said he always wanted to go.

Lyon,
Do you think you'd ever want to meet up in New Orleans? I know, it's a huge thing to ask . . . But I would love to see you.
Let me know what you think!

Ps. I forgot to tell you my last name is Descartes - and not related to the great Rene Descartes but "I do think, therefore I am" ;)
Amelie xx

I hadn't heard from Lyon in a few hours, it was nearing later in the afternoon here and started to feel anxious. Had I totally blown it? I spent almost every minute of every day talking to him and now he'd gone cold. I sighed frustratedly, deciding to go to the cafe and sit by the fireplace to relax with my book or maybe look up some crystals or tarot decks to buy on my phone. I needed to gain some sort of control over myself. I made this move to better my life, not get trapped in old habits of worrying and chasing people. I used to put so much stock in wondering how the other person felt about me, or wondered what they thought, that the old habits and anxiety started to creep up into my body, my palms got sweaty, my heart beating wildly. I really hoped that I didn't fuck up with Lyon. I took a deep breath, closing my eyes, remembering how to meditate and allow the negative energy to leave me. As I got comfortable in the café, a message came from him.

Amelie,
Please forgive me. I've been so busy with work. Night time seems to be the best time for me to talk – but I don't want you to think I'm ignoring you. Would you like to chat more this evening? As for your offer . . . I'd love to, but I can't right now. Hmmm.. maybe we can video chat or something? Would that work for you? I'm up till 5:30am most nights anyway. A total vampire ;)
Also, great last name! Ha ha, I should hope you think, would be a killer if your brain stopped working ;)
Looking forward to hearing from you,
Lyon xox

A sigh of relief. I hadn't totally fucked things up. Nighttime, huh? Well, I guess I'll have to change my nightly habits. As I read his response to my last name, I couldn't help the laugh that left me. A smile spread across my lips. He always had a way of putting me at ease even with dark humor. At least now I could focus on my business during the day before seeing Lyon tonight. I was starting to let things slide since I got so involved with him.

Lyon,
That sounds good! I'll just have my other lover over if you're okay with sharing. ;)
Amelie xox

I smirked at my own joke and sent it to him. I was so content with my latte, my Anne Rice book, and the fireplace. A ding on my phone showed me Lyon's name.

Oh, your other lover? Should I be jealous?

I chuckled at his response, he always was the one to enjoy the banter and tease me even further. I loved it. I had finally found someone who could keep up with me intellectually and stimulate my body and soul.

Non, Monsieur. Do not be jealous . . . otherwise you'll be jealous of an inanimate coffee cup touching my lips, instead of yours. Now wouldn't that be silly?

We could be so silly and downright stupid with each other, but it was always with the best intentions and loving remarks. I sent him back the message and ran a hand in my hair, now I had to come up with a time to video chat with him, and to look present-able. *Mon dieu!* As Lyon would say.

Ha! You are too adorable. I can imagine you blushing. And yes, I'd much rather kiss you than your coffee cup. So, date and time for video chat?

He was really getting down to business. I found out through the past week that he was a November Scorpio and most Scorpios I knew were logical, down to business and didn't fuck around. My Aries heart (March 21 birthday) was more on fire than ever with this man. He was going to be the death of me. Quite possibly literally.

Wow, you don't waste any time, do you? I love it! How about Friday night? I'll stay up extra late just for you ;)

After I sent him the message, I kept my eyes on my phone screen browsing through Amazon to clear my mind. I had found myself so obsessive with my thoughts of him. I knew that soon I would have to call Ru. She is a witch too; with amazing psychic abilities and magical powers I've never seen on anyone before. She was of Creole descent so that made a lot of sense. I remember her telling me stories about how there was voodoo magick in her family that she really didn't want to touch for fear it would lead her down a bad road. Though she stuck to the witchcraft practices she felt safe with. I'd have to ask Ru to move here, I think. Firstly, I need my best friend, and second, she would fit right in! The sound of my phone going off alerted me that Lyon had replied.

Yes, Friday night sounds good. Oh, you will, will you? Hmm, I feel special. Haha ;) Well I look forward to it! Though . . . You might not like what you see.

I had read his rather cryptic message. Not like what I see? Is he saying his pictures aren't him? Is he a fraud? My mind started spiraling. The anxiety in my chest started again. I heard Spirit say to me, 'Trust him.' So, I did. How could I not? Even when everything in my physical world seemed to betray what my soul and intuition knew.

What do you mean, Lyon? Are your pictures not truly you? Is that what you're saying???

I couldn't seem to stop going down my anxiety rabbit hole, almost demanding he tell the truth. His response was immediate.

No, no darling. I am exactly as I say I am those pictures are me. I just know that people have a certain . . . image of me in their minds. I may not be what you expect, but I'm hopeful you can see past my . . . quirks. Darkness if you will.

My heart melted. Beneath this gothic rock star confidence was a man who was just as insecure as anyone else. I loved him even more for it.

Well, I'm not going to judge you, love. Everyone puts on an image. You might be disappointed in me. I know I'm only 29, but I'm a lot more than just a young pretty face. We all have darkness, Lyon, but I think we do what we can from what we learn. I think we'll be fine! I hope I don't offend you by what I'm saying. I just speak the truth :)

I didn't expect this conversation to get as deep as it got, and I was getting a bit frazzled. Luckily, I didn't have to wait too long for his response.

Oh darling, you could never offend me. Honesty is something I admire. Thank you for your kind words and I can feel the loving energy from you. Yes, we do learn from our experience, don't we? Well, Friday night it is! I'll message you once I am done with work.
Bonne journée, Amelie! <3

I saw his message and smiled; a warmth enveloped my heart. He was the sweetest man I had ever met. At least I could speak my truth to him, and he wouldn't be offended. I had too many people in my life who I felt like I had to suppress my truth or my feelings just to placate them. Lyon wasn't that way at all.

"Friday. It's a date." I whispered to myself and got up to head to my newly opened shop, which wasn't far from my apartment or the café I started frequenting. While looking for places to live I happened to find a little shop for rent that had been abandoned for at least a year and nobody was taking it. I managed to obtain a bank loan for all the business expenses, which included my move to New Orleans and so I was able to open my metaphysical shop sooner rather than later. Between Lyon and I conversing over the last two weeks I registered my business and booked a couple of clients for a reading which I was beyond excited for. I wondered if Lyon would like a tarot reading sometime. Maybe once things moved forward between us, I could ask him? I couldn't help the grin on my face, I finally felt like I had a boyfriend, someone special in my life.

Friday night came the night we decided that we would try to video chat and it had been a week since I last heard from Lyon. I had set up my laptop, got my hair done, make up done and I wore a cute red halter top with black jeans. A gothic cross adorned my neck. A cute gothic, vampiric style, for our first online date, I wanted to make the best effort I could for Lyon. I poured myself a glass of wine and waited for his message to tell me when he was ready. I waited, and waited, and waited.

I felt such anxiety that I thought I was having a heart attack. I ended up calling Ru and speaking with her about how I was feeling. Her voice soothed me through the speaker phone as I laid on the couch.

"It honestly sounds like a twin flame connection. The energy you two feel is very powerful. And I know people talk about soulmates all the time, but twin flames are specifically made to challenge each other, to heal and to love each other. The anxiety you feel shows how much you love him. I don't want you to worry though. We'll figure this out, I promise. Just relax, take time for yourself, love. I'll be booking a ticket there soon. I always wanted

13

to go to New Orleans and find out more of my heritage as a Creole witch anyway!"

I could hear her excitement and I smiled at the same time as taking a huge breath to relax, "You're right. I'll take a bath to calm down. He missed out. I can't wait for you to come! I've missed you and I think I could use my best friend here." I heard her chuckle.

"I'll be there sooner than you think, girl! Don't worry, I gotchu." She said reassuringly. We hung up after our farewells and I took another sip of wine, my eyes slightly clouded from intoxication. "Fuck." I whispered.

It was almost 11pm New Orleans time. I was giving up hope. Was I not good enough? Or was he just busy with work? He seemed so excited to meet me. What happened? My mind was spiraling, heart racing and I downed the last bit of wine I had – thoroughly tipsy. I then heard a knock on the door.

Bang. Bang. Bang.

The sound made me jump, breathless and startled. I wasn't expecting anyone and in New Orleans anything was possible, I always heard people say that you were never alone here, and spirits were alive in old buildings like mine. I moved towards the door, my bare feet hitting the cherry hardwood floors as I walked. I looked through the peephole and what I saw had me terrified and yet excited.

I gasped as I took a step back from the door. My heart racing, my throat slightly closing up. I had to swallow and take a deep breath to recover. Opening the door I saw the most beautiful man: tall, blonde, blue eyed, standing graciously outside my door. *Lyon.*

I couldn't breathe momentarily as he smirked down at me. "Bonsoir Amelie. I believe we had a date tonight, no?" He cocked his head to the side with an amused grin. "I'm sorry I did not message you, I wanted to surprise you."

What the fuck?

"Well, yes, we did. I thought you changed your mind or bailed. I was worried about you." I felt it was very easy to be vulnerable with him. He disarmed all my defenses and normally I would have told a guy to fuck off and leave me alone at this point. He wore his rock and roll attire which was very attractive. His beautiful face, smile . . . wait was that fangs?

His eyes were concerned and somewhat sad, "No, darling. I'd never bail on you intentionally. I just knew I had to see you; it is much better this way than video chatting. You did say you wanted me here in New Orleans." His face was questioning, almost confused.

"Y-Yes, but you knew where I lived?" I took a slight step back feeling nervous. *Was he stalking me?*

He was gauging me, wondering about my reactions. I could see it in his face. It was like he could read my mind, predict my movements. He caught my arm with his left hand as I stumbled while his right hand caressed my cheek softly. His fingers felt electric on my skin, cold to the touch, yet my body felt like it was on fire. I could sense he was like me – supernatural. I didn't know how I knew; I just did. Claircognizance was one of my main abilities, the ability to know things before anyone else did, or know details about a person before they even told me out loud. He smiled again; his fangs more prominent. The pieces starting to come together, his fangs, cold touch, nighttime habits . . .

Oh. My. God. I am not hallucinating this is real! It's not just the wine. This is happening!

My heartbeat was so loud I could hear it in my ears and nothing else. I felt one of his arms around my back, as his right hand ringed and beautiful caressed along my neck. I never felt such intimacy before. Our eyes locked together, never leaving each other. My breath caught in my throat before he lowered his gorgeous mouth to my ear.

"I told you; I wasn't what you were expecting."

I felt my body go limp in his arms from a mixture of all kinds of intoxication before I felt a piercing pain in my neck. A growl left his lips as I felt myself going deeper and deeper into a pleasure I'd never known before. I wondered if this were how I would die, by a mysterious stranger who changed my entire life around. My twin flame. I'd be a headline by tomorrow morning, and nobody would know what happened to me. Fear replaced the intoxicating pleasure. Next thing I knew the pain stopped; black was all I saw.

2

Thumping. Beating.

Poison. Hating. Loving. Wanting.

The pleasure of the unwanted, the obscene erotic heat between my teeth.

I hate myself for it. I hate her for it. Yet, I love her for it.

The taste was exquisite, divinity in my veins, as it was in hers. Her magical essence can be detected and yet she has not disclosed it. I could see thoughts . . . no memories. Her memories? Or my memories? Or is it both? I cannot tell in this present moment - as we are united in a bloody, erotic dance. Her thoughts mixed with my own. I felt the vibrations of her heartbeat against me, and I realized with quick intuition that if I didn't stop, I would kill her - or be forced to turn her. I don't think I can do that. *Keep her fragile, that's how you like her*. The monstrous demonic voice in my head whispered. The demon that lies beneath all vampires, the one we must keep at bay. No! I like her as she is. Beautifully Divine.

I stopped drinking from her breathlessly. Her heart fluttered softly underneath me, her body limp in my arms, but she was still breathing and that made all the difference.

Blood began trickling down my lips and chin, dripping onto the hardwood floor. My tongue moved to lick her wounds, to clean her and heal her. The saliva of a vampire is very powerful in healing minor wounds and reducing pain. As I did this, I wished that I could take back what I did, to confess my sorrows. My old Catholic ways rearing its way inside my body.

Unfortunately, I would have to explain myself when she came to and face the impending judgment that might befall me. *Mon dieu, Lyon. What have you done?*

I picked up her small body and laid her down on the couch, placing a fluffy white pillow behind her head. I turned on her electric fireplace and moved to grab a cup of water from her kitchen. The cabinetry was exquisite like how it was in the 1700s. A sense of familiarity washed over me as I moved through her space. Of course, some modernity showed with the stainless-steel refrigerator and the gas range. I came back and placed the glass of water down beside her on the wooden coffee table then sat beside her. A sigh left my lips as I took in her silent beauty.

Please wake up, darling.

It was as if she heard me, (my thoughts potentially penetrated her mind) her green eyes opened and began looking towards me. I watched as she frowned. I could hear her heart speed up slightly as she tried to sit up.

"Lyon? What did you do to me?"

Her voice, so fragile, soft, innocent and questioning. My heart hurt to hear these accusations. "I'm so sorry, Amelie. I did not mean to hurt you. I don't know what came over me. Your essence is very . . . addictive to me."

Great now she was going to think I was this psycho-stalker from France. Way to be romantic . . . *imbecile.*

"I know you deserve all kinds of explanations. I just want you to be ready to hear them." Her eyes searched me for the truth. I read her thoughts, and she was scared, mystified and quite in love with me.

I watched as she sat up and grabbed the water. "So, are you a vampire?" She asked. I chuckled darkly, "*Oui*, I am. I detected you are somewhat of a magical being yourself, *chérie.*" She nodded as she put the glass down and snuggled into the blanket on the couch. "I'm a witch, I come from a long line of witches, but my family basically rejected it for centuries. They won't even acknowledge their psychic powers like I have. I was the only one who embraced it. I wanted to tell you earlier, I just was worried you'd think I was some sort of freak. But it looks like you had your own secret too."

I nodded in understanding. "Hmm, I can understand that. After my turning I had to embrace my new life with the fact I was to be rejected by society as well. And that I wouldn't have a normal life anymore."

I took her hand in mine, my heart beat with love for her. Yes, vampires did have a beating heart, it is just undetectable to human ears, and it sounds more prominent while feeding from living beings.

"I am sorry I inflicted this on you, Amelie. You did not deserve that. I got lost in you - it would seem." I smiled gently.

She smiled softly back. "Yes, I've been lost in you since we met. I've been in love with you from the start, I think."

I caressed her cheek lovingly, "Well, at least we feel the same way. Though I know the witch community hates my kind. Even the fact you are not French probably brings some . . . complications."

She looked up at me confused, "Why?" I noticed she moved even closer to me, and I bridged the gap by sitting on the edge of the couch, her hand still in mine. "My friends and family are very . . . *traditional* in the French way, they want everyone to fall in line with the old ways, being with our own kind solely and never deviating from that. I am a free spirit though; I love whoever I please." My eyes staring into hers, her hues the perfect earthy shade of green. I was falling more in love with her every second. *I want to protect you.*

She smiled, "I hear your thoughts. I guess that means we can telepathically speak?"

I nodded, "That's how I found you. I can read minds and I'm very *observant*, which allows me to predict people's actions," A smirk forming on my lips as I continued, "Though it takes great deal of energetic focus in order to do it. And you are the only one who has been able to telepathically converse with me, apart from certain vampires. Most vampires can read minds, pick up subtle body language that the human eye cannot detect. But some of us may not be able to telepathically speak like we seem to do . . . Also, I do apologize for showing up . . . the way I did." The words were flooding out of my mouth before I knew what to do with them.

She laughed lightly and it was music to my ears. The most beautiful music. "My best friend Ru, who is also a witch, told me we're twin flames. We're destined to be together, apparently. Maybe that's why we both felt that pull? It could also be the reason for our telepathy. I too haven't been able to telepathically communicate with anyone other than you. As for how you showed up . . . I do want you here, just maybe next time *tell me* you're coming."

I smiled amused, "Oh, so you're talking about me now?" I teased, "I have to compete with your other lover *and* your best friend, hmm?" It was nice that we could talk openly, she did not judge me and was no longer scared, I gained her trust. "I promise, I will tell you everything from now on."

Liar. Katerina is still a secret you keep. Knowing Amelie could read my mind I made sure to block that out. Another trick vampires had was that we could shield our minds from other vampires or supernatural beings from invading our mind, and it allowed us to control what people heard for our own protection. Since the war between witches and vampires it was imperative we kept that level of defense up so that no one would be attacked without notice.

"Well, only nice things. Though I did tell her I thought you bailed on me."

I nodded, "Ah yes, the illusive Lyon, King of the Connards, *oui*?" I smirked; her smile followed. "You're not an asshole, Lyon. You are different. We both are. I'm just glad you didn't kill me, and that you told me the truth of who you are. We can't have secrets anymore, and need to be honest for this to work, okay?"

I nodded; it was a fair request.

"So, what now?" I asked, not sure what to do from here.

She grinned up at me, "Can I get a kiss?"

I laughed, *"Oui, Mademoiselle,* you can." I leaned in, cupping her cheek lovingly before pressing my lips to hers with a loving, passionate kiss. All my love was being energetically sent to her in this exchange.

I pulled back from her, my eyes locked on hers as I took her hand in mine, "I want to show you something." I said before helping her up slowly so she could get her bearings back. I then led her to the rooftop of her building. Ironically, it had a rooftop garden that she didn't even know about.

"This is beautiful up here!" Her face lit up like a Christmas tree, an innocent look in her eyes and a smile as big as a child. "Did you know this was up here?" She asked me as I stopped in the middle of the roof.

"No, not originally, but you do now, I found it on my way here." I winked and took a breath. The moon was full, glowing in its full power. I loved the moon; it always guided me in times of trouble, and it lit up my world of darkness. Much like Amelie did.

She looked up at me, the moon behind me, the look she gave me was that of wonder and love.

"You're so beautiful, Lyon. Even the night can't extinguish the beauty within you. You're like an angel."

I laughed darkly, "I think I'm more of a devil, darling."

She giggled, "You're both. Beautiful like an Angel and the temperament of a Devil."

I nodded, "Ahh I see. Well then, don't think me too hedonistic if I'm devilish with you." I smirked, pulling her hands to my chest, "Really though, please don't judge me. Many people do, they often don't understand me and I - I don't want to lose you, Amelie." My brows furrowed with worry.

With a squeeze of my hands, she looked up at me with nothing but pure adoration, "I could never judge you. And you won't lose me, I'm yours to keep." She smiled reassuringly. I nodded and moved back from her to show her some of my powers. Even in the vampire world some gifts were best left dormant unless needed. It's like the English say: *Never bring a gun to a knife fight?*

Well, that's what our vampire culture is like, one does not just show off extremely powerful gifts at any given moment, not only is it considered arrogant, but if one is in time of war, one musn't show off all the cards in their deck.

I focused my breath, allowed myself to feel free, calm, and relaxed. Almost meditative. I then felt a weightlessness that always made me feel better, clearer. I opened my eyes to see her reaction, her mouth shaped in a little O like she didn't know what to believe.

Was I a devil that was to take her away, or an angel sent for her salvation? Only she could give me the answers I sought.

"It's a gift I don't show many, I use it to get away from every-thing, to feel more at peace." I showed her I could go higher by allowing my body to ascend. She laughed as she watched and then I landed in front of her. "So, tell me. Am I your Devil or your Angel? Do I bring darkness or light?" My eyes intensely searched her anxiously awaiting her answer.

I felt her fingers lightly brush my cheek, "Lyon, you are the perfect depiction of both. There is no dark without light, no demons without angels. I see you as you are, brilliantly magickal. I love you as your devil and angel. You are uniquely you."

I smiled at her, I felt so much love in my heart. I didn't know I could feel so human in anyone's presence but hers.

"I want to show you something too." She said and took my hands in hers, "Close your eyes." She whispered, it was innocent and yet seductive to my ears. I obeyed immediately, feeling the soft warmth of her hands, the blood flowing naturally under the skin.

I don't know how long we stood there but it felt like forever before she said "Open". My eyes fluttered open watching in won-derment at the magick she befell me. All the lights in the rooftop garden were lit up, all surrounding us in a beautiful luminous glow, like a million candles, I could hear the hum of the lights, it was a comforting sound.

"This is beautiful! How did you do it?" I was amazed! I have never seen or experienced a witch do magick before. Of course, I always knew witchcraft existed but since the racial divide I never witnessed such a marvel till now.

She smiled while blushing, "I learned how to do it when I was a teenager. I loved playing with candles, still do, and I practiced on them by lighting them with my mind. Then I turned to lights, probably mastered that most recently."

I smiled down at her; she was truly amazing. "I love you, Amelie - and I am not ashamed to say it. I know it's only been a week or two, but I feel it's been so much longer. I think we were meant to find each other."

She nodded in agreement, "Me too. Everything happens for a reason. I love you more than you know." We both smiled, she wrapped her arms around me, pressing her body into my chest. I laughed lightly into her hair, "Hold on tight." Before she could comprehend what was happening, we were both suspended high above the ground, above the twinkle lights of the garden, below the moon and the stars.

"You are impossible." She gasped, "Jesus! Lyon!"

A jovial laugh left my lips at her reaction, "I won't drop you; I promise." I soothed her, "You are always safe with me."

3

The smell of coffee drifted into the room as my eyes fluttered open with the morning light streaming through the window behind the curtain. I must have passed out in Lyon's chest last night after he took me up in the clouds. I removed the blankets, and saw I was in my plaid pajama pants and a rock t-shirt. Lyon must have helped me into my clothes. I pulled my hair up into a messy bun before shuffling to the kitchen. He was standing at the island in all his beauty, wearing the same ensemble as last night.

"Good morning, coffee smells good." I smiled sleepily as he looked up.

"*Bonjour*, darling! Yes, I made it for you, I hope I did it right." He smiled. I swear if he could blush, he probably would have. I moved over to hug him and take the cup,

"Thank you." I said appreciating all his efforts. He kissed my head and let me sit across from him.

"Um, so you helped me with my clothes last night? We didn't –"

I was cut off by his laughter which sounded like angelic church bells, "No! I knew how tired you were, so I helped you into your comfortable clothes. You were so wiped out from last night; you were hardly awake. I made sure you got to bed though," He replied.

I smiled with a blush, "Oh. Well, thank you." I took a sip of coffee and realized it was 8am and Lyon was still up.

"Um, shouldn't you be in a coffin somewhere, Paris Boy?" I asked with a quirk of my brow and a smirk.

He laughed at the nickname, "Paris Boy?"

I shrugged, "It suits. Just deal with it." I challenged, and he just shook his head with a smile.

"*Oui, Mademoiselle, c'est la vie* . . . " He chuckled, "And to your question, technically yes . . . But I closed all the drapes last night. As long as it's closed, I'll be fine. Is it alright if I stay with you for the day? I can leave tonight."

I reached for his hand with my free one, 'Of course, babe! You're always welcome here. If you want to sleep in my bed, you can, I'll close the door and try to be quiet."

He smirked again, "I sleep like the dead, don't worry."

I laughed at his humor and leaned in to kiss him, "Well then, I won't stop your slumber. I have to clean up and get things done for work. Also, my best friend Ru wants to come into town. Since you're here, maybe you two could meet? Or is that too much?" I didn't want to spring anything on him too soon. Especially with how things went down last night.

He smiled softly, "Sure, that would be nice. A witch too?" He asked with a curious gaze, I nodded with a sheepish look. "Ha! Well, I shall be on my best behavior, no promises though." He joked with a smirk.

"Okay, *Monsieur*, go sleep before I make you." I teased, wiggling my fingers in a magickal way as a joke.

He got up and moved around the island to hug me, "Be safe darling. Oh, I also plan on taking you out for a date night after, so make sure you have some energy left." His eyes were brimming with amusement.

I blushed, "Uh, okay. But wasn't last night kind of a date?" I was half-joking. "Ya know, wine, blood, the rooftop garden. Was *pretty* sexy and scary." I joked. Though him biting me was terrifying, I knew that deep down he didn't have a malicious way about him. I felt it in his energy, the way he spoke to me, the way his eyes showed his love, and his deep regret of what happened.

He swatted my butt before kissing my forehead, "Stop it." He chided as I giggled.

"Okay, go sleep. I'll be around if you need me or text me."

I moved to write down my phone number since we hadn't traded that yet. I ran to make my bed, take out my clothes for the day, and headed to the bathroom to change as he moved to my bedroom and closed the door.

The rest of the day went by pretty smoothly, I cleaned my place, went to get groceries, and went to check on my shop. I spent a few hours at the desk sending emails, organizing stock, and I met with a couple of clients who came in for a tarot reading. I didn't have enough income to hire more people or to gain a lot of traction yet, but I had to start somewhere.

After a couple hours at the office, I headed to the coffee shop to grab a latte when Lyon texted. It was about 4pm in the afternoon, the sun hadn't set yet, and since it was summer, it was still very sunny. I sipped my coffee slowly as I enjoyed the cafe experience. It was my time to relax, and I figured he'd be sleeping. I lit up with joy at his little message.

SMS Lyon: *Hello darling! Just checking in to see how you are. If you need help with anything let me know. I couldn't sleep any longer, restless, I think. Miss you xx*

He might feel a bit cooped up with nobody else there . . . I grabbed my phone to text him back.

SMS Amelie: *Hi love! Oh, I'm fine, I did some work stuff and errands. I just popped into the cafe for a drink while I waited for you. Don't be shy to turn on the tv if you want, or you can read any of my books in the living room. I should be home within an hour. Are you okay?*

I wanted to make sure the sun wasn't getting to him and if he needed my help I'd go home immediately. Otherwise, I wanted to have time to myself before tonight. A good recuperation of my energy was definitely needed for whatever he had planned. My phone buzzed again notifying me of his message.

SMS Lyon: *Yes, I am fine. No sunlight is getting in, nothing I can't avoid. Enjoy your other lover, I'm jealous. ;) See you soon.*

I laughed at his message and typed back:

SMS Amelie: *Don't be jelly! Good! Being safe and not bacon is good! I'll be home soon. Kisses! xx*

I stayed at the coffee shop for a little while longer as the sun was starting to set. I headed back home with my groceries, luckily nothing that would go bad while I was out. I took out my phone to text Lyon again.

SMS Amelie: *I'm heading back! The sun is setting yay! :D*

Grabbing my things I headed towards the nearest bus. I then felt my phone vibrate again.

SMS Lyon: *I wish I could come get you! You shouldn't be carrying all your things by yourself. >.< Glad you're heading back though, I'll make sure you're fed and taken care of when we head out.*

I smiled at his message, he was so attentive and caring. I loved him so much because of that. My heart always beat a little faster with him, but my soul felt so comforted by him. Finally, the bus came, and I was soon home in my apartment where it was dusk enough that Lyon at human speed raced down the stairs to help me carry my items up.

"Such a gentleman, thank you." I kissed him quickly on the lips before allowing him to head up.

"Oh, this is nothing for me at all, so I should help." he said over his shoulder as we climbed the old staircase to my apartment and settled into the kitchen area. "I'll put this away, you settle in, get ready and we can go."

"Demanding." I joked with a little sarcastic yet amused tone, with a laugh I headed off to my room to do what he said. "Where are we going? What should I wear?" I yelled to him standing in my bra and underwear looking at my closet.

"Darling, you don't have to yell, I can hear you. You look fine as is." I heard him closer and noticed he was standing in my doorway leaning against the frame, arms crossed with a smirk on his face.

I rolled my eyes, "Get!" I threw a pillow at him. He laughed and backed out from my fierce pillow throw.

"Okay, okay! But honestly, wear what you like. Casual but nice."

I sighed and with magick closed my door. I moved through the closet and found high waisted skinny jeans, black boots with a chunky heel and a white lace cami tank top. I did my makeup and with my magick touch I curled my hair. *Who has time for hair appliances anymore?* Once I was done fussing with myself, I followed Lyon out of the apartment and towards the street.

The summer air was soft and inviting, yet one could detect a hint of a cool spell (no pun intended). I could tell that spring was still clinging to the air. He grabbed my hand and pulled me down the street, neon lights humming, streetlights buzzing and honking horns filled the air. "So, where we goin' *Monsieur*?" I asked in a casual drawl of my voice, clearly the Louisiana hospitality rubbing off on me.

He laughed with a soft smile, "We, *ma petite*, are going to a nice restaurant." He wouldn't tell me what else was in store, typical November Scorpio, they were logical and secretive. I rolled my eyes at him with a smile as he chuckled in amusement.

"Lyon?" He looked over at me, with a bit of concern at my question.

"Mmm? Everything alright?"

We stopped for a moment so he could fully look at me, taking both my hands in his. His leather jacket looked remarkable on him. "When do you have to go back to France?" He gave a soft smile and kissed my hands.

"I don't have a set schedule right now, so for now I don't have to. Why?" He moved to brush my hair out of my eyes, my bangs covering them slightly.

"I just don't want you to leave, that's all." He sighed, pulling me closer, cupping my face.

"Darling, nothing will take me away from you - even when I am away, I'll always be with you. In here." He pointed to my heart, "and here." He pointed to my temple. "Telepathic gifts allow us to always speak to each other even when we're apart. I'll always hear and feel you."

I nodded with a soft smile, "Okay. What am I thinking now?" I grinned. He looked down at me, focusing on my thoughts. *Kiss me, Kiss me.*

A grin on his face as he heard me, he moved forward and kissed me tenderly on the mouth. He left me breathless in one fell swoop – just his kiss and voice alone could take me to higher places.

"Damn Lyon. You're impossible."

He laughed and took my hand, taking me to the little place he had in mind.

Once we got to the Italian restaurant we grabbed a booth by the window, a candle on the table, low lighting, hardly anyone there. "You did good, Monsieur." I commended him, he helped me sit before sitting across from me.

"Well, I had to take you somewhere nice, *non?*" He was definitely an incredible man who was always ten steps ahead. I definitely wouldn't want to be his enemy, but I'd gladly be his lover. I looked him over with more focus.

His leather jacket was off to the side, beside him in the booth. He was wearing a long-sleeved black shirt, like last night, rolled up slightly to show off his beautiful forearms. His hair was down, curling in a wavy sort of way, it framed his face beautifully. His eyes, a deep blue like the darkest of oceans in contrast to the lighting, the flame of the candle casting low-light shadows that made him look like an angelic devil.

He looked back at me with his signature smirk, I blushed. "I'm admiring the artistic beauty that is you." I admitted without him having to ask me anything.

He chuckled, grabbing my hand, "You're just as beautiful, if not more. Though I am pretty damn attractive." He winked. He knew how to tease and joke with me, using his own vanity to his advantage to make me feel better. How the fuck does he do that?

The waiter came and asked what we'd like to order, I hadn't even looked at the menu yet. I knew Lyon couldn't eat so I wasn't sure how this would go. Though I knew what I wanted to drink. "I'll take a glass of your best rosé." I ordered. Lyon, taking my lead, ordered a vintage red wine.

"Good choice." Lyon said smoothly with his French accent as the waiter took our drink orders and walked away.

"How are you going to get away without eating Lyon?" I was a little worried.

He reassured me again with his smile, "Don't worry. I can drink alcohol like humans do. I'll just say I'm not hungry."

I nodded moving to let go of his hand to grab a menu, "Are you though? I mean . . . " He gave me a pointed look.

"*Oui, je suis.* It's not something I can't handle, *chérie.*" I looked up from the menu to meet his gaze and nodded in silence. I trusted him. I went back to the menu and chose gnocchi. One of my favorite classic Italian dishes. The waiter came back with our drinks, and I gave him my pasta order, he asked Lyon what he wanted, and Lyon politely declined. Once alone again we clinked glasses, "To our new romance, and to adventure." He said before we took a sip.

"Amen to that!" I said happily and took a sip before putting it down.

"So, Amelie. I feel that even though we know each other on such a deep emotional and spiritual level, we hardly know anything about each other. How did you end up here?"

My eyes went wide as he asked me. I looked between him and the table, leaning over I grabbed a napkin and played with it in my lap, a nervous habit. I hated talking about my past.

"Um, well there's not a lot to tell. To be honest, not something I want to get into here. But I moved to New Orleans to be more unified with myself, I guess. I wanted a change from my old life, I wanted a fresh start somewhere where nobody knew me or knew people that knew me. I wanted to find my own path, forge a new life and heal from the past. I don't talk to my family really; I ran away from them if I'm honest. My best friend Ru, the one I want you to meet, she's the one I tell everything to and she pushed me to come here. To learn about the craft, to gain more abilities, start up my tarot and metaphysical shop. So, that's basically it. Then I met you." I smiled and looked at him again.

He had soft eyes on me now, "I'm sorry you went through so much hardship, from the sounds of it. It's always nice to start fresh. Since meeting you, I feel this is my fresh start."

I quirked a brow, "Did you have a previous relationship before?"

He nodded, "Yes, it didn't work out. I – I needed to stop going for the same type of people that hurt me. A vicious cycle really."

It was my turn to reach out to him, my hand on his, "It would seem we both had similar things happen. Before you I was sort of with someone, but they put me as a second choice all the time. If it wasn't for Ru, I'd still be in that cycle of chasing someone to love me . . . I wouldn't have met you." We both smiled and he leaned forward carefully not to spill our wine glasses, he kissed me sweetly.

"I'm so very grateful that we met too, Amelie." I blushed and pulled back to drink some wine and as I did my food arrived.

"Oh! This looks lovely! Thank you." I grabbed my fork and began to blow on the gnocchi to cool and eat it. "Oh my God! Lyon, thank you for taking me here, this is amazing!"

He grinned, enjoying his wine, and watching me eat. "*C'est bon!*" He stated with a grin, happy that I was enjoying my meal.

I laughed, "*Oui, c'est bon.*" I replied in what little French I knew.

When we finished dinner he paid the bill, insisting on being a proper gentleman. We then went outside into the fresh air, my arm linked with his. It felt so natural to be with him. It was like I could breathe for the first time in my life, I felt safe in his presence. It wasn't just that he was a vampire, but I knew that no matter what he would always have my back.

I looked up at the sky, the moon lighting our path, the streets busy with honking horns, passersby, dogs in the distance, just like before but somehow after our discussion in the restaurant things felt different. I felt more vulnerable with him and that was scary, but it felt good at the same time.

He looked down at me and smiled, "You're beautiful, you know."

I blushed and chuckled lightly, "Thank you. So are you." I leaned into him more. "You know Lyon, I don't want to get stuck in the past by constantly talking about it or reliving it emotionally. I just want to be free, and I feel that with you. Though I will admit life hasn't always been easy for me, and I know I act very differently from how life has actually treated me."

He nodded, "I admire that about you, Amelie. Life isn't always fair, but it seems you never played the victim but always tried to be better." He held my hand tighter, and it felt right to be here in this moment with him. Every moment was special, and I never wanted to take it for granted.

"Tell me about your family." I said to him looking up at his magnificent beauty, we kept walking along the moonlit streets of New Orleans – bluegrass music could be heard from nearby pubs and restaurants, even on some street corners.

He chuckled, "My family? Well, do you mean my old family when I was human or my vampire family?"

I blushed, "Oh well, I guess I mean your current family." I smiled sheepishly as he smirked at my innocence.

"They are from France. They're very highly regarded, and they like to keep up with the rules of vampiric society. They prefer I marry a French native, but as we can see, you are not that and I love it." He bent down to kiss my cheek.

33

I giggled. "Rule breaker, huh?" I asked as he laughed with me.

"Yes. Always. But my family is my refuge if I ever need something they're always there. My brother is kind, very business oriented and always wished I could go into business with him, but it was never my thing. Music, songs, singing. That is my passion. Other than you." He grinned, I blushed again.

"They sound nice." I smiled up at him. "Do you think they'd like me?"

He looked down at me, looking a little hesitant. "Yes, but they might take issue with you being a human, a witch and not of old French lineage." He rubbed the back of his neck, "It's all political Amelie. Which is why I stay away from it all. However, I think once they get used to the changes, they'd love you." I nodded. There seemed to be a bit of an awkward tension but the love we share will overcome anything. I just know it.

"Hey, you like music and singing. Why don't we check out that bar?" I pointed towards the karaoke bar with purple and blue neon signs. "I'd love to hear you sing."

"Ah, okay?" He seemed embarrassed somehow, like it was too intimate. I laughed and pulled him along.

"It'll be fun I promise!"

He laughed, "I thought I was supposed to take you out for a fun night!"

I grinned back at him, "I am having fun!"

He followed me into the bar, we moved to get some drinks, I learned quickly that Lyon loved his alcohol especially when socializing, but it wasn't a bad habit. It was to help him blend in and to curb his blood cravings.

We took a seat in a little corner booth, it was a bit quieter from the rowdy crowd. We sipped our drinks and sat beside each other, laughing at the others. "Honestly, half these people are horrible, but it's fun to watch."

He said, "I don't want to show them off."

I looked up at him, "Love, don't be silly. You can't help that you have crazy talent. Maybe you'll get a fan base here in America!"

He smirked and chuckled, "You don't give up, do you?"

I giggled, "Nope." I kissed his sculpted cheek. "I want to see you have fun and do what you do best. I think everyone deserves that."

He leaned down to kiss me softly, "You're impossible." He whispered to me.

I giggled again knowing he used my own words for him against me but in the sweetest way. "I love you." I beamed. Finally, the awful person on stage got off and went to their table.

"Go, Lyon, Go." I ushered him out of the booth.

He sighed, "You're so demanding." He winked, again using my own words against me. I stuck my tongue out at him and then smiled while sipping my drink. He went to request a song and I wasn't sure what it would be – but when it was an 80s rock ballad I was not surprised. I recognized the familiar tune of *'I Want to Know What Love Is.'*

His voice was like melted chocolate and sweet honey. It was beautiful and he hit every note flawlessly. I looked around to see the other patrons stop what they were doing and listen. He commanded the crowd as if he were on a stage of a crowded amphitheater. His eyes eventually found mine, as he sang, and I could feel the love he held for me. The vibrations of our energy were so palpable it almost made me dizzy. My body shivered in chills of love and high vibes. Once he finished, he moved towards me. "There, how was that?" He grinned, knowing he did well but wanting to act like he was humble.

"Okay, okay Rockstar, sit down before you light the place on fire."

He laughed, "So, it was good?"

I nodded, "Very. I think the singer is in love with me."

His eyes roamed my face, biting his lip lightly and moving to kiss me passionately. "That's because he is."

We were in a state of bliss that I never had with anyone. After a couple more drinks we headed back to my apartment. The heady sexual energy was tantalizing, and a slow burn carried itself up my spine. When the door closed, he grabbed my face and all but ravaged my mouth. I could feel the sharpness of his fangs which made me moan and whimper at the same time. He pushed me against the wall, tearing his leather jacket off and throwing it to the floor before kissing my neck, his fangs teasingly grazing against my neck.

I wrapped my arms around his shoulders, "Lyon." I breathed out, my heart racing. A deep growl left his lips, but it wasn't threatening in any way, more a way he expressed he was turned on.

"Amelie, you drive me crazy." He whispered.

I chuckled, "That almost sounds like a song title."

He pulled back to look at me and smiled softly, "It does, doesn't it. I might have to write one about you then." He grabbed my hand and pulled me along to the couch. "Did you want another drink, or should we keep going?" He asked not wanting to go too far if I didn't want to. I took a breath, "Um, maybe one drink would be okay. I should drink some water too."

He nodded, kissing my forehead, "Coming right up."

He moved to grab us a glass of wine each and me a glass of water. "Have you been with other men before?" he asked, probably picking up on my nervousness.

"Um, no, n-not really." I blushed madly and thanked him for the wine as he passed it to me and put the water on the coffee table. He sat back down beside me, moving to have his right side towards the couch, his knee bent under him slightly. He took a sip of wine and moved to touch my hair, tucking it back slightly.

"Don't worry, I'll go slow and gentle, I promise. I won't ever do anything you don't want me to do. Okay?" He smiled softly and grabbed my hand.

"Okay." I smiled back and took another sip. "I-I never really had a boyfriend . . . Most guys wanted to just fuck and dump me. I always wanted a boyfriend, but I knew I wasn't going to give myself up for anyone who wasn't serious so . . . I just . . . Never did it." I felt so embarrassed and nervous. What late twenty-year-old hadn't had sex? Me!

He moved into me and caressed my cheek, "That is extremely noble of you, and you *should* protect yourself. I'm proud of you for waiting. Not many do and it's best to have these experiences with people who care and love you. Too many people are into cheap thrills and not about actual relationships."

His eyes locked on mine, and I felt like he could see into my soul – well I guess he could, Ru said that he was my Twin Flame so we were the same soul separated into two bodies. He understood me better than anyone else. "Do you trust me?" he asked softly. I nodded. "Do you love me?" I nodded. "Good, because I love you more than anything in this life, and I trust you too. So, going forward, just know we love and trust one another. If there's anything you don't like, tell me. Anything you want more of, tell me. I might be able to read your mind, but I'd rather hear it from you." He said before kissing me softly.

I hummed back in that blissful state. "How do you do that?"

He pulled back his brows furrowed a little in confusion. "Do what?"

I smiled wide, "You do this calming thing where whenever I'm anxious or scared or whatever, you have this ability to calm me down."

He laughed lightly, "I think that's because we're safe with each other. You feel safe and therefore calm. I've also been told I have a very calming energy. Even if one might look at me and think otherwise." He grinned.

"Bad boy." I teased.

He quirked a brow and smirked, "You think so?" I put my glass on the table and bravely moved towards him to straddle his lap. "Maybe you're the one being bad." He whispered, his eyes lustfully looking up into mine, though I could see how much he loved me too. It wasn't just superficial desire or lust – but a love-based desire.

He picked me up which made me gasp and then giggle as he moved us to my bedroom. He gently closed the door with his foot and laid me on the bed. I watched him take off his shirt as I reached for the hem of my shirt lifting my top, showing him the lacy bra, I bought, before putting the shirt on the floor.

"Well, you thought this through." He teased me further.

"Yes, I thought of you when I bought it." I bit my lip before he crawled on top of me, kissing me, biting my bottom lip, before kissing and biting my neck. I relaxed against the bed and ran my hands in his hair. A delightful purr left his lips as I did this.

"Oh, you like that?" I asked with seductive amusement.

He nodded, "Yes."

I smiled up at him, my fingers tracing his jawline, his lips, before leaning in to kiss him again. "You're adorable when you're turned on then." I grinned, blushing.

He rolled his eyes, "Gee, thanks Amelie." I laughed and tugged his hair which made him growl.

"Okay, that was hot." I admitted with wide eyes.

He smirked, "Ha! See, I'm not adorable, I'm sexy."

He had this way about him where he could be sexy and adorable at the same time. My eyes followed him as he moved to kiss down my body, his lips between my breasts, magical hands down my body to my waist. He unzipped them and pulled them down. He was so gentle as not to scare me and I really appreciated this softer side of him. His eyes were brimming with desire and love. The corners of my lips softly turned upward as my eyes followed his every action. I was now in my lacy underwear, and he was staring at me like I was the most delicious dessert of all New Orleans.

"You are heavenly." He whispered before kissing my hips. My hips inching towards him, biting my lip. He grinned, "You want this?"

I nodded, "Yes."

He smiled moving to kiss my lips, "Good, I'm glad you communicated. I don't want you to ever say yes to anything you don't want. Understood? I really don't want what happened the other night to ever repeat itself."

I nodded, "Yes, *Monsieur.*"

He growled lowly again, "I love it when you call me that." I gave him a saucy grin before watching him stand up to take his pants off so that he was in his Calvin Klein underwear.

"Wow." I said admiring him. He was beautiful and should be an underwear model. "Can I keep you like this?" I asked shyly.

He grinned with a laugh, "You wish."

I beamed up at him innocently, "I do."

He moved to crawl on the bed and get comfortable between my legs, his hands in mine. "I love you." He whispered.

I nuzzled his nose, "I love you too." His lips found mine again before he moved down my body, but this time kissing my feet, my toes, my ankles, up my thighs to my hip bones again. My breathing getting heavy.

"Are you okay?" He asked, his brows furrowing in concern.

I nodded. "Just a little nervous." I replied.

He gave me kind eyes before smiling softly, "I'll take care of you, I promise." Immediately, I felt myself get calm again.

He moved to kiss my inner thighs to my most sensitive spot. I gasped. "Lyon . . . " I grabbed his hair gently as he peeled my underwear off and his mouth started in on me again. "Oh my God." I whispered a moan, "That feels so good."

Closing my eyes I felt him lick and lap at me making me wanton for him. My hips bucking up into his mouth, his hands gripping my hips to keep me steady. He didn't want to hurt me with his fangs, I knew that. However, before I could get any release he stopped.

I pouted, "Why?"

He smirked, "Because I want to make this last." He said before climbing up to meet me, his mouth on mine and I could taste myself on him.

"Damn." I whispered and blushed.

"You're so sweet, I love it." He admired that about me and always did. He kissed my nose and my face, moving to grind himself against me. I moaned and wrapped my arms and legs around him. He wasn't even inside me yet and I was ready to just come undone right there.

"Breathe, Amelie. Just take your time, okay?" I nodded as he caressed my face with his gentle hands. He sat me up to take off my bra and put it to the ground with everything else. His hands cupped my breasts. They were a perfect fit for his slender long fingers. "I think we were made for each other." He whispered, admiring my body. I gasped, biting my lip, my skin flushed with desire and nerves. His fingers pinched my nipples which made me absolutely feral, my head tossed back in pleasure. "Oh fuck . . . " He chuckled low before kissing me on each breast, his tongue and lips teasing each one. My groin was on fire with desire, and I could feel how wet I was.

"Lyon . . . I need you." I whispered, a pout on my lips as I looked back at him. He cupped my head, fingers entangled in my hair softly and kissed me again, more dominant.

"You're too impatient, darling." He chided gently.

A sigh escaped my lips, "I know I just really want you."

I was almost childish in my petulance but not in a negative way.

He smiled, "Come here." He moved us so he could get up, to take off his boxers and I could see all of him. He was a well-endowed man to say the least but so perfect in his stature.

"Um, wow. I – I uh . . . How is this gonna work?"

He could see how worried I was. He moved to sit with me. "Shh, it's okay. This is why I need to take my time with you. So, you can enjoy it as much as possible. It might hurt a little but I'm going to try not to."

He kissed my forehead and stroked my cheek as he lay beside me, and his right hand moved to touch me. He pulled my legs apart gently before touching me in the places I needed most. "Just relax." He said brushing my hair back with his other hand and allowing me to feel him.

I felt him move down the bed so that he could be more level with my center, two fingers slowly pushing inside of me. The feeling of his fingers was foreign but began to feel better the more I trusted in his movements. "That feels good, I want more of you Lyon." I whispered. I felt him smile against my skin, his lips kissing and his fingers thrusting. My hips buck up into him more but before I could finish, he moved away again, his fingers leaving me.

He got himself ready and steadied himself above me, positioning us both before slowly going inside me. A loud gasp left my lips in shock of how this felt. Part of me felt like I was being ripped open, not sure how to react to something so foreign inside of me.

"Are you okay?" His tone immediately concerned.

I licked my lips slightly breathless, "It hurts a bit . . . " My eyes met his blue ones.

His voice was so soft and gentle, "Just relax baby, you need to relax against me. It'll feel better."

I nodded and tried to relax my muscles into the bed. He kissed my lips and my neck. "You're doing really good, I promise."

I smiled and wrapped my arms around him, "Okay."

His lips were soft against my temple as I felt him move inside me slowly, my hands gripping his waist as I felt him thrusting at a steady pace. Not too fast but where I could feel every inch of him. The pain subsided into pleasure. I moaned in his ear, my breath gently blowing the tips of his wavy hair. He groaned against me, spurred on by my moans.

"You feel so good." I whispered; every thrust now was like magick to me. I could feel the energy in my body build up, not just sexually but magickally too. He moaned and bit my neck gently; I could hear a growl deep in his chest.

"Are you okay?" It was my turn to ask him this now. He pulled back licking his lips,

"You taste so damn good and I'm trying to keep my composure here." He was just as breathless as me, and I couldn't help but blush and smile.

"Let's try this." I said while moving us, so I was on top, with him in a seated position. It was the perfect angle to be inside me, and yet I could help him with his Blood urges. I cupped his perfect angular jaw, "Stay with me." I whispered to him, my hips moving up and down on his length. He groaned and bit his lip. I smiled and wrapped my arms around his shoulders, my nails in his upper back. He groaned and growled. It was so sexy.

"Lyon . . . " I moaned a breathy moan in his ear. He moved to clutch my jaw gently and kiss my lips.

"You're so perfect." He whispered, his other hand wrapped around my hips to pull me closer on top, both of us moaning in each other's mouth before his mouth made its way to my neck, his fangs softly piercing my neck in a love bite. I sensed he didn't want to do too much when it came to feeding from me considering our first meeting.

"I'm so close." I pulled back nibbling his ear lobe and then moved to kiss and bite his neck like he did with mine. He moaned loudly, pulling his head back from my neck, desire evident in his blue hues. It was clearly something he liked as well.

"You're too much." He teased before moving us back to where he was on top of me and thrusted faster at a pace that drove me wild. The pain from before no longer a worry. My back arched against the bed; head thrown back against the pillows as he continued his lovely intoxicating rhythm. The room filled with our very own melody of moans and gasps. He was the finest lover, knowing how to touch and kiss me. I held the iron bedframe as he continued faster but trying to be gentle, his fingers moving to touch me in all the right places, which had me in a tangle of moans and breathless words.

"Lyon! *Oh my God!*" I practically screamed, he muffled it with his own mouth kissing me, his fangs against my tongue. It was only a few more thrusts of his body against mine that we were both coming down from our climax together. Forever marked each other's body inside and out.

I held him tightly to me as my body shuddered to a stop, my breathing heavy, sweat in my hair and I giggled. "Wow . . . " I said as he looked down at me with pure love and admiration.

He moved my bangs out of my eyes. "You're a vision of perfection." He said before kissing me sweetly from my forehead, down my nose, my cheeks, my lips, my chin. I giggled again and blushed as usual.

"I love you." I whispered, brushing some of his hair out of his face, which looked so beautifully messy, I adored it.

He nuzzled my neck before speaking, "I love you too, *ma amour.* Always." His thumb caressed my cheek before he moved to pull out, to which I groaned.

"Are you okay, darling?" he asked, his brows furrowed in concern.

I nodded, "It's just sore."

He nodded back in understanding, "It'll get better in time. Give it a few days. Sit on some ice, maybe take tomorrow off work."

Smiling, I took his hand in mine and kissed it. "Okay. I wanna spend more time with you anyway."

He smiled softly in return. "That sounds lovely. By the way, when will I meet Ru?" I could tell by his expression he was eager to meet my best friend.

"I'd love to get to know her, I know traditionally vampires and witches aren't exactly friends but she's your family. I want to try."

I grinned, "Yay! You'll love her. She's a lot like me. I think she'll love you." I inched towards him to kiss him as we lay beside each other. The blanket curled around us, pillows propping us up as we gazed at each other. I ran my fingertips up and down his arm. "Lyon, when do you think I'll be able to come to France?"

He cocked his head slightly, "Whenever you want, darling. I just need to prepare the family for it. Traditionally vampires mate with other vampires. Especially the old French line, they're very . . . particular."

He wanted to be as gentle as he could in explaining this. He moved me closer, him on his back and me in his chest. "So, you have to go back soon?" I asked.

He was silent for a moment. I knew what he was going to say before he said it. I could see a somewhat pained expression on his face, "*Oui, ma chère.*" He sighed, "But let's not let that spoil the night, alright? I really enjoyed tonight. And I will enjoy tomorrow with you." He hugged me with his one arm and kissed the top of my head. "Rest, my love. Then we can talk more about everything. Just know I won't ever leave you."

I nodded and kissed his heart then his lips. "I love you." I think the fear showed in my eyes because he moved more hair out of my face before cupping my chin in his finger and thumb.

"Nothing will take me away from you. Trust me and trust that."

I gave him a watery smile, "Okay."

He softened and kissed me, "Shhhh, don't cry baby. Get some sleep, I'll still be here when you awaken."

I loved his old way of speaking. It always soothed me.

"Bonne nuit." He whispered as I started to fall asleep in the loving arms of my dark angel, my Dionysus.

The next morning, I awoke with the smell of an amazing breakfast and of course coffee. Turning on my back, the sheets wrapped around me like a Goddess, my hair splayed on the pillow. I smiled thinking of last night's love making and the way he held me as I slept. A twinge of sadness was in my heart knowing he'd be leaving soon but I had to enjoy what we had right now.

I got up, legs feeling a little stiff, hobbling over to my robe. Lyon wasn't kidding. I needed a bag of ice! I wrapped my silk black kimono on and went out to see him. *A vision of perfection* he says . . . well that's what he is, especially in the morning.

"I could totally get used to this."

He turned around and grinned, "Good morning, darling!" Moving over to me quickly to kiss me. "I'm making you breakfast and coffee. I hope it's alright."

I could tell he was a little embarrassed and he hoped he didn't mess up my coffee. I smiled up at him, "I see that, and it smells amazing. But I was also talking about you, waking up to you every day, I definitely can get used to that." I smiled with a blush. He chuckled and went back to doing his thing. He wore a black sweater with jeans, very 80's cozy rocker style.

"I'm going to go shower and get dressed. Though I do need a bag of ice or frozen peas . . . " I felt my whole-body flush as I told him this. He sensed my embarrassment and moved to hug me gently, "Don't worry, I got it covered. Let me know what you need, and I'll see to it. I told you you'd need it."

He pulled back to kiss my forehead sweetly, "Don't be embarrassed, *chérie*. It's perfectly normal to feel this way." I nodded before quickly going to shower.

The warm water was heavenly on my skin, I felt like I was being cleansed by the Gods. It was beautiful. I washed up as quickly as I could and got dressed in my favorite underwear, a pair of black leggings, and a white Henley top with buttons on the bust just under the collarbones, leaving my chest somewhat exposed but in a modest way. I did my hair up in a messy bun. Once I was happy with my appearance, I quickly brushed my teeth and washed my face. As soon as I finished, I found breakfast and coffee on the island table. "Oh, this looks beautiful, thank you."

He moved to sit beside me and kissed my cheek. "Anything for you."

I smiled and sat down, flinching a little bit. "Hmmm, you need that ice huh?" He rubbed my back affectionately before moving to the freezer and grabbing a bag of frozen peas, wrapping it in a towel and letting me sit on it.

"Ahhhh, thanks." A sigh of relief left me while I smiled. Digging into my food, I moaned at the taste of everything, "Are you sure you're not human? You cook very well for someone who's dead . . . " My eyes went wide at what I just said. "Oh, I didn't mean . . . "

He laughed and smiled, "No, you're quite accurate. I watch a lot of cooking shows. I actually loved cooking when I was mortal. I grew up in a rich household though and didn't have the *luxury* of cooking. That sounds totally backwards . . . " He chuckled. I nudged him playfully, "It just shows your humbleness. You can cook for me any time!" I commended him on his efforts, "It's really good." Pancakes, eggs, sausages, toast, and coffee. It was like a Bed and Breakfast but at home.

"So, what's the plan today?" I asked, turning to look at him.

He looked over, "Hmm, well I do need to rest soon. How about after you finish breakfast I go to sleep for a while, you can relax too, do what you need to and then we can figure out plans for tonight?" He moved a stray piece of hair behind my ear. I noticed he loved being physically affectionate and it was really sweet.

"Okay, sounds good to me." I leaned in to kiss him and nuzzled his shoulder. "I wish I could cuddle with you while you slept." I literally wanted to soak in his scent, and touch him all the time, afraid of losing him. His chuckle vibrated deep within his chest as I rested against him, "If you were a vampire that might be possible, but vampires are known to be quite . . . agitated in their sleep, it's best I protect you from that."

I nodded in understanding, moving to eat more, he smiled softly. I could tell he liked taking care of me in this way.

I felt his hand on my back, stroking it gently, like he was absentminded and enjoying the silence between us. As soon as I finished, he took the plate and began to clean up.

"You don't have to do that."

He turned to look at me over his shoulder, "I know, but you need to relax."

I blushed. It was true. "Okay, I'll go sit on my bag of peas and drink my coffee like a good housewife." I commented with joking sarcasm, he laughed and turned to do the dishes. I found that to be super attractive. Grabbing my coffee, I got up and moved to the couch, frozen peas in hand. I got myself comfortable as best I could. The sun began to peek through my living room window.

I kind of wish I could open the curtains.

"If you want to, I can go lie down." I jumped at his voice being right beside me, turning to see him sitting on my right side.

"Oh." I blushed again, not sure what to say. He took my hand in his and smiled, "It's okay. I read your thoughts, and you don't have to feel bad about it. It's life." He shrugged and kissed the back of my hand gently. "I'll go lie down; you do what you need to and then I'll get up when I can. I am able to go out at sunset, when it's not too light out."

I nodded, "Dinner time, got it." I winked at my double meaning.

He chuckled and kissed me. "See you soon." I nodded sipping my coffee.

It still blew my mind he could read my thoughts, and I must have zoned out to not even notice. I really should learn mind control . . . I don't want other vampires being able to read my mind, or *any* other supernatural being.

As the hours went by, I had managed to walk around the apartment with my windows open, clean up, do laundry (sneaking into my room to grab my basket so Lyon didn't wake up), and prepare dinner for myself. I had taken the day off work, so this was a nice change of pace. As the sun began to set, I smiled knowing my beloved Prince would wake up soon. I don't know why I thought of him as a Prince, but knowing how old he was I wouldn't be surprised. It's like I knew things about him he hadn't even told me yet. It didn't bother me at all. I rather enjoyed it. I embraced that part of myself.

At dinner time, while I finished making my steak, baked potato and roasted veggies, I heard the door open. Lyon walked in, in all his loveliness. My eyes took in his shiny blonde hair, stature of a God, and his sweet endearing energy. I loved him more and more every minute we spent together.

"Hi." He simply said, walking over to me with a grin.

I blinked a few times, "Oh sorry. Was I staring?"

He nodded, "Mhm."

I blushed as he came to hug me from behind as I prepared my food on my plate. "I missed you." He whispered.

I giggled, "Miss me? You slept in my bed, babe."

He kissed the back of my neck, and rested his chin on my head, "I love how small you are, it's adorable."

I snorted, "Shut up if you know what's good for you, Monsieur."
My failed attempt at threatening him only rewarded me in getting
a kiss and a squeeze of my hips. "I love you." I whispered.

I felt his nose nuzzle my neck just under the nape, "I love you
too." I hummed, closing my eyes, relishing in the feel of him
against me.

The energy felt so joyous, calm, and loving. I then felt my
stomach growl with hunger pains which made me open my eyes,
"Okay, I gotta eat." I told him gently, swatting him away so I could
put everything on the table.

"Want me to get you some wine?" he asked as I carried my plate
and utensils to the table.

"Please." I said, getting comfortable at the island table watching as he graciously grabbed the wine and a glass.

"So, what's the plan tonight?" I asked him curiously digging into
my food. He poured the glass and then set it at the table, moving
then to sit across from me.

"Well, I thought we could take tonight to get to know each
other. It's nice outside, we could sit up on the roof, bring some
wine and enjoy the night?" I smiled softly, a giddy feeling in my
belly starting.

"That sounds really nice actually. Um, but how are we going
to sit up there? There's nowhere to sit." He smirked at me, and I
knew there was some other plan or way around that.

"Darling, are you not talking to a vampire?" he asked with a tilt
of his head. I nodded; my mouth full of food. I grabbed the glass
of wine and sipped it listening to him. "New Orleans is not new to
me; I've been here before. I know the man who owns the antique
furniture shop and I'm sure he'd allow me to take some things off
his hands. I'll carry it up."

I laughed, "Okay, that's kind of awesome. Do you need help?"
He caressed my cheek, "Always the helper." I didn't say anything,
because it was true.

"Says the man who is basically serving my every whim."

He nodded, "We're the same, that's why." I nodded and continued to eat. He then swiftly made a move to get his leather jacket, "I'll be back. You eat." He pointed sternly but in a loving way.

"Okay." I said putting my hands up in surrender. He smiled and then left.

I had no idea what to expect, but whatever he had in mind, I knew would be amazing.

4

The New Orleans's breeze was intoxicating, and I couldn't help but fall back in love with this city. Just as I was falling in love with Amelie. Looking around me, feeling the supernatural energy of this city, it had been at least thirty years since I'd been back. Was I stuck in France for that long?? Some days it didn't feel like it, until I met Amelie. I realized I had been living a stagnant life for so long and I was craving freedom again. She gave me that. I just hoped I wouldn't crumble it all down. Life wasn't so kind to me; mortal and immortal alike.

The moon lit my path, the sounds of people laughing, jazz music in the background. I smiled and took a deep breath. *You're safe Lyon.* Yes, I was safe in this city, with Amelie, and nothing could take me away from her. Not even my responsibilities in France.

I found the old shop and saw the owner, much the same man I met thirty years ago, now less mobile. Grey haired, a little pudgy, but sweet and kind all the same. He was glad to let me take the furniture off his hands. It was cluttering the shop with all the little knick-knacks, baubles and random items people left behind here. Along with some antique witchcraft stuff. Many people didn't believe in our superstitious tales. Yet witches and vampires roamed the earth just like them.

The old man shook my hand as I paid him for all the things I picked out, he even offered me the truck to transport it back to Amelie's. I greatly appreciated his kindness at this late hour – late for humans who ran businesses that is. I gave him enough to cover the cost of the rent and some for himself. He almost wept. I enjoy helping others who are kind to me. Much like Amelie.

Stepping out into the night again I loaded the truck in the back where nobody could see me, and then drove back to Amelie's apartment. 80's rock music on the radio which I enjoyed more than any other music, and turned it up enjoying the beat, the anthems got my undead heart pumping. Although, I knew I needed to feed soon. I planned on at least getting this done first and then maybe going for a Small Pint before spending the rest of the night with Amelie. I didn't want to go back to France yet but I knew my family would worry, I'd been gone for at least three nights and without a word. I hadn't even turned my phone back on since I texted Amelie the other afternoon.

Shortly I was in the back of her apartment building. Quickly, swiftly and quietly taking an old antique couch using my Flight gift to reach the rooftop. I set it down in the middle of the rooftop garden where the twinkle lights were overhead on electrical wires. I repeated these two more times grabbing a few chairs and a small table up there. It was starting to look like a little Paradise in itself. It would need some plants, maybe a small firepit, one that would be safe to use. Yes, definitely a firepit for Amelie in the fall and winter months. I went back down to bring the truck back to the old man, and next thing I knew I was back on the rooftop. Grabbing my iPhone from my pocket turning it on, I noticed ninety new messages from my mother and brother. I ignored them and texted Amelie. I wasn't in the mood to deal with them.

[SMS Amelie]: Come to the rooftop. Xx

I smiled awaiting her reaction. I had hoped she wasn't busy or still eating but I had a feeling she just finished. Within seconds my eyes beheld the radiant beauty of my beloved Amelie, her hair in a messy bun, a long cardigan sweater over top of the white long-sleeved shirt she wore from earlier, a wine glass in her right hand. She must have been feeling the spring chill which was why she was layered up. She smiled up at me, her Converse sneakers adorning her small feet. I adored this petite woman.

"How did you . . . ?" She looked shocked and amazed, her green eyes growing wide in amazement before drinking in the space with her eyes. "I love it! It's cozy, and kinda gothic . . . antique."

I nodded, "That's the point, darling. And now we can have a cozier night up here. We should get you some plants. Though I'm not a big plant person, I don't know what you'd like."

She laughed, the sound ringing in my ears to delicately. "That's okay, Ru knows plants pretty well, when she comes over to visit then I'll get some."

In that moment we both glanced at one another, a knowing between us that I wouldn't be able to meet Ru. I had to go back to France, there was this nagging energy calling me back there, and my family literally pestering me on my phone. I hadn't been able to tell her when I was leaving, and the departure was drawing near.

Her beautiful face fell. I moved to wrap her up in my arms, "It's okay darling. I'll come back; you know that." My hands reached up to touch her beautiful face, my thumbs brushing against her cheeks as she started to cry.

"Hey, hey, please don't cry." The sobs leaving her lips and into my chest as I held her. "I just . . . you've done so much for me already Leo."

I frowned in confusion at the nickname, "Leo?" I asked.

She nodded, sniffling while looking up at me, "Like Leo the Lion. You're courageous, strong, passionate, driven. Leo."

I smiled and kissed her, tasting the wine on her lips. "I love it, thank you." She smiled back softly.

I sighed, "Look, we both know what's to come, but I want to make this a good night. Let's sit up here, have some wine, and just be with each other."

She nodded, "We need to clean that first though." She pointed behind me with her wine still in hand. It seemed that her crying had ceased for now and she was focusing more on spending time together. I was happy for that.

"Why not use your magick skills?" I asked her. She looked perplexed, her delicate eyebrows furrowing. "I've never done that before."

I nodded, caressing her face, "I know, but try it." Standing behind her I placed my hands on her shoulders gently to show support. She finished her wine and handed me the glass. "Okay, here it goes." She took a deep breath and focused.

5

I had not expected Lyon to do all this for me. He truly changed my life in such a huge way, even in the small things he did. When he's not here anymore I will truly miss him. The idea that he would meet my best friend was slowly fading. I thought we'd have more time together, but I could feel the anxious energy that surrounded him. He was trying to be as present as possible, but I could see that he was distracted with worry.

However, the rooftop was starting to become my own little haven, my little place to just be in nature, to be in my own space and just *be,* much like the apartment I currently have. The garden was an extension of that now. The furniture was something I appreciate, old, antique, gothic, and cozy.

As we spoke, and I cried, I held onto him for dear life, fearing the inevitable. He bluntly told the truth of what was to come, however, we didn't have to succumb to the negative feelings. We could just be together and that's all that mattered. He was right. I needed more wine though; I was not able to handle this soberly. I'll stay up all night with him. I won't even think of falling asleep. Thank God for coffee!

Coffee and wine? Good combo. I inwardly scoffed at myself.

He then asked me to do something I had never in my life even attempted.

"You want me to do magick on this?" I asked him, he nodded. I had never even tried it. The only thing I did before was light candles and the biggest thing was lighting the twinkle lights above us – but maybe because he was here I could muster up the strength and power to do this. He had the ability to awaken the power within me, to seek out my own Goddess-like nature.

I felt him move behind me, his hands on my shoulders supportively after he took the wine glass and put it somewhere. Inhaling a deep breath, I closed my eyes focusing on the sounds around me. The wind was warm on my face, the crickets and frogs humming and chirping in the background. Jazz music. Laughter. Cars. Like New Orleans' very own soundtrack. I then thought of what my intention was – *I want to clean the couch*. I surrendered to the buildup of energy within me, my hands outstretched, the magickal current at my fingertips, unseen, but felt. Pushing my hands outwardly towards the furniture I felt a release of that same energy exit out of my palms and fingertips. Opening my eyes, I noticed the dark green couch looked not only clean, but it had been buffed, polished and brought back to life!

Holy shit!

"Whoa!" I gasped, moving to grin at Lyon behind me, I could hear his soft chuckle at my excitement. "I did it!"

"You did! How do you feel?" He asked, placing his chin on my shoulder.

I took a moment to ponder this, "Well, I felt a lot of energy build up in my body. Focus is definitely needed," I was thinking more out loud than to him. "Afterwards I just felt all the energy direct itself into my fingers and palms, then outwards like a release. I didn't expect it to actually work, and not like this." I motioned towards the couch that looked almost brand new out of a 1900s shop.

"Do you want to try the others?" He asked me.

I thought, biting my lip. "I think I should save my energy. I just want to drink and talk to you."

He barked a little laugh, "Okay, you sit, I'll bring out the bottle and another glass. Do you want me to make you a cheese plate?"

He was the best boyfriend ever! *"Please."* I grinned as I picked up the wine glass I had out here that he put on the ground behind us as not to get knocked over by my magick. He nodded, looking at me adoringly.

Sitting on the newly cleaned couch, I noticed it was comfortable, more than I had expected for an antique couch, but it had some spring to it. The material was that of a soft velvet, the emerald green color was soothing and majestic. As I got settled Lyon was back with the extra glass of wine balanced on the cheese board and bottle in his hand. "Damn, that's impressive." I said with raised eyebrows.

"Vampiric balance, my darling." he said while putting everything on the rustic wooden table. "Sorry it's not cleaned off yet." He apologized.

I waved my hand dismissively, "No worries, I don't mind. I'll clean everything later. Honestly, knowing how to clean by magick, will make my life so much easier. I wonder if I will be able to do it faster?" He topped up my glass and passed it to me, before he took his own glass, sitting beside me.

"It will, in time. Just practice."

I leaned against his chest as he wrapped his arm around me. "Thank you, Lyon, for all of this, for everything." I meant it. Every moment I cherished. He kissed my head and smiled,

"You're welcome, *chérie*. Anything for you." I knew he meant it. We sat in silence for a moment with our wine.

"So, you said you wanted to talk tonight." I stated moving to sit cross legged making sure to take my shoes off first. My body facing his. Wine glass sitting in my lap with both my hands. The moon and stars above were so bright, illuminating our faces along with the twinkle lights creating ambient mood lighting. Things were getting serious now. Our eyes connecting. I could feel the heat between us that naturally occurred even in intimate conversations.

He leaned forward, "I wanted to get to know you more, and to explain more about my life. It's only fair." I nodded, moving to take a piece of cheese and sipping my wine. "What do you want to know?"

He smiled brushing his hand along my knee, "What city did you move from before New Orleans?"

I smiled with a chuckle, "Right to the point. Um, New York City." I blushed, he smiled encouragingly. "I always had a pull towards New Orleans for some reason, and I love the French culture, so . . . "

He grinned, "You have a thing for the French it seems." He teased squeezing my knee.

I nodded, "It would seem that way, yes." I took another piece of cheese and ate it as he sipped his wine. "Have you always lived in Paris?" I asked.

"No, I have for the past ten years, I lived in Lyon, my namesake, for a while in the south of France. It's beautiful there, you'd love it. I want to take you there some day."

My mouth hung open slightly, "I've always wanted to go there, besides Paris!" He laughed again at my excitement, his eyes twinkling in amusement.

"Well, then. Once things are more settled at home, I'd love to welcome you to France."

Silence invaded us as we looked at each other, feeling the anticipation of sexual desire and love between us. I drank more wine and poured more into the glass.

"Do you ever feel like you know more than you should about a person?" I asked.

He looked a bit taken off guard by my question. "How do you mean?" He furrowed his brows a little in confusion. I took his hand interlacing our fingers.

"Sometimes it feels like I know more about you than I actually know. Like, my soul knows before my brain does?"

He smiled, *"Ah, oui. Je comprends."* I loved when he spoke French and he knew it.

"Okay, so I keep getting this feeling like we've been together before, or something. I know that you've been living for a long time, but maybe my soul reincarnated to be with you? I feel like New Orleans drew me here because of you, maybe because of my lineage." It all was so confusing and made no sense, but I could see in his face he understood what I was saying.

"I get you." He whispered. I leaned in closer to him, our knees touching.

"Have you fallen in love with a woman before?"

He sighed, hesitating slightly. "That's a touchy subject, but yes."

I made a sympathetic face, "I'm sorry. If it was me, if I hurt you in another life."

He gave a small smile. "I don't think it was you, I think that maybe we were always connected spiritually, like our souls . . . until you incarnated in this life. I don't know for sure. I'll have to look into this further. All the women I'd been with, were *nothing* like you." I could sense his bitterness.

"I'm so sorry they hurt you like this." I cupped his face and kissed him, "I'd never do that to you."

He nodded, "I know."

I pulled back, "How do you know if I'm not lying?"

He chuckled, "Your heart and blood pressure tell me a lot. I know when your sad, scared, angry, in love." He teased me with a grin. I blushed. "See. Right there." He pointed to my face, I giggled.

"So, my turn to ask a question." He said, pouring more wine for himself. "Why did you leave your home country? I know you mentioned toxic family and friends, but was there another reason?"

I sighed, silent for a moment before answering. "Not all my family is toxic, my mom and I are really close. She encouraged me to come here, to find myself. She knows I'm a witch, though that's something she doesn't fully understand yet. She's trying though and that's what matters. And it's more of a dysfunctional type of relationship. My family isn't inherently bad, but they just never coped through their trauma properly. Being away from them made me see that. Ru and I are inseparable best friends, she also encouraged me to come here. I just needed a new start, a new life. To be somewhere different. I never expected to come here, but it just happened. And I'm so glad that it did." I smiled up at him. "It led me to you, my Rockstar."

He would have blushed if he could. "Speaking of." He said, "Not to interrupt, but when I go back to France to deal with my family, I plan on touring again in the summer. I'll make sure to come here."

I gasped, "Really?! Oh my god, Lyon that's amazing." I moved to kiss him, almost spilling our wine. "Sorry, I just – I love that idea. *The Devil and Desire*." I teased, "I want to hear that for sure."

He laughed and it was so nice to hear him laugh like this especially with all the pain I felt from him as we opened ourselves up tonight.

"Okay, and I promise to dedicate you a song." His fingertips touching my bottom lip,

"Okay." I said and he moved to kiss me, biting my lower lip. I moaned. "Leo . . . " I sighed.

He growled softly. "I want to taste you." He whispered.

He then pulled back, realizing what he said. "Amelie, I'm sorry, I –"

I smiled and hugged him, "It's okay. I trust you. You can if you want."

It was his turn to gasp and be surprised. "Really?"

I moved to look at him, putting the wine glasses to the side, mirroring what he did the other night. "Yes." I held his hands in mine, the contrast of his big ones to my small ones was endearing. I appreciated our differences. "I want you to bite me."

He took a deep breath, "I don't want to hurt you." He whispered. The backs of his fingers now brushing my cheek,

"You won't." I said, putting all my faith and trust in him. "It's okay." I whispered. He nodded. I knew he felt bad from when he showed up only a few days ago and bit me, almost killing me. It felt like forever since that happened. It was strange to think that we got this close in the span of only a few days, less than a week.

He pulled me into his lap, my legs wrapped around him. I put my hands on his shoulders. Our eyes met, green on blue. I kissed him softly, his fingers brushing the skin of my exposed neck, his mouth moved from my lips to my jaw, to my neck. I gasped, my heart quickening. He had his left hand on my back bracing me against him. I felt his tongue on my skin before the inevitable sharp sting in my neck. I groaned, but it was a pleasurable pain. Unlike anything I'd felt before. Just like that night in my doorway. I heard him moan at the taste of my blood, moaning against him at the sound of him. I felt the urge to be closer. Sexual tantric energy between us.

"Lyon, I need you." I whispered, feeling my body hot, wanton with passion and desire for him.

He pulled back licking his lips and cleaning the wound on my neck, "You taste amazing. I've never had blood like this before. You're absolutely Divine."

I blushed, "Well I am a witch, so yes, I am a Divine being."

He smiled, "You said you needed me." I nodded.

"Yes."

He smirked, "Well it would be my pleasure to give you what you want." I felt my whole-body flush.

"When you bite me, it gets me lustful." I admitted. I looked away feeling embarrassed.

He tilted my chin to face him, "Don't be ashamed, darling. It's just me and you. I don't judge you."

I hugged him again, feeling a warmth of love for him. "I don't want you to go." I admitted, feeling emotional all over again. The pain of his departure burrowing itself into my heart. My eyes were pricking with tears already. I knew he felt it too.

"I know darling, I know. It's only temporary and it's just so I can smooth things over for the family before telling them, alright?"

I nodded. "Say it." He said with a stern tone.

I pulled back to look at him "I understand." I said. *Damn he is hot when he's demanding.*

He smirked again, "I heard that."

He lifted us off the couch and carried me into my bedroom. "What about the cheese and wine?" I pouted.

He shook his head, "I'll take care of it; besides I don't want you falling asleep on me."

I snickered, "Well that's not the plan, I plan to stay up with you all night!" I said in a childlike playful tone as he put me on the bed, shut the door and began to undress himself. My eyes going wide. "Are you stripping for me?"

He chuckled. "Maybe." He tilted his head teasingly.

"You're impossible!" I groaned and fell back onto the bed, feeling hot and bothered and tipsy. I felt him move to lay between my legs, his hands intertwining with mine.

"Hey, I love you." He said kissing my lips.

I opened my eyes and grinned, "I love you too." I then got brave and sat us up, taking off my shirt, pants and socks, only in my bra and underwear.

"Well look at you beautiful." He complimented me in my lacy underwear.

"Hehe." I giggled and took my hair out of its bun. Dark auburn locks tumbling down my back in natural curls.

"You're so gorgeous." He whispered huskily kissing my back, shoulder blades, his fingers running up and down my arms.

I turned to the side, "Bite me again." I smirked at his hesitation, "You don't have to like do it hard. But I wanted you to bite me on other parts of my body."

He cleared his throat, "Amelie, you're playing with fire here."

I moved to look at him, "I trust you and I think it'll be fun, sexy. Like . . . vampiric foreplay."

He gave me a surprised and exasperated expression all at once. "Do you have a kink or something?" He teased.

I nodded, "Only with you though."

He pulled me close, again me in his lap, legs around his waist. "Darling, this could end badly. I'm already intoxicated by your blood."

I cupped his face to show I wasn't afraid, "You won't let it get that far, I *know* you. Even if people think we're rushing or don't know each other – our souls know more than people realize. Besides, magickal blood it seems, regenerates faster than normal human blood, at least from what I've experienced after you bit me, my energy levels seemed to have recovered super quick. And from all the esoteric books I've read on witches while at work, that seems to be the case. I'll be okay, if I get tired or lightheaded, I'll tell you."

He sighed, a little frustrated. "I'll try it, but . . . "

I squeezed his hands in mine, "I trust you." *How many times did I have to tell him this?*

"A lot." He said answering my thoughts with a smirk on his beautiful lips.

"Get outta my head, weirdo!" I slapped him playfully on the arm.

"Ow!" He feigned being hurt. We both went into a fit of laughter.

Between giggles he brushed his thumb along my mouth, across my bottom lip and then cupped my face with his hand gently, leaning in to kiss me deeply. I wrapped my arms around him, feeling his body against mine, and how much desire he held for me. I could feel his fangs against the inside of my cheeks, but it didn't bother me, it only enhanced the erotic feelings dwelling within my core. My fingers running along his shoulders, down to his shoulder blades. He moved to kiss my neck, down my collarbone to my shoulder, I felt a sharp pain when he bit me, but it wasn't overwhelming. I dug my nails into his back out of reflex and he growled into my skin. He obviously liked that.

"Is this, okay?" I asked him. He nodded. I could feel his tension as he focused solely on being careful. He was restraining himself.

"Don't be scared." I whispered running my right hand in his hair softly. I wanted to soothe him, nurture him. He deserved that type of love. He looked up at me and the look he gave took me back. It was a look of pain, sadness and love. He had never been loved this way. I could see it. Feel it.

"Hey, it's okay." I cupped his face again, "What's wrong?"

He moved to hug me tightly, not crushing me though. "I just – I love you. And the way you love me, it scares me sometimes."

I frowned slightly, again running my hands in his hair as he hugged me. "Why does it scare you?" I pulled back to look down at him, his eyes turning a grey color. I noticed when he felt certain emotions his eyes would change. He sighed and tucked some hair behind my ear,

"Because it's not something I'm used to. I've never been loved in this way, *cherie*. Not by anyone." I felt a deep hurt in my chest, I wanted to cry. My empathic nature taking its toll all of a sudden.

"Oh baby, I'm so sorry. You deserve all the love in the world." He scoffed, "Do I?" My heart sunk in my chest at his words. Oh no, now things were turning dark. "No, don't do this. Not on our last night, Lyon." I commanded, my divine feminine nature taking over. I needed him to listen.

It was then he untangled himself from me, gently pushing me away on the bed. He ran a hand in his hair and stood up. "Lyon?" I asked, fear enveloping my chest, my very being. Was he pushing me away? He looked at me and sighed in frustration. "I can't . . . "

I looked pleading up at him, "Don't go Leo, please. Whatever it is, we can get through it. If I said something to upset you –"

He shook his head, "No, you did nothing wrong. It's me."

I had no idea what was going on, my heart breaking in two already. He could sense it. "Darling, I just – I need time, I think. I'm scared to lose you and to hurt you."

I stood up. I could feel the wound on my shoulder was almost healed now. "Then don't go. Don't run away from me." I went to grab his arm and he looked at me as if I shocked him.

"Amelie . . . " He said in warning.

Tears were welling up in my eyes. "What the fuck?" I whispered angrily. Why was this happening?

He checked his phone before looking at me again, "Amelie. I can't right now. I need to go home." He got his clothes and began to get dressed. The whole night was supposed to be a perfect send-off. This wasn't what I wanted.

"Lyon, please, stay with me. Leave tomorrow. If you want to do something else, just tell me. We don't have to be intimate; we can watch tv, or talk, or –" I was trying to come up with anything to keep him here. He snapped his head at me and took me by the shoulders.

"I can't! Just leave me be, Amelie."

I felt my gut churn, my heart fell into my stomach. Tears started to pour down my cheeks. I couldn't believe what was happening. As soon as everything was going well, it was taken away just as quickly. I began to get dressed too. I couldn't fathom him leaving.

"Why do all of this then?" I argued back. I wasn't going to let him walk away like this.

"I love you. I do." he said, softening slightly but keeping his distance as he went to grab his things and his leather jacket, exiting my bedroom. "Things are complicated right now, I'm sorry for that. I just – I really do need to get home to France."

"You'll be back, right?" I sniffled.

He looked at me. He himself looked torn. He came closer, cupping my face and kissing my forehead.

"When the time is right. I promise." And with a blink of an eye, he was gone.

I couldn't fathom this at all. My chest started heaving. I immediately grabbed my phone and called Ru.

"Hey, Ru? I need you to come to New Orleans. Lyon left . . . He . . . He's gone." I sobbed into the phone. Ru's sweet and calm voice on the other end was reassuring.

"I'll be there in a few hours, sweetheart. Okay? Just hang tight till I get there." I nodded, "Okay." I moved to go outside to the rooftop garden. I cleaned everything that Lyon and I had left up here. I tried my magick but I was too upset to focus so I did things the old fashioned way. Cleaning helped. All I could think of though was him. His scent was everywhere in this apartment.

"Fuck!"

I was angry, hurt, scared, heartbroken. What the hell was happening to me? I wanted to chase after him, to text, or call him. It would be useless but it's what I wanted. I knew I was going down a rabbit hole that I couldn't come back from without Ru to set me straight. Thank God she was coming. Thank God I had her.

Within a few hours Ru was at my apartment, a bag on her shoulder, she had quickly packed a carry-on for a few days. She didn't need much, and I always let her roam my closet if need be. When I saw the gorgeous tall, brunette, with curly hair down to the waist, her two different colored eyes, one brown and the other blue, the warm complexion of her mixed heritage - I smiled.

Ru had been brought up by a single white woman of Scottish-British heritage, but she had Black Creole roots here in New Orleans as well. Her father was Creole but abandoned her when she was a baby, all she knew about her father was that he was Black Creole from New Orleans and was never seen again. As I've said earlier, she is a witch, like me, though she has Hoodoo and Voodoo in her background. Although, she preferred to stay away from that. It wasn't in her nature, and she wasn't initiated into that community of witchcraft anyway. Either way, I loved her for who she was, and she made my life so much brighter in the darkness. Just like Lyon had, before he snuffed it out like a candle, all that was left was the smoke he left behind.

I hugged her immediately in the doorway, my face red from crying, I'm sure I looked quite the sight.

"Hey, babygirl. It's okay, I got you." She said in her urban city accent. I could almost hear a hint of Southern in her now that she'd come to New Orleans.

I sighed, "Hey." Pulling back to let her come through the door, "You can put your bag in my room. Also, don't mind if you see any blood, nothing bad happened. Lyon and I were experimenting with something . . . before . . . he . . . left." I choked up again. Ru put her bags down and noticed what I was talking about and used her powers to clean up the sheets and set the bed back to normal.

"There, no trace that anything happened." She gave a soft smile, and I grabbed the bottle of wine, two glasses and took her upstairs to the roof.

"Lyon and I made this together. But I think it'll eventually be a nice hang out spot." I turned on the twinkle lights with my mind, it was getting easier to do that now. We sat on the couch, and I poured us two glasses.

I cuddled into her side. We had that kind of friendship where we could be close. She wrapped her arm around me, "What happened?" I moved after a moment, sitting up to take a drink of wine and start my story.

I told her everything from the moment we met, to when he showed up at my door (which now felt like ages ago) and bit me for the first time. She almost interjected, I could see she was about to start yelling but I put my hand up. "Let me finish." I told her before taking another sip of wine. She warily agreed, taking a sip to stop herself from talking. I continued my story to where Lyon left.

"So, that's everything . . . It feels so much longer than it has been. I feel utterly shattered. I don't know what to do. He said it's not my fault but then, why did he leave?"

Ru sighed, moving to squeeze my knee.

"Girl, I think he got scared. Remember I mentioned the Twin Flame connection?" I nodded.

"Well, a lot of times the Divine Masculine will run. There's a runner and a chaser. The Divine Feminine will chase him, physically, emotionally, energetically. What that does is activate you both to ascend and heal all core wounds of the past. Past life karma, things from your childhood, etc. It's complicated and can be scary for the both of you. He's obviously never been loved the way you love him, but you also need to focus on yourself more. You don't *need* him. You *need* yourself. You two essentially are the same person. Two bodies, one soul. That's why you're the same, that's why this love feels otherworldly. And I mean – he's a vampire, you're a witch. So super-supernatural."

"Wow." I said, nodding, trying to process it all. It was nice to talk to Ru about this and her being super relaxed about it and supportive was exactly what I needed. I drank more wine and poured another glass. "So, what comes next?"

She turned to face me, "Well, stop crying over him for starters. If you're obsessed with thinking of him or trying to figure it all out, it'll only create more chasing, which will push him away.

The best thing you can do, is focus on you baby girl. I'll help you. We can do a reading with the tarot to see what's going on for you both. But don't obsess over it, I know it's hard. I know you miss him, and you'll continue to miss him. But it's the only way to get him back. *Seriously.*" She gave me a knowing stern look.

"Okay, okay. So, how can I start?"

Ru smiled, "Right now, by just hanging with me. Maybe take a bath? We can go for a walk? Have you explored New Orleans?"

I shook my head, "Not really. Except to get groceries and see a cafe." I had spent the last three to four days with Lyon."Well actually, Lyon took me out on a date, and we walked around a bit. We went to a karaoke bar." I giggled. "He sang me a song."

Ru smiled softly, "Awww, that's adorable. He loves you, clearly. Hold on." She moved to go back inside. I looked up at the moon and sighed.

"Spirit, if you have any messages for me, please tell me. Tell me what to do. I love him so much. I know you brought us together for a reason. I just need the faith in you to eventually get him back."

Ru came back with another bottle of wine and tarot cards. I grinned, "Oooo, fancy." She poured us more wine and then started to shuffle the cards.

"What are you asking it?"

Ru looked over at me, "Shhh, I'm focusing. I'm trying to get you a message about Lyon."

I stayed quiet and the cards started jumping from the deck. She laid them out on the table in a simple spread.

Eight of Swords. Three of Swords. The Lovers.

"Well, the man is clearly in pain. He is in his head thinking about all of this and he's heartbroken, but he loves you. He sees a future with you, and he knows that this relationship is Divinely guided. I'm picking up on the fact he's afraid he'll get hurt again and be disappointed. That's why he walked away."

I nodded, "That sounds about right. He did say it was him, not me. He said that *'he couldn't'* . . . I don't know what that meant."

Ru nodded in understanding, "He *couldn't* because he can't love you the way you need him too. That's why you gotta focus on you, love yourself in the way you want him to. I know it's confusing and makes no sense right now. But, this relationship, this connection, is about fulfilling yourself first. Then he'll eventually do the same and come back."

"Okay." I sipped more wine, "He did say he promised to come back when the time is right. He had something to deal with back in France. Which we already spoke about, but he was supposed to leave tomorrow, not tonight. He got spooked."

Another nod from Ru, "Yes, because he's scared to hurt you and be hurt. In the Twin Flame journey there's three core wounds: Fear of Abandonment, Self-Worth, and Rejection. So, once those three things are healed, then it will bring you two closer together. There's a thing called "Mirroring" where you two mirror each other. If you heal something in you, then he'll do the same. Even if you don't know it in your logical mind, you'll feel it. Everything you think and feel, he'll feel it too."

I nodded a bit more excited now, "Oh! Well, we have telepathy too." Ru smiled at my excitement, "Well that's pretty normal for this type of connection but even especially since you're both supernatural beings."

I reflected over the cards and all this information. "So, we're Twin Flames, for sure? It's more than soulmates?"

Ru nodded, "Yup, soulmates are two separate souls who grow and love together. This is considered a "One Soul" relationship because you both are the same soul, just in separate bodies."

I nodded again mulling over what she said. "Okay, my brain hurts now. But this makes more sense."

Ru laughed, "We can talk more about it tomorrow. But the important thing is, don't dwell on what was said, and what wasn't – or what he meant by anything. It'll drive you crazy. Also, do these things for *you*. Not him. You gotta heal for yourself. I know it doesn't feel like it right now, but you'll feel better in time. Don't obsess over when you'll get back together, or how. Focus on what you want. You want him? Think about all the things you'll do together; think about the life you want to have with him. And find ways to heal yourself. Journal, mediation, maybe even find some witch friends here."

I nodded more and more excited. "Okay, okay. I mean, it still hurts like a bitch, but maybe tomorrow we can find a cool bar and have fun?"

Ru laughed and smiled, "That's my girl! And we can do some witchy stuff while I'm here. I've been wanting to check out New Orleans forever. So, I'm kinda glad this happened. Though I hate you got hurt."

She hugged me and I held on tightly. "I'm so glad you're here Ru. Hey, if you want to stay a while you can. I'd love it if you moved here."

She grinned as she pulled away to look at me, "Aw, man! I'd love to. Let's see how things go. Oh! I can help you with work tomorrow."

I gasped. "Oh fuck, I forgot I was supposed to work tomorrow. I took today off, I was umm . . . Ahem..recovering from last night."

Ru made a joking disapproving tone, "Girl, what did you guys do???"

I laughed, "We had sex. Obviously. Which was so good! I've never felt like that before in my life. He's so good to me . . . Was so good to me." I trailed off. Ru took my hand, "Hey, we'll get him back. I'm in this now, the three of us. I'll help in any way I can."

I smiled softly, "Thanks Ru."

I was so happy to have Ru here for tonight, she came all the way from New York City just to be with me. It was so nice not being alone, to understand this connection between Lyon and I more. I was starting to understand myself with the support of my best friend.

The Separation Part I: Lyon's Dilema

6

What the fuck had I just done? I left the woman I love behind for what? My own selfish reasons: because I was a coward who couldn't face his own fear? I knew that I had to get things sorted with my family first but - would they even understand? Probably not. *Mon dieu!* I felt like such a fool, an idiot. Again! *Connard.*

What would Amelie think of me now? She already had been heartbroken in her life over and over again. Now I was just the same as the trauma that hurt her. I did promise to be back, and I fully meant that. *I will be back Amelie.* I don't make promises lightly.

I sighed, looking at the millions of text messages from my mother, my brother, my . . . the person weighing me down. I was supposed to be with someone else, someone fit of the Beauchene name . . . and I had squandered that for my own love, my own freedom. Amelie made me feel free and I wasn't going to let that go for someone else's marriage agreement. It was between *that* family and mine. Not me and *that woman.* Of course she'd catered to my every whim, but I didn't want any of that. I wanted Amelie. I needed to make my family see sense. As I headed towards the clouds with my Flight gift, I quickly called my mother.

"Good evening, Mother." I said in the sweetest tone. She was worried and a little angry. "Don't worry, I just needed some time away. I am coming back now." I said in French "I will be there in a few hours. Goodbye." I hung up, pocketed the phone and then headed towards the sky higher and higher moving against the wind and dense clouds. The moon was full and bright lighting my way, not that I couldn't see without it, but it made me feel a little less alone. I wondered how Amelie was doing, and I couldn't think of anyone else.

Within a few hours I landed back in Paris. I couldn't face going home just yet, so I called my brother. We got along well, and I told him to meet me in a cafe that was open late by the Eiffel Tower. I checked the time. 1am. I still had a couple hours till sunrise.

I sat at a small booth table, beside an electric fireplace, a view of the lit up Eiffel Tower in the background. I loved Paris, but it somehow felt foreign without her. I wished she was here. I wished I had told her everything. I had a cup of coffee in my hands, mostly to blend in. I wasn't a fan, but the smell reminded me of Amelie. It was like she was here telling me everything would be okay.

I looked up to see my brother, not as tall as me, in business casual attire. A long grey wool coat, his hair was blonde but cut short, blue eyes same as mine and a soft face. I smiled at him gently.

"Hello." I said, getting up to hug him. He hugged me tightly before we sat down.

"We were so worried about you." He said in his most elegant French. We weren't from Paris, but not too far away. Our dialect was a little more sophisticated than the average street French of Paris.

"Ah yes, I know." I sighed gripping the cup. "I needed to get away. It was just getting suffocating."

My brother looked at me, "You fell in love with someone didn't you, Lyon?"

I went to argue but seeing the smirk on his face I chuckled and nodded. "I did. But she's not what you think. I really love her, and she loves me. I just didn't have to heart to tell her the full truth and I wanted to bring her into the family. That's why I came back. I need to tell Maman and get her to see the truth." I ran a hand in my long hair.

"Alex, I don't know what to do." I was clearly in despair and out of my mind. "I feel her, the girl I was seeing, everywhere. For instance, she's a coffee lover, and well now I love the smell of coffee." I chuckled darkly.

Alex's eyes lit up. "I've never seen you like this, brother. Tell me about her and I promise I won't tell anyone until you're ready."

I smiled, feeling confident to tell him the story of how Amelie and I met. I told him everything from the online flirtation, the idea for a video chat, the whole thing.

"You bit her??" He was almost exasperated.

I threw my hands up in surrender, "I didn't mean to hurt her, I got overwhelmed! I've never had such an intense feeling towards anyone. Least of all a human. Oh, uh, she's a witch too."

Alex gasped, his eyes as wide as saucers, *"My God!!* Lyon, you can't date a witch. For centuries vampires and witches never mixed well. And mother's not going to like she's an English American girl."

I frowned, "I don't care what Maman thinks. I love Amelie. Who cares what her race or background is? She treats me well. Besides, she's learning French." I countered back and took another whiff of the coffee. Amelie and I had many conversations together between the passionate sex and our dinner dates and that was when I found out she was learning French.

Alex looked out the window to see passersby before turning back to me. "What's she like? I mean, considering her nature and status."

I smiled fondly, "She's sweet, kind, caring. She's funny. She has been through some really horrible things in her life. I feel like by me walking away just added to that, but I promised her I'd be back. I mean it."

Alex sighed and gripped my wrist, "Brother, you can't just desert the family for her."

I glared at him, "*I* will do whatever *I* want. I plan on bringing her into the family, I don't care what anyone thinks. Please try to put aside the elitist vampiric bullshit for now."

Alex nodded, "I want things to work out, I do. I just worry for you." I could see I wounded his ego slightly by my outburst.

I sighed looking down, "I know. Thank you for hearing my side of things before it gets warped by Katerina once she and mother find out."

Alex scoffed, "Katerina. You know I once thought she was a good person. Thought you two would be amazing together. Now that you tell me all about what you and Amelie went through and how you feel for her. I really hope you get what you want Lyon. I'll help however I can."

I smiled, "Thank you."

He smiled with a nod. "Well, what are your plans now?"

I shrugged. "I honestly don't know. I guess face Maman's wrath?"

We both smirked and giggled. "She loves you Lyon. You're the youngest, she'll see sense. I think she just wants what is best for you and the family."

I nodded in silence. I knew that to be true. She cared for us all. I was the rebel and the chaotic one. She had to deal with all of my shenanigans.

I checked the time and realized we'd been talking for over an hour. "I guess it's time to go home, see Maman and face the music . . . "

Alex smiled, "Speaking of music. When are you going back out on the road?"

I shrugged again, "I don't know. Soon. I promised Amelie a song." I winked. He laughed and we together left the cafe and headed home.

It wasn't long after I got home that I was bombarded with questions of where I was, who I was with, why didn't I tell anyone. It was exhausting.

"My God, stop, please!" I growled at everyone. "I'm tired. Let me tell you all when I am ready. The important thing is, I'm home, I'm safe. Nothing bad happened." *Except I got my heart broken and potentially ruined the life of my beloved witch.* I kept my thoughts shielded from everyone. Vampires could read other vampires' minds after all.

My mother, Bridget Beauchene came to greet me. She was short, but feisty, much like Amelie. She had blonde hair, blue-green eyes, fair skin. A stern look but a small smile adorned her face when she hugged me.

"I am glad you are home, son. Yes, we will talk tomorrow. You must rest. Your bed is made for you."

I smiled softly, "Thank you, Maman." I said and headed up to bed.

I went up the steps of the Manor, it was ornate with gold, white, blue, and peach colors. Much like Versailles. It had been in the family for a very long time. My room was one of the largest, of course I was the youngest, so I was spoilt. A brat one might say.

I sighed, opening my door and closing it behind me. A four-poster bed was in the middle, a chaise lounge in the corner, an ornate golden tub behind a screen divider, the windows were covered with heavy curtains to keep out the sun. I didn't like sleeping in a coffin anymore, I preferred the comfort of the bed.

I took a deep breath, closing my eyes and when I opened them, I noticed Katerina on the bed, beautiful, with her dark hair and dark eyes, her skin a tone darker than my own. She was a Goddess to some, but to me, she was a pain in the ass.

"Katerina . . . " I warned. "You need to leave."

She pouted, her full lips on display, trying to seduce me. "Lyon, you've been gone for so long –"

"Three days . . . my dear that's not that long." I objected. I wasn't up for her games. "Now leave so I can sleep."

She pulled herself back on the bed, her elbows resting on the deep red comforter. My room was adorned with more gothic blacks, reds and golds compared to the rest of the house.

"Well, I thought sleep was for the wicked." She flirted.

"Um, that's not how that goes. Look you need to leave, now." I was fed up and moved to push her, but she bested me in strength as I was weary and tired. She made a move to be on top of me. All I wished was for Amelie to be the one in this position. Not Katerina.

I moved my hands to Katerina's thighs, then her hips, my fingers gripping them before I chucked her off me.

"I SAID LEAVE!" I yelled. Just then the door burst open, and Alex was standing in the threshold, "Katerina, my brother said for you to go. Respect him and this family. Now!" Katerina nodded and took her leave with a sigh. She was vexed, I could sense her emotions.

Looking towards my brother, a small smile pulling on my lips, "Thanks."

He nodded with a good-natured salute and exited my room shutting the door. I rested back against the pillows, my clothes and shoes still on. I really didn't need the bombardment of Katerina. It threw me off. I sighed looking at my phone. I could text Amelie, but what good would it do if I told her I needed space? It wouldn't make sense. No. Best to rest up, get myself prepared for tomorrow night and then face everything. I kicked off my shoes and curled up into the lavish silk pillows against my skin, pretending it was Amelie's soft skin, before I passed out.

I don't remember the dreams I had or if I dreamt at all. I just knew that eventually I was being woken up with a knock at the door. Urgh . . .

"Go away!"

I could hear the door open a crack from my position in bed, "Psst, brother. It's me."

Sitting up I allowed my brother entrance, "Come in." I said, rubbing my eyes.

Alex quietly shut the door, "I'm up before everyone else. I wanted to give you some fresh clothes." He said quietly and sat beside me on the bed.

"Why are you whispering?"

Alex shrugged, "It felt appropriate; besides I don't want anyone hearing us. Look, I thought it over last night, and after seeing how Katerina accosted you – I want to help you and Amelie get back together. We need a plan to get rid of Katerina. You know once you tell everyone everything, she's going to try her hardest to get rid of Amelie. Might even resort to death . . . "

I felt my gut wrench. I didn't even think about that. "Fuck . . . " I ran my hands in my hair, "What do you have in mind?"

Alex clapped my shoulder, "Be brave, brother. Pretend you love Katerina, take her out, dress nicely for her. Just do what you need to. Understand what I'm saying? Once we figure out how to kick her out of the family arrangement, then we tell mother about Amelie. I know it sounds fucked up, but it might be the only way. You need to drop Katerina's guard."

I groaned again, "I have to sleep with her?"

Alex gave a sympathetic look, "Yes, I mean . . . pretend it's Amelie? Just give it a few weeks, okay? At least one thing is clear about the agreement, *you* have to be the one to propose. So, it's in your power. You can delay the proposal a few weeks. But anything longer than a month, and maman and Katerina's father will become suspicious. You've already wasted enough time in their eyes . . . "

How is this my life?

"Fine . . . " I gave up in defeat. "Let me get ready now."

Alex gave a reassuring look, "Just keep me posted if she does anything fishy. I'm trying to gain evidence she's not fit for the Beauchene family. As long as I can prove it with the Vampiric Court, we can get you out of this arrangement."

I wondered in that moment what my father would do. He died several years ago and now our maman was in charge, she was the eldest of the vampire clan besides my brother. If anything happened to her, then my brother would have been the next of kin to rule the Beauchene family, yet he abdicated recently, so now it all would fall to me.

"What would papa do?" I asked. Alex shrugged. "Don't know. He had a soft heart; I think he'd tell you to do what you think is right. You always have done, anyway. Just trust yourself." He then got up to let me get bathed and ready.

As soon as the door closed, I got up, running the tub to make a hot bath, hoping to God that Katerina wouldn't try to assault me in here too. Then again, I'd have to go along with it now, wouldn't I? This was horrible. Three weeks Lyon, just three weeks.

I got into the hot bath, the warm water soothing and inviting. I enjoyed these little moments, and it made me wonder how Amelie was doing. Was she having a bath too? Was Ru there to help her? A big part of me wanted to message her but I felt it would be too cruel to do that. Especially knowing I had to seduce and go along with Katerina for a short time. It wasn't fair. Yet, some urge was pulling me towards Amelie again . . . Maybe if I just let her know I was safe it might ease up her worry. Then again it might cause more pain if I disappear again. A frustrated sigh left my lips. This was so messy and complicated.

After some reflection in the tub, I got out to get dressed in black jeans, and a black button down rolled up to my forearms. I wore a chain necklace and leather strap bracelets. I put on my rings and tousled my damp hair that was curling naturally before heading down to the sitting room. It was often where we had drinks and family meetings.

My mother, brother, sister, Katerina, and a couple of family friends were there.

"Good evening, Lyon. I hope you slept well." My mother said handing me a drink and pulled me to sit beside her. Katerina on the other side of me. I inched towards my mother more, which she noticed. Her soft touch adorned my face as she moved my hair out of my eyes. "My sweet boy." She could see me pleading with her, there was something there I couldn't detect as she was so good at hiding her true feelings. Probably where I got that from.

"So, what are we all talking about?" I said moving to clear my throat and take a sip of whiskey. Alex was sitting in an armchair and his wife beside him. They smiled affectionately. "Well, you. We were wondering where you were off to, and what your plans were with Katerina." Alex said, giving me a glance that told me to play along.

I nodded, smiling softly, "I was just exploring. I needed some fresh air; I went to New Orleans. I thought maybe my band could play there in the next tour. I should speak with them soon." Which was true. Only my motive was more about Amelie than anything else.

Katerina gasped with excitement, "Oh, darling that's wonderful!" I smiled which felt more like a grimace.

"Hmmm, yes." Katerina touched my shoulder and I felt myself shiver out of disgust. I hate myself.

"What's in New Orleans though? I mean other than bugs, and humidity." She asked.

I rolled my eyes trying to make it playful, "Well, there's French culture there. It's one of my favorite cities. The Southern *cuisine* is pretty amazing." My eyes alight, thinking of Amelie's blood briefly before closing my mind to everyone. "The music gets me inspired. Which is why I think The Devil and Desire should play there this summer." I looked at everyone who seemed to be liking this idea. Good.

"But –" I heard Katerina interject, "Summer? That's in three weeks!"

I nodded. "Yes, is there something wrong with that?"

Katerina pouted, "Well, you'll be gone a long time. I'll only see you for three weeks."

I had to cut this off before she went on about engagement parties. "Darling, as you've stated you don't like New Orleans. So, it's best I go and spend time with the band, get our name out there, and then I'll be back. It'll be good for us. Besides, I can get you something nice when I come back, and we have three weeks to spend together." I brushed my thumb against her lip, she was all but trembling with desire. I looked to Alex. He smirked.

Fuck you. I said to him telepathically.

Katerina smiled and leaned into kiss me. I wanted to gag. I made it look as real as possible. I was the best actor of the family being in the arts. My mother smiled but she put her hand on mine and squeezed it. I knew that she knew something was off.

I moved to sip my drink. "Well, now that you know where I was, why I was there, can we get on with life please?" I tilted my head and stood up. "I need some air."

I went to the back garden to just get away from everyone. I was all but ready to throw up. I looked out from the back wrap-around porch to the gardens. Rose bushes, lilacs, and other beautiful flowers adorned hedges, like the garden of Versailles.

"Marie Antoinette how I wish I was you right now." I downed the last of my drink.

"Beheaded?"

I turned around to see Alex behind me. "Yes. Stick a poker in my eye, drown me, burn me, behead me. Anything but *this*." I motioned towards the house. "I hate myself for this Alex. I *cringe*."

Alex hugged me, "I know, I know. It's just for now. I witnessed Katerina's first attempt on you last night, so there's one strike. We just need two more. Then we prove to the Court she's unfit." I nodded.

"But then how do we convince them of Amelie?"

Alex put his hands up, "That's all you."

I sighed, "Right."

Well, getting one complication out of the way would make room for the next I suppose.

My eyes looked at him properly now, how he wore the finest waistcoats and oxford shirts like it was the 1900s. "I commend your style but is this modern?" I teased.

He laughed, "Hey, I like the vintage look. Besides. It's business attire now." He winked. We shared a laugh before I looked up at the sky.

"Whose going hunting tonight?"

Alex shrugged, "No set schedule. I think it's fend for yourself night." I nodded, giving him my glass and bolting at vampiric speed to go off and find something to eat.

I found myself at a vineyard in the South of France. The warmth reminded me of New Orleans. Fuck. *I wish you were here Amelie.* I thought. One day soon I would share the rest of my life with her, and I would bring her into my family name. I wasn't going to give up. It's only been one day but it feels like forever.

As I walked along the vineyard, some young drunk punks were trying to mess up the yard. Well, here we go. I lured one young man away and pulled him behind a tree, compelling him for a small drink of blood. The other college boy was getting drunk and being stupid in the middle of the field. They weren't criminals or evildoers, so I didn't think it was fair to kill them. What was the harm of a little taste? I patched them up before leaving them feeling disoriented, while I got the high of whatever alcohol they consumed. Blood trailing down my lips as I licked at them, wiping my mouth with my hand and savoring the taste before cleaning myself up as I headed home.

"Lyon!" I heard the familiar voice as I entered the house, Katerina lunging towards me for a kiss. I felt disgusting but was now in a drunken stupor from the college kid to not care.

"Where is everyone?" I asked.

She grinned suggestively. "Gone. They wanted to go hunting and give us privacy." She pulled me by the hand towards the stairs to my room. *Fuck my life.*

As soon as the door was closed and locked, she was on me like an animal. Kissing me, biting me (which wasn't all that sexy without Amelie), she grabbed my clothes, pulling at them.

I had enough of her trying to have the upper hand. "Mm mm." I shook my head before pulling her hands off and grasping her wrists. I moved her against the wall and took over.

She giggled. "You're so dominating I love it."

I really wish she'd shut up.

"Darling, I have an idea." I said pulling away. Her dark eyes big and eager to serve me.

"What is it?"

I moved to sit back on the bed and crossed one leg over the other. "I think there's some handcuffs in the basement. Wouldn't it be fun to try that?"

She gasped, "Oh my God, just what I was thinking. Yes, I'll go get it right away." She moved to leave and go downstairs. I rolled my eyes and let out a breath before grabbing my phone and texting Alex.

SMS Lyon: *Bro! Need help, she's trying to make me have sex with her. Please. I can't do this. Come home soon, save me! PS. Don't ask why we used handcuffs. It's not entirely what you think . . . I need her off of me . . .*

I hit send and then ran a hand in my hair. I hoped he'd respond before she got back. I bit my lip nervously before being notified of a reply.

SMS Alex: *Haha! Too funny. Sorry it is! But yes, I'll come home soon. Almost finished the hunt. I'll make an excuse and come save you. Stay safe!!!*

I snorted at his response. Of course he'd get a kick out of this. Maybe it if wasn't me in this situation I would have laughed too. I put my phone away beside the bed so that she didn't get suspicious before she came back.

"Okay, I got them! Took me a bit to find them. I think this is so cool you want to try this Lyon. We've been dating a while and it's nice to get to know each other's kinks and interests."

I nodded with a small smile. "Mhm." I motioned for her to come closer to me. "Now, I think you should lie on the bed, get yourself relaxed - I want to show you how much I missed you while I was away."

Total lie. I had much self-loathing.

She grinned, "Okay!" She was so eager to please me, which in one way I felt bad for, but the only person who could ever please me was Amelie. I kept my mind clear, no thoughts of anything for anyone to read.

Katerina moved to take her shoes off, and settle against the sheets of the bed, her peachy pink dress hiking up her smooth thighs. She truly was beautiful. Anyone else would be happy to have her. I wasn't. This was the tragedy of it all. I wanted my sweet witch. Katerina paled in comparison. No pun intended.

I knew I had to be brave for this. Like Alex said. I moved to hover over Katerina, her legs spread for me. Grabbing the hand-cuffs I put her arms above her head, wrapping the handcuffs around the iron bedframe. Once I got her in them, I kissed her neck, she pressed herself against me. A groan left my lips, though I was wishing it was Amelie.

"Lyon." She whispered. It was wanton and husky, but not the way Amelie was; sweet and innocent. Fuck, I need to focus. Moving from her neck down to her collarbone, her chest, my hands moved down to the swell of her breasts. I placed kisses down her stomach, my fingers inching up her skirt, revealing matching pink lace panties. They were sexy and adorable, but it wasn't the same.

Amelie invaded my mind so many times. She never left me. How I ached for her. Please hurry up, brother. Katerina moaned against me. I could smell the desire racing in her veins. "It's been so long since we did this." She whispered. I stayed silent, trying not to throw up. I kissed her feet, up her calves to her thighs. She bit her lip with anticipation of where I'd go next. I gripped her hips, pulling her down slightly and pushed her dress up above her waist. My lips pressing kisses to her hips. I didn't want to do anymore of this.

Bang.

I gasped and got up. "What was that?" I asked, looking warily towards Katerina. She gave me an apprehensive look too.

"I thought everyone was going to stay away for a while. Maybe if we're quiet, they won't know were here?"

I pinched the bridge of my nose. She really wasn't the brightest girl. I then heard footsteps.

"Lyon?"

It was Alex. Thank God!

I looked at Katerina. "I'm sorry, we'll get caught." I rushed to take the handcuffs off her when Alex walked in the door, right on time. He pretended to be shocked, "Oh shit! *Fuck!* Sorry, Sorry!" He covered his eyes. I appreciated his performance.

I sighed, "Sorry we were trying something new . . . " Katerina rushed off the bed to fix her dress, blushing slightly.

"Please don't tell anyone." She said embarrassed. She grabbed the handcuffs and shoved them in my dresser drawer.

"Uh, bye Alex." She said before rushing off to leave the house. I sighed in relief as Alex shut the door.

"Thank God. I was trying so hard not to have sex with her." I admitted. He laughed lightly. "Shut up, it's not funny." I threw a pillow at him.

He laughed harder, "It's a little funny."

I smiled and rolled my eyes before an idea popped into my brain. "Oh, can I show you Amelie? I know you wanted to see her."

He nodded in intrigue. I pulled up Amelie's webpage for her tarot business and showed him the picture on my phone. "Here."

He raised his eyebrows, "Wow! She's beautiful." He shook my shoulder with his right hand affectionately. "I can see why you love her. There's a softness to her, genuine. Something Katerina doesn't have." Katerina had only ever loved me for my beauty and status. Her family was powerful but not as powerful as mine.

We laughed at that. Then an idea came to mind.

"I was thinking . . . You know how you mentioned wanting to get another strike against her to prove to the Court?" He nodded. I made sure Katerina was actually gone before opening the door and bringing him into the library where the grand piano and my guitar were. I loved playing when nobody was around as it soothed me.

I made us each a drink from the bar cart, passing him a glass before moving to sit down.

"So, my idea," I said as I sat on an armchair and he sat opposite me, "What if we plant something on her. Like she stole something of mine . . . something valuable? Pretended like we didn't know about it, and there, strike two."

Alex nodded slowly. "Wow, you really do think of every-thing . . . but how are you going to get everyone to believe you?"

I smirked, "Who doesn't believe me? I'm a famous rock star, with loads of cash, fans, and a rich family. Besides, I'm quite convincing. Plus, I have you the big CEO of the finest winery in France, which humans and vampires can both enjoy. She doesn't have that except for her family name."

Was I savage? Yes. Did I care? Not particularly.

"I cannot do this for another three weeks. I need to get to New Orleans as soon as I can. I promised Amelie I would."

Alex quickly fixed himself another drink and mulled it over, "How would you get all these people on your side?"

I smiled, "Simple. I wear a prized possession at the concert in New Orleans. Where everyone sees it. I give it to you, you put it in her purse or something. I ask through the media who has seen it, and then boom, you find it, call a lawyer and it's done. Look, I trust you to come with me, not her. And you can get to Paris and back before me. As long as we keep our minds clear from her being able to read it, it'll be easy. Nobody can say no to thousands of fans who could see it happen and the media. She'd have no one on her side to account for it. I'm seriously desperate . . . "

Alex nodded, "I can see that."

I gave him a pleading look, "I know this sounds bad and I know it's elaborate. It's to keep Amelie safe. As you said, Katerina is volatile if I just tell her everything, she could hurt Amelie."

Alex sighed and looked at me with a serious look, "I'll do it. Because I love you. But know if this goes badly . . . "

I nodded, "I know but I'm willing to take any risks right now."

"Okay, brother. You've got me. So, now what do you want to do between now and the summer?"

I pondered this for a moment.

"Well, is it possible that your wife can take Katerina on a girl's trip or something?"

Alex chuckled again, "I'll ask her. They are kind of friends, which is surprising."

I groaned, "I don't like it."

"Hey, she's, my wife. I can't not support her." Alex chided. Just as we were finishing our drink and conversation everyone had come back home from hunting.

"Looks like everyone's back. Thank you for helping me. I really appreciate it." He hugged me again. "Anytime. I want to see you happy. I'll defend Amelie as well, if it comes to that."

I smiled, "Thank you."

It wasn't going to be easy, but I felt I had no other choice in order to defend and go after what I wanted in my life. If it meant being deceptive, savage and standing up for what I believed in, then I was willing to do it. For Amelie. For myself.

7

Three long weeks had passed. It was always the same cycle: I avoid Katerina and find ways to get back to Amelie with Alex's help. I did manage to have a band meeting, and everyone seemed on board to tour again. New Orleans hadn't been a place we played before, and it only seemed fitting to make a USA Tour. We had announced it in the media and were getting prepared. It made me feel a whole lot better knowing I'd get to see her again and to do something that I loved. On Friday evening I started packing up band equipment, outfits for the road, and organizing when a knock came at the door. It was Alex.

"Brother?" He asked.

"Come in!" I replied. I was folding some things into my suitcase as he came closer to whisper in my ear.

"Katerina's coming. She knows, I think. About Amelie. She's been suspicious of you for a while. Whatever happens Lyon, I've got your back." He clapped me on the shoulder, lifting my head to look at him, our eyes meeting.

"I've got yours too." I also clapped his shoulder with my own hand, a brother in arms gesture. Alex then went downstairs to join the family in the sitting room. I finished packing and zipped up my suitcase. Taking a deep breath. Whatever was coming, I was ready. I needed to protect Amelie, and I would with my whole heart.

With a sigh I sat on the bed. A light knock came, and the door opened. Right on schedule . . . Katerina walked in the room.

Beautiful in that superficial way, but I was no longer interested in superficiality.

She smiled softly. "Getting ready for the trip?" I nodded. She moved to sit beside me, taking my hand. "I'll miss you. Promise you'll be safe?"

I looked at her and saw she seemed to care but I couldn't be bothered. "I always am." I took my hand back from her, placing it in my lap. She frowned. I could feel her heart elevate in anger.

"Why don't you love me Lyon? How is it I'm not good enough for you?"

"Katerina, I'm not doing this." I warned her.

Her hands clutched my arms. "No! Fucking tell me! I've slaved for you for years, always the polite girlfriend to your family, always wanting to be in with you and them. How is it I'm not enough?! I'm beautiful, I'm rich, I have a name that suits yours!" All of this was pretense. All she cared about was status and how she looked, how we looked to the Court and to our families. It wasn't real love. It wasn't the same type of love I received with Amelie.

I barked a laugh, "Katerina, you are a superficial bitch! You only pretend to care because you think I'm attractive. You pretend to everyone around you! Your name and beauty mean *nothing* to me when all you are is a plastic Barbie doll. Cold, hard, plastic and unfeeling. I've felt nothing for you for a long while and you were too stupid and stubborn to see it!" I was enraged and everything was coming up. "I can't do this anymore, I don't want to marry you, I won't be forced. Not by you, your father, my mother, nobody! I want to be free to choose who I love!" All the years of repressed emotion and feeling trapped was coming out of me like hot lava.

She gasped, tears running down her face, but anger was underneath the tears. "You love someone else! WHO TOOK YOU AWAY FROM ME?!" I growled and opened the door, running out of it, her behind me. "WHO IS SHE?" She screamed. Everyone downstairs heard it, I was sure. She grabbed me trying to stop me. I pulled away and jumped over the mezzanine banister and landed on the floor below. I went to the sitting room. Katerina's footsteps close behind me.

"It's over, mother." I said before Katerina pushed me against the wall. I could hear my family gasp at the contact of my body hitting the wall.

She took my phone punching in the code, "Oh, this little human?! She overpowers me?? She's nothing, a nobody from fucking America . . . It's pathetic." She said scrolling through my phone, grinning maliciously, "I will have to go to New Orleans now, as that's why you're going right? This whole thing about the band, it's a ploy to go see her." She looked at my mother who was shocked by this whole ordeal. Yet Bridget Beauchene was known to stay calm and calm she stayed. Alex came over to us and plucked the phone out of Katerina's hand.

"Strike one, two and three, Katerina. You assaulted Lyon, stole from him, and threatened someone he cares for. And it would seem you stole his passcode to his phone as well. I don't think the Court will like this one bit." Alex winked at me.

My mother got up and went to us, "Enough." She pulled us apart and sent Katerina to the foyer of the house. "Katerina, I'm sorry but you must leave now, and I do not wish to see you back here. Get your things and leave. This marriage arrangement is over. I will deal with Lyon myself, and the Court *will* hear of this." She then looked at me, "All of it." I gulped. Was my mother going to sell me out?

Katerina grabbed her things and glared at all of us, "I will see you in Court."

I shrugged. I really didn't care. My mother squeezed my hand and pulled me into the meeting space. She looked at the friends we often had over and silently excused them with a look. Once they left Alex closed the door and then it was Maman, Alex, his wife, me, and my sister Gabrielle. The soft features of my sister's face lightened as she smiled at me, supportive and kind. It was nice to know I had family who truly cared about me and what I wanted, even given the circumstances of Vampiric Law and

Tradition. I knew I hadn't been my best self lately and I hope that she wouldn't judge me too harshly.

"Maman . . . " I went to say but she silenced me with her hand. "Let me speak."

I nodded, fearing the worst. I really hoped my own mother wasn't going to punish me for my desire to be free and love someone of my own making.

"Lyon Beauchene. I am shocked. You have been the rebel of this family, you never listened to the rules, you squandered that marriage . . . " I was bracing for it, the horrible fate I might endure. I peeked up at her behind the curtain of my hair. She smiled. "I am proud of you." I looked at her in disbelief.

"Sorry?" I asked in French.

She laughed, "I am so thankful you didn't marry that wretched woman. I am proud of how you shook her off, how strong you've been this whole time. You are the rebel of my heart, Lyon. My darling boy. I want nothing but the best for you."

My eyes started to well up with tears. This was beyond what I thought I would receive, wrapping my arms around her in a hug. "Thank you." I cried in her shoulder as she hugged me and stroked my hair.

"I should have said something centuries ago, I'm sorry Lyon to have seen you suffer for the Old Traditions. It wasn't fair." She pushed me gently to look at me and wipe my tears. "Alex has been watching from afar, telepathically communicating with what he's been seeing. As discreetly as possible. I have eyes, son. I could see it. Especially when you came back from New Orleans. I know that you did not wish to ever marry Katerina. I don't want to hold you back any more. Now, you must tell me all about this girl, Amelie, was it?"

I nodded and Alex threw me the phone to show mother the photos. It was strange to go from such a tense moment with Katerina to speaking about Amelie so candidly. "This is her, she's a human. But she's the kindest person I've ever met, maman. She treats me unlike any other person. She truly *sees* me. I've never had that. I felt an instant attraction, not just sexual but this other-worldly energy. I can't explain it."

Maman looked through the photos, "She has kind eyes. A sweet smile. I can see why you feel for her."

I smiled and took my phone back, "I know that we've never met before this, but I feel like we have. Is that weird?"

My mother squeezed my hand again, "Meet me in the library tomorrow. There's much we should discuss. For now, you don't have to marry Katerina. You can focus on the band and seeing your girl again. Then when you come back, you *must* face the Court. We need to prepare for this case. Katerina won't make it easy, and you know the laws about mixed race relationships. The Court has been very strict on its traditions for centuries. They don't like change."

I sighed, "Mother . . . I have to confess one more thing."

She looked at me with weary eyes, "What is it, son?"

I took a deep breath, "Amelie is a witch . . . "

The shock on my mother's face was exactly what I expected. I knew this wasn't what she wanted entirely, though she wanted me to be happy.

"I know it's a lot . . . " I said to her, Alex came over and stood by me.

"He's happy with her, Maman. The very least we can do is meet her. As you said, Lyon has always been the rebellious one, it's the least surprising. I think." He grinned with a wink.

My mother sighed and stood up, fanning herself almost like an aristocratic woman of the 1700s. It made me laugh a little. Gabrielle smirked at me and sat closer. "Can I see her?" she asked, reaching for my phone. "Oh, she's gorgeous! I can sense her genuine energy. Maman, you have to allow this union. I want her to be my sister!" A pout left Gabrielle's lips and I laughed.

"Well, I'm glad you guys approve. Makes me feel better."

My mother stopped her pacing and put her hands on her hips. "You are impossible, Lyon!" Her stern demeanor was back.

"I know." I replied with a smirk. "Amelie told me the same thing." We all laughed. "You'd like her, Maman. Just let me do this tour and see what she thinks of all this." I pleaded.

I could see her considering this, "Alex go with him, please."

Alex nodded, "Of course. I'll keep him in check." He nudged me playfully. I rolled my eyes.

"Okay, well now that this is settled, can I go hunt now and relax before tomorrow? I have to go on the road, I want to be prepared." I was antsy to get out of there. My mother nodded. I moved to hug her and kiss her cheek. "I love you, Maman." I said and she smiled caressing my cheek.

"I love you too, son."

Gabrielle, Alex, and I went hunting together. Stalking the streets of Paris. We were like wild, drunken college kids. Just being together. Happy. I was finally *free.* Well, almost. For now. I felt that a huge weight had been lifted since the Katerina incident at home. I knew I had a lot to answer for later, but for now, I was going to enjoy this time with my siblings.

I was to be in New Orleans within the next 48 hours and it felt exhilarating. I couldn't wait to see my beloved Amelie again. Three weeks felt like eternity. We sat with drinks in our hands from the bar on the top of the Eiffel Tower. The lights of the city illuminating our playground. I missed Paris. I just now missed New Orleans so much more knowing Amelie was there.

I gazed at my phone looking at Amelie's name in my contacts, maybe I should text her . . . Gabrielle looked over at me, her beautiful long blonde hair in a braid, a fur pink coat with a pink dress. She was such a little porcelain doll. It was cute. She had a heart of gold though.

"What are you worried about, Lyon?" She took my hand before sipping her wine. I looked over at her, while pocketing my phone. Alex was standing above us, leaning his elbows on the railing, his gray wool coat blowing in the wind. He looked down at us listening.

"I missed Paris, didn't even realize it till I came back home. Now, I miss New Orleans more because of Amelie. How can I make both places my home?"

My sister hugged me tightly, "You'll always have home here Lyon. Wherever you go. You can come back anytime. And maybe you can bring Amelie here? You can spend some time here and in New Orleans. Like . . . uhh . . . How do the English say? Summer home?"

I smiled at my sister trying to speak both languages. Even as an immortal she kept to her French roots as close as possible. She definitely would want to try for Amelie though. "Yes, a summer home would be nice in New Orleans. Get away from the snow." I nudged her playfully with my shoulder. I looked out at the city with nostalgia and finished my wine. "Let's go home, sun is coming up soon." The streetlights started to dim as the light of the sky took over the horizon.

We all headed back, Alex wrapping an arm around me brotherly. "Well, we're on the road tomorrow! I'm excited actually. I've never gone on tour with you before. I get to see all the action." He grinned.

I laughed, "Yes, just don't take it to heart if I'm everyone's affection." I teased.

He pushed me playfully and I pushed him back. "*Asshole.*" We joked and then once we were home we went to sleep in our separate rooms.

I felt so content to be free to live the life I wanted. Of course, I worried about Amelie's safety, but the Court wouldn't stand for violence. I think that's the only reason Katerina wouldn't do anything. I prayed to God for Amelie's safety. I may be a vampire, but I was Catholic at one time in my life, I felt the need to practice it again, to protect Amelie when I physically couldn't. I asked God to protect her with guardian Angels and that we would reunite soon. As I finished my prayer, I kissed the crucifix I often wore (crucifixes do not hurt vampires, that is a folklore myth due to the Catholic belief that the cross could hurt us due to our 'demonic' presence) and took a few deep breaths. No contact was killing me, and I wanted to try to reach out telepathically. I steadied my thoughts and heart on Amelie. The oddest sensations overtook me, I felt pulled towards her energy, I could feel her feelings. She seemed scared. Was she okay?

"Amelie. I'm here. You're safe." I whispered in her mind.

"Lyon? You-You're here? Am I going crazy?"

I laughed lightly, "No, I'm here, telepathically anyway. I had to make sure you were okay. I miss you."

"I miss you too. I'm out at a bar there's some creepy guys staring at me but I'm out to make friends."

I felt a sense of urgency and jealousy well up within me. I knew that Amelie was bisexual and knowing she was around beautiful women on top of creepy guys hanging around, I felt the need to mark my territory, to protect her.

I didn't say anything, but I knew she'd feel my anger, frustration, and jealousy through our telepathic link. We not only spoke in words, but in feelings and sensations. I had never experienced telepathy to this extent, and it was quite fascinating to me.

I hated the fact that I messed up so much that I could not be with her physically. But I needed to organize myself by getting out of this conflict I had with Katerina before going back to her.

As the night went on my jealousy got the best of me. I needed to sleep too but I couldn't leave the night without giving Amelie some sort of explanation as to why I left her. When she had finished her night out, I felt her tapping into my energy again, a pulling sensation on my heart and in my mind.

Her beautiful voice rang in my mind as she asked me what happened. I began explaining everything from Katerina to the struggles I felt with having all this conflict in the midst of our love life. I felt a huge weight lifted as we telepathically spoke. It seemed so silly now as to why I didn't just reach out in the first place out of ego, pride, and fear. With this I was able to sleep somewhat peacefully knowing I wasn't holding back secrets anymore and maybe I could get back to New Orleans much easier than I thought.

The next night was full of goodbyes, but there was something my mother wanted to tell me. I had completely forgotten. I met her in the library like she requested, it was just her and I. She looked regal in a deep emerald, green gown, her blonde hair in a French braid. A royal beauty. I stepped closer to her humbly. "Maman, I'm so sorry, with everything going on, I forgot you wanted to see me before I left."

She had been sitting in an armchair towards the fire, a book in her lap. She looked up at me with kind eyes. "Lyon." She said closing the book and standing up to greet me, placing her hands in mine. "There's much we need to discuss when you come back, but I wanted to get you prepared now." Her words confused me to say the least. A frown began to form which expressed what I felt. She caressed my cheek and then pulled me silently towards a table with a huge tome on it.

"What is this?" I asked curiously looking at the old thin pages, some looked burnt on the ends.

"This is our family history and all its magickal wisdom."

My eyes widened in wonder and awe like a child. "I can't believe I never seen this before."

Bridget smiled and nudged me, "We kept it from you till it was time, darling. We were human once, then came our immortal lives and with that history comes a lot of shame, guilt, and trauma. I didn't wish that for you. When you became part of this family, I knew there was something special about you. Which is why I turned you during the Revolution. I knew you'd change the world Lyon and now Amelie is a part of the picture, it is all coming together."

I looked towards her, the low ambient lighting casting a glow upon her lovely face.

"What do you mean?"

She turned to me and sighed, "Amelie and you – I think were meant to be together. To bring the two cultures together. Magick was always a part of our story. All of us. Back in the ancient days it was how we all communicated and bonded. We all knew that we could thrive as long as the mortals didn't get in the way. Witches and vampires did co-exist at one time. But it was greed, power and envy that separated us all. It is why both our communities hid in exile, creating our own government. To keep that power at bay. It's why the Court forbade a mixed lineage. Witches began hunting vampires, in retaliation, vampires began hunting witches, and then humans were hunting us both. No one is certain as to why this came about – but I would guess that someone from the witch clan was jealous of our immortality and power and sought power themselves. Back then vampire hunters were very real, unlike today, but we must be careful in case one ever arises again. Nobody truly believes in vampires even if we rule the country. I think humans of today's age are somewhat ignorant, getting lost in their own worlds to care what is going on around them. Oh, it was an awful time Lyon. Your father and I never wanted this to happen again, which is why he worked so closely with the Court. We didn't want you, Alex, and Gabrielle to ever see that."

I nodded pondering over everything. "And now, what's changed?" I asked.

My mother looked at the book and flipped a few pages. "This is an ancient prophesy that was foretold by an old Seer." The book told the story of a woman who gave birth to a child, a daughter, and that daughter grew up into a beautiful woman, the woman fell in love with a man – a vampire.

"This is Amelie's lineage, and that's you." She said pointing to the images in the book.

I gasped, "No wonder I feel so strongly for her. She mentioned something about Twin Flames . . . "

My mother nodded, "Yes, it's not very common and many people put that label on relationships but it's actually more rare than people realize. You two were chosen to be together. It had to happen exactly this way, even with Katerina involved. Otherwise, you would not have met. Katerina in a way had to teach you what you did not want."

I could not believe what I was hearing, but it made a weird sort of sense. "Why keep this from me?"

My mother's soft blue eyes met my own. "I'm sorry I did. I didn't want you to get scared and I think I had to wait until you actually met Amelie. Maybe a part of me wondered if you ever would. This prophecy is old as time, and the Court doesn't know about it. Even if they did, I doubt they would believe it. It is an ancient prophesy foretold before the Court was even established. But this is your chance for change. To bring about change to both supernatural beings and bring peace. It might even change all of humanity."

I shook my head, "Mother, I'm not some beloved savior. How is this even possible?" How could I, Lyon Beauchene be *this* man?

She closed the book and put it away before anyone else could see it. "It is what it is Lyon. You either have to accept it, or not. If you don't then I don't think Amelie and you have any chance of being back together. It is Divinely orchestrated." She shrugged. "Either way Lyon, I know you'll make the right decision and I know you love her. So do right by her, and by you."

I nodded. I wanted to tell her about my telepathic conversation with Amelie but kept it to myself for now. She came to give me a hug. "Now, go with your band, have fun, be safe. Keep me informed, alright?"

I nodded with a small smile. "Okay. I will."

We hugged again and she saw me to the front hall where I said goodbye. Gabrielle and Alex came with me to the car as we took off, the band in a bus behind us, on our way to the airport to America finally and it would only be a matter of time before I reunited with Amelie again.

Within hours we landed in New Orleans. The smell of the humid nighttime air was deliciously floral and warm. The magnolias and jasmine smelt divine. The temperatures were already rising in early June. I missed this place and the one person in it that I craved.

My brother and other crew members were putting up the outdoor stage. It was going to be an intimate gathering of a few hundred people, not the thousands I had been used to in France. I wore black leather pants with boots, silver chains on my wrists and crosses along my neck, a three-quarter length sleeved black shirt, that was open at the chest. Silver rings on my fingers. I looked at myself in the mirror of the backstage trailer that was rented for me. Blonde hair curly and sitting perfectly around my face, blue eyes staring back at me. I hadn't been on the road in a little while, I was excited but mostly, I missed Amelie.

It took everything in me to not skip the show and go to her. She should have heard of us by now, media splashes were everywhere. *The Devil and Desire* had many fans. I hoped she'd show up tonight. I hadn't heard anything from her in my mind since last night, so I assumed she had been busy with work. Surely, she'd know I was here.

I could hear the crowd getting excited for the show. My heart pounding as I looked through my phone, finding her contact and writing out "I miss you . . . " - after a moment or two I plucked up the courage to hit send, though I didn't know what would happen after . . . I didn't hear her heartbeat or smell her lovely scent I missed so much. She wasn't here. Maybe she'd come later? A lonely, defeated sigh left me as I put my phone down.

A knock at the door came and there entered my brother. "Well, brother, it's all set up. The crowds almost all packed in here. Looks like it's going to be a great show." He smiled and leaned on the little table in the trailer. He tilted his head and looked at me.

"What's wrong? I thought you'd be thrilled?"

I turned around to face him, crossing my arms. "I mean, it's nice to be going back out. But I thought Amelie would be here. I thought I'd see her again. I was hoping she'd be front row, center. You know?"

Alex laughed, "What makes you think she's not coming? She loves you."

I shrugged. "I don't feel her energy at all, and I know her, we spoke about her coming to a show. There's no way she'd not know about us tonight."

Alex got up and hugged me, "It'll be okay. Maybe she's sick? Or is busy with her job? You can always go by her apartment when it's over. For now, be the rock star that they love, and that she loves. Pretend she's there."

I rolled my eyes and chuckled, "Okay . . . " I could hear the crowd go wild as my guitarist and drummer started to tease the crowd with some opening notes.

"Good luck." Alex said and patted my back as I went out to the stage to greet everyone and put on the show of my life. The crowd was electric, the lights, the sounds, the hundreds of heartbeats. It was driving me wild, and out of hundreds of people all I wanted was the one heartbeat that could bring me everything I desired.

After the concert, I ran off the stage as fast as I could. People were screaming my name wanting autographs and photos, but I wasn't thinking about any of that. My brother told them there would be a merch table for anyone who wanted a T-shirt, pins and other types of things. I ran backstage and back behind the trailer making sure nobody saw me before I used my Flight gift to head to Amelie's.

I remembered the rooftop garden hangout I made for her. I had hoped maybe she was sitting there having a cup of tea or enjoying a good book with the twinkle lights we set up. I was almost out of breath by the time I landed on the rooftop. My eyebrows pulled into a frown. She wasn't here. No lights, no book, no tea. I went to her window, and peaked inside, lights off, no tv on, or anything. I checked the time. 11pm. Maybe she was sleeping? I knocked a few times. I heard absolutely nothing. This was strange. All her things were there but she wasn't.

I focused on my breathing, going inward and listening. No heartbeat, no breathing, no scent. Amelie simply wasn't here or in the surrounding area. So, where the hell was she? This wasn't like her. I sighed and sat on the old couch I had bought her. I texted my brother to let him know Amelie was nowhere to be found.

My heart was breaking, my mind worried. What had happened and where could she have gone? I thought about the people that knew her best. Would Ru know anything? With a frustrated sigh, I decided to just try Amelie's phone. I found our old messages and texted her quickly seeing if she was alright. After a few moments of sitting on the couch I double checked my messages, it appeared she hadn't seen my message at all. Normally she'd text back right away or within a few minutes. This was becoming ominous . . . It was as if she disappeared. Trying to contact her again might bring about danger if she was in any such situation. A frustrated growl left my lips. If only I hadn't left . . . This wouldn't have happened. *Fuck!*

Wracking my brain, I thought of any other locations she could be. She had a favorite cafe, but they'd be closed by now. Her tarot shop maybe?

I quickly used my gifts to head over there, using my phone to type in the address of her workplace. Once found, I frowned again, no lights, no neon sign that flashed. Descending down to the ground I looked through the old windows. The front and the back windows all revealed dusty books, boxes of unopened deliveries and other knick-knacks and witchcraft tools. No Amelie though. I could pick up another scent along with Amelie's, someone supernatural as well. I had a feeling it was Ru. Yet both witches weren't here. It seemed Amelie hadn't been to work in the last few weeks either. So, if she wasn't at work, or at home, where did she go? There was no use sticking around and getting into trouble.

I took a walk in the Lafayette cemetery, somewhere fans or others wouldn't find me. It was quiet, I could think. I lay under a big tree, the moon shining brightly. I looked up with childlike eyes, "How do I fix this? How do I get her back?" I asked the moon as if she had some kind of answer for me. The moon reminded me of Amelie because she too loved the night sky, the moon and the stars. They gave her answers as a witch.

Maybe that's what I needed to do? Think like a witch. Her best friend Ru might know what's going on. I just needed to find out how to contact her. She was back in New York most likely, and I didn't have the time to go there and back before I needed to leave in a couple days. I texted Alex and asked if he could do some digging on how to find Ru. For the rest of the night, I meditated and went to go feed to calm my overwhelming thoughts of fear.

Three days had passed, and I was on my way back to France. Within those three days I had played in New Orleans, Texas and Boston before I had to come back home. I was going to play in New York City to find Ru, but my emotional state was getting worse I couldn't think straight and I knew I had to go back home to plan something out. My mother might know where to look.

I pulled the USA tour, which many fans were upset about, but I said it was due to severe mental illness while I was on tour. I could not perform like this. I would refund all tickets and give them special passes for the next concert. I had enough money to do that.

Alex had been worried. I was getting agitated, depressed, frustrated, and anxious. My mind was in overdrive trying to figure out what the hell happened to Amelie. As we took the night flight home, he had been searching for any information he could on Ru, but nothing was coming up. She stayed hidden and she wasn't 'out' in the witch community like Amelie was.

Alex patted my knee, "We'll find her brother. For now, there's nothing we can do. Just relax, you'll need your mental and physical strength for the Court, remember? Katerina hasn't gone away."

I glared. "Thank you, Alex, for reminding me why my life has officially taken a shit." French sarcasm leaving my lips. Alex removed his hand and sighed. He was getting frustrated with me.

I rubbed my eyes, "I'm sorry. I just . . . I am really worried, and I miss her. Maybe maman can help us?"

Alex nodded, "Yeah, I'm sure she can. She's got tons of books and things that we don't even know about. Maybe something can shed light on Amelie's disappearance, or she might even have the manpower to track her down."

I nodded. I would have taken the whole three days to do it myself but seeing as I had other obligations, and my mental state was horrible I couldn't do it. Not right now.

As soon as we were back in France, a few hours before sunrise, I went home to go sleep in my coffin when I was feeling particularly agitated, I would lock myself up in my coffin instead of sleeping in my bed. Nobody spoke to me as I entered the house. Gabrielle and my mother observed me warily. Alex had to keep them informed of my '*state*' as he called it. I trudged up the stairs to my room and locked myself away from everyone. As I looked around me, the curtains had already been drawn and my bed freshly made, yet what I wanted was the old coffin I used to sleep in. I didn't know why, but it made me feel safer.

Changing into track pants, I found the traditional looking wood black box and climbed in. I closed the lid and let the world slip away.

I kept having weird dreams, or memories, or both. I could see myself in the 1700s, blue frock, lace and trim, the fashion of France of the time. I was in this house, but it was less modern, and I was in the ballroom, people were laughing, dancing, drinking, eating. I looked around the room and Katerina was there; she was trying to get my attention, but I ignored her. I could see my siblings dancing together in a waltz and my immortal mother and father were speaking in hushed tones. Humans and vampires were mingling together. I felt human, my skin felt different, my heart beating wildly. I hadn't felt this human in such a long time.

My eyes searching for someone . . . I saw by the drink table a beautiful brunette woman wearing a white dress, her hair done up as beautiful as Marie Antoinnette, strings of pearls in her curly hair. She turned to look at me and smiled. It was Amelie! I walked over to her, "Amelie, darling. Are you alright?"

She smiled and cupped my face, "Yes, of course! I do miss you though." She looked just the same but had the attire of someone from the 1700s, my era.

"You look beautiful." I said, taking her hand in mine.

Oh, how I missed her touch. She made me feel more human than any other person in the room.

Katerina was glaring not far from us. I pulled Amelie away from the people and out onto the balcony, the moon and stars shining brightly. She giggled, "What's this all about, dear sir?" She tilted her head with a soft smile. "You're acting rather odd."

I laughed, "Sorry, *Mademoiselle.* I just feel like you're going to slip through my fingers." I told her, my French accent thick and smooth.

"Lyon, I'm not going anywhere. I told you that. You're my forever. Always. You just need to find me. But to find me, you need to find yourself."

I frowned in confusion. "What does that mean?"

Before she could answer I woke up, gasping and I bolted out of my coffin, turning to see that Alex had broke down my bedroom door.

"Oh, hello. Why did you break my door?"

Alex sighed and ran a hand over his forehead "Because you were practically screaming in your sleep! We were worried, you locked yourself in here . . . Wait . . . You *never* sleep in your coffin . . . "

I saw my mother and sister behind him. "I just needed to be on my own, in my own company . . . I had the strangest dream." My fingers running in my messy hair to try and tame it.

My mother came forward to hug me softly, "I know, we could see flashes of it. Darling, take a bath, get dressed and come see me afterwards. We should discuss things further about Amelie."

I nodded, blinking back tears, "I - I miss her."

She nodded too, "I know. We'll sort this out. For now, get yourself levelheaded and together. She can't be helped if you're losing your head."

They all left me to my thoughts so I could collect myself. I closed the coffin and went to the closet figuring out what to wear. Everything seemed to be happening so fast and confusing to say the least.

I decided on black pants and a red shirt. Drawing a bath for myself, the heat felt heavenly, and I needed the time to mull over what I had just dreamt. Was it a past life memory? Or was this a mix of insanity and reality? Hopefully maman could help me figure this out. My chest where my heart was, felt so empty and I could hardly hear it beat. I felt that when I was with Amelie, she made me feel more alive and more human, just like my dream. I felt empty, numb and confused without her.

After some time to myself I got out of the tub, dried off and went to see my mother in the library. It was often a place for her, my siblings, and I to have vulnerable moments together. It was calming and peaceful.

Alex and Gabrielle went out to hunt to give maman and I privacy. I knocked on the big oak door and she gave me permission to enter. Taking a deep breath, I opened it. She looked up at me from a big oak table with tons of books, some as far back as the medieval ages. She smiled, "*Bonsoir*, Lyon. Please close the door and come here."

I did as she asked and moved to kiss her cheek, "*Bonsoir,* maman." She held my hand gently and pulled me to all the books. I noticed two glasses of wine on the table and the fireplace roaring.

I smiled, "Hmm, wine and books. Sounds like a peaceful night."

She laughed, "Yes, I'm sure you and Amelie do the same?" I nodded, looking a little sorrowful. She passed me the wine glass and smiled, "I even put a few drops of your favorite blood in there."

I arched a brow, "*Really*? Well, now I think I have a new favorite . . . "

My mother looked at me with a knowing look, "You drank from her, didn't you?" I nodded, shrugging, unashamed. She gave me a reproachful look.

"What?" I asked looking innocent, "She asked me to, she liked it just as much as I did." I shook my head chuckling at my mother's reaction halfway between chastisement and amusement as I drank from the wine glass.

To keep a low profile, we aimed to not kill humans as much as possible. Either drinking from blood bags, blood donors (some people would volunteer to give us their blood), or we would skillfully have small drinks from person to person to keep us fed. The older the vampire as well, the less they had to drink. I would only kill in a last resort situation. I was too moral, too Catholic to take a life just because it was my "nature" to do so.

"It is good, but not as good as hers."

She slapped me across the arm playfully, "Lyon . . . You are -"

I smirked, "Impossible. I know. She tells me the same thing." I heard her laugh and it was such a soft and beautiful sound. It wasn't often I heard my mother's laughter. "Anyway, why have you summoned me?" I asked with amusement in my tone, she scoffed,

"I *asked* you here, because I have some information on what you saw in your dreams. As I told you the story before you left for New Orleans, there is a prophecy here - and that woman you saw? That *is* Amelie, from the 1700s. She was a French woman, with some renown, but not like us. Or like you. Yet, I remember how you doted on her. I wanted you to be happy. Katerina was always trying to get in the way. Including her father. That's why you could never be. You were ripped apart by them . . . By us. Your father and I were forced to accept the arranged marriage proposal, otherwise, Katerina's father would have destroyed us. I don't know how you managed to evade marriage for this long, but it seems to be Katerina was willing to go along with whatever you decided knowing that you have more power than she does. Now that her family has no power left after the raids . . . We can fight back . . . They didn't recover as well as we did with status and financial gains. Yet, they seem to think they can beat us in Court, which is quite arrogant . . . I'm so sorry Lyon that I got in the way, you have to understand that Katerina's clan were far more powerful in numbers and strength than we were back before the Revolution . . . I won't let it happen again." She paused a moment before continuing, "Amelie must have reincarnated to finish what you two started. She just doesn't remember. And of course, she came as someone slightly different than before."

I stood there in shock, awe, and a bit of anger. "Mother, how could you? You knew how happy I was with her. I don't even remember if I was a vampire then or not. Everything seems so hazy, and I don't understand why!"

It was my mother's turn to give me a sorrowful look, "I am so sorry, my darling. I didn't want to hurt you; I was trying to save the family. And, you were a vampire then, why?" Her brows furrowed in confusion.

"Well, I felt human in my dream, or memory, whatever it was. I *really* felt human. I think she's the only thing that makes me truly feel alive. Like *myself*. I'm starting to feel like everything in life is a lie, like my dream world and real world are mixed. Why don't I remember?"

My mother reached out to take my hand that was free, "I promise never to stand in the way again, unless it is to protect you, and Lyon, back then it was. And it was to protect her. She wasn't a vampire; she was a human girl who I didn't want to see killed by Katerina's father. And I believe after Amelie's past self left you, you repressed those memories so far back that you can't remember until now. I've heard it said that with Twin Flame relationships they often forget who they are until they meet each other again. I think Amelie awakened your memories and now everything is coming up to the surface. That humanness you felt, that is how she makes you feel on the inside. Vampire or not, she loves you for who you are, not *what* you are."

I scoffed, "Well now mother, isn't that interesting . . . Seeing as Katerina wants to kill her, herself." I glowered and pulled away finishing the wine and looking at the books. "So, what? Now how can I find her and help her? Or does she even need saving?"

All these self-fulfilling prophecies were doing my head in. My life was a mash-up of memories of hundreds of years ago and this life. It's starting to feel like I'm living in two different realities melded together.

My mother sipped her wine before showing me another book, "This book tells the story of the line of witches she came from in New Orleans. It says she came from France and immigrated to New Orleans, once you were both separated in the 1700s, then through reincarnation ended up in New York. Now she's gone back to where she feels most called to. Witch covens are very powerful especially in a place like New Orleans, there's something there that's different than any part of the world I've ever known, some deep magickal tie and it's possible she might have met a coven somehow. There's no way of knowing entirely. We need to dig deeper. This book is a mix of the history and lore that's past, along with prophetic tales, but you can't just go on a whim Lyon. These witches are descendants of the ones who were against us in the raids. It won't be easy, and you can't just go there alone."

I nodded realizing what she said was true. "What's the plan then?"

She grabbed my wrists, "The best thing we can do now is to find out about her friend Ru. She could get you in, or closer to the Coven. Maybe she knows something."

Silence overtook us for a moment before I moved to hug her, "Thank you for helping me find her. I know it's not easy and I know you were only doing what you thought was best at the time." She cried softly in my chest, "I wanted you to be happy, my dear, boy. I hated seeing you so unhappy just for the sake of politics. For centuries . . . I lied to you about her ever coming back . . . I'm horrible. Please, let me make it up to you now. And to Amelie."

I nodded, pulling back to look at her, "I'm listening." I might be angry but I'm not heartless. She smiled and wiped her tears before taking a much-needed drink from her wine and I poured myself another glass.

"I have a friend, she's a witch, but one that can be trusted. She wanted all of us to co-exist peacefully, she left her coven and decided to become a solitary witch. She might know Ru's family, or her lineage. I can get some information and see where we can go from here. Be patient. It will take time. We are figuring it out and I will let you know as soon as I hear from my friend." I sighed, nodding in silence.

It then dawned on me, we are in the age of technology, "Mother, why don't we just try to electronically reach out? I know you don't like a lot of the human advancements, but Alex and I could always figure it out. Wouldn't that be faster? And less of a pain for everybody?"

My mother seemed rather embarrassed as she gave a little bit of a sheepish smile, and if she could blush, I'm sure she would have. "Oh, yes, I suppose you are right. I'll still see if we can gain more information outside the internet, as you've said Ru seems to be a little "off-the-grid" at least with witch covens, but if you think it's best maybe there's a way to connect." I laughed lightly taking her hand, "Let me ask Alex and see what we can find."

The rest of the night Alex and I researched Ru's whereabouts. Although we didn't have her full name, there weren't many New Yorkers named Rouge. We hoped this would narrow down our search. Yet, my mind would drift to thoughts of Amelie and how she was doing. I needed to know she was safe. I wondered if telepathy would work again, since texting didn't seem to do anything. I needed to let her know I loved and missed her, and that I was going to come back for her. I just needed to know where she was. I really hoped that Katerina hadn't tried anything, though if she was afraid of the Court then she'd stay clear of Amelie. Yes, our government kept strict laws to keep us from going feral, ever since the Revolution and raids we couldn't keep piling up bodies and expecting no fallout. I was determined to do what I had to do to find the love of my life and to keep her out of harm's way.

The Separation Part 2: Amelie's Demise

8

It had been two days since Lyon left. Since my heart shattered in two. Ru was here with me, sleeping on the couch. We had gone out a couple nights ago in New Orleans to check out the bars and walk around the streets. I could feel all the energy here, the ghosts, spirits who never left the earth. Yet somehow that made me feel a little less lonely. It was like I had friends on the other side, ones that wouldn't judge me, that I could tell all my secrets too and they'd just listen. My heart felt a little less empty and having my best friend here helped a lot too.

With a yawn, a messy bun and freshly brushed teeth I went to make coffee. The sweet sounds of the coffee percolator and the smell of freshly ground coffee permeated the air. It roused Ru from her slumber. A soft moan had left her lips as she stretched and sat up.

"Mornin'" she smiled groggily and got up to meet me at the island table.

"Morning to you too, sleepyhead. I hope my couch was okay, I know it's not the best accommodation."

Ru shook her head and gave me a hug, "No, it's great. Better than spending on an Air BnB." She grinned before going to the bathroom to freshen up. I waited for the coffee to brew, my eyes scanning over to the window. The sun was beautifully illuminating the trees, the plants and nature all around. It was a warm day; summer was finally upon us. I sighed looking at my phone. Part of me wanted to text Lyon or send him a message on the blog but I kept fighting with myself. Ru said I needed to not give in to the temptation of chasing him. She knew as well as I did, if not more, that he would come back when the time was right.

It was hard to even agree with the Divine at this point, I was hurt, angry, and confused. I loved Lyon with my whole heart, and I didn't ever want to let him go. I had never been in love like this before. Ru promised to help me understand it, so we planned on going to my work. I needed to organize some things and I had a few new shipments coming in for the coming weeks.

The percolator beeped which made me jump, taking me out of my thoughts. Ru came back out of the bathroom freshly changed and cleaned up. She had her hair down in her beautiful curls, a simple white T-shirt and ripped jeans. "You okay girl? You look startled." she asked me with a quizzical look.

I shrugged. "I was just thinking . . . " I turned to pour the coffee into the mugs and put them on the island for us to add sugar and oat milk or cream.

Ru sighed sliding into the chair across from me, "About him?"

I nodded. I grabbed two teaspoons and passed one to her, before adding my own sugar and oat milk. "Yeah . . . I just miss him."

She smiled and patted my hand, "Hey, it's totally okay to miss him. He's your guy, your twin flame. You can't ever forget him. You just gotta start working on yourself, that's what he's gotta do too. This is completely normal for twin flames. I know it hurts, it sucks, but each day it will get a little easier. It'll feel less painful and get a bit brighter. But it's up to you to put your mind and per-spective where it should be."

I nodded again grabbing my mug and sipping my coffee. *Ahhh.* It tasted so good.

"I know Ru. I just need to wrap my mind around everything. It's a lot."

She nodded in response, "It is. But honestly, you're lucky. Not everyone gets a twin flame, not everyone gets that type of rela-tionship, or that healing. It's predestined and nothing or nobody can stop it. So, if you look at it like that, it's not so bad. As long as you research, do the work on you, everything will work out as it's supposed to."

I smiled softly, "You're right, it's easier said than done, but he's worth it. Every tear, all the pain, all the love, he's worth every bit of it."

She smiled back, "And so are you."

We spent the rest of the morning chatting, having coffee and getting ready for the day. I wore black ripped jean shorts, converse and a purple tank top, my hair still in my messy bun. I paired my outfit with a couple of vintage and ornate necklaces and rings. I wanted to try and look my best in case anyone came into the shop wanting a reading. Lyon was right. I did need to catch up on my work.

Once at the shop, I unlocked the gate, and the door and turned the lights on. Ru looked astonished, "Wow, this is amazing! All Victorian and gothic! Very you."

I grinned up at her, "Yup, and all mine. I love it."

There was an old chaise lounge couch against the wall on the right side, a old antique mirror above that, old pictures of witches and Victorian families on the walls. A witch's hat in the corner above a shelf with all kinds of books, spell books, ornaments, and pendulums hanging from the wall. Other shelves had an assortment of tarot and oracle cards, pendulums, spellcasting items etc. It was a home for a witch, a psychic or a person who was into that sort of thing for fun.

I sat at my oak wooden desk and started to organize the cash register and debit machines. Ru perused the shelves and then came back wearing a witch hat. "How do I look?"

I laughed as I looked at her, "Perfectly witchy. You can keep it on while you're here if you want. I think it would be fun."

We both chuckled and started on organizing. She helped dust the shelves and put things back where they were supposed to. She then sat with me to help me understand things more with the journey I was on with Lyon.

"Ru?"

"Yeah?"

"Can you do a reading for me? I want to know what he's going through. How he feels about me. I'm too afraid to do it myself. I'm too anxious."

She smiled and nodded, "Sure." She grabbed an open box of tarot cards that I had for myself. We moved to the back of the shop where I had a table set up for readings.

I took a deep breath as she shuffled the cards and splayed them out onto the table.

3 of Swords. Judgement. The Lovers reversed. 4 of Cups.

I watched as she arranged them and then sighed, "Well, it looks like he's going through a hard time. A breakup of sorts. He's not interested in any kind of offer right now. It's potential that he's seen someone before you, or at the same time as you." A pang of pain entered my heart as she said that. I had no idea he had someone else. "He's not happy." She added. She then looked at the bottom of the deck.

"On the bottom is the 3 of Cups . . . I'm hearing '*third party*'. I think Lyon and you have a third-party situation he's trying to get out of. It seems with Judgement, that he's asking the Divine for help or something. He might be balancing karma right now, which is why you needed to separate for now."

I nodded, wiping my silent tears. "Okay, okay . . . That makes sense, I guess. I just don't know why he didn't say anything. He told me he wasn't used to being loved the way I loved him . . . He also said he had matters at home to attend to."

Ru nodded in a pensive way. "That could be what he was trying to express." She rubbed my back before putting the cards back into the deck and reshuffling. "Let's see what his feelings are for you." she said as she continued to shuffle. I bit my lip nervously as she did so. My hands gripping the wooden chair I sat on. Cards started flying out everywhere.

The Lovers upright. The Star. Knight of Cups. The Empress.

"Wow!!! Girl, he loves you! He sees you as a Star, a Goddess. You're definitely on his mind and he cares a lot about you. He wants to make you an offer of love, but I think he feels you're out of his league. This all makes sense. He wants to be the man you need, and you both are going through some karmic releasing. Don't worry. He will be back; I can feel his energy. He's very sensual and strong."

I smirked, "I know." I laughed a little and smiled down at the cards.

"Regardless of this third party situation, he's really trying to get out of it, he's heartbroken but he is working his way back to you."

She checked the bottom of the deck. "Justice. Yeah, see? Archangel Michael is this card, and he's bringing in balance, truth, clarity and protection. You both just need to balance things out. You need to focus on you, your healing and your work."

I sighed with a nod. "Yeah, I know. Lyon said the same thing too."

She packed up the cards and put them back on my desk. I went back to the front and turned on my open sign and started to research more about twin flames on the computer I had at work.

"It says here that telepathy can happen, smelling their scent, having lucid dreams can happen. I started having telepathy with Lyon while he was here . . . but these other explanations haven't happened yet. If they do, I'll let you know." I said looking over at Ru who was reading a book about witches and covens.

She looked at me over her book, "That's good! Well, I was thinking . . . " She closed the book and put it beside her. "Why don't we try to find you some friends in the city? Maybe some witch friends? I'm only here for a short time and I think finding a community of likeminded people would really help you."

I thought on this for a moment as I leaned back in the computer chair, "Yeah, that might be nice. I'll definitely check out some groups online."

She smiled approvingly. "Alright, it's a start. Just remember, focus on yourself. It's okay to miss him, but try not to stay stuck in the pain. Release and heal. There's lots of meditations and journaling you can do. I recommend both, and as you know, crystals are healing too. You have tons here."

I smirked, "Maybe I can yoink a few."

Ru let out a laugh that filled the air, "Hey, it's your business. It's technically not stealing."

I went to grab a little satchel bag and found Citrine, Amethyst, Obsidian and Rose Quartz. All to help with healing, confidence, self-love, protection, and cleansing. I grabbed a couple of candles and put them in my bag.

"Let's go have lunch. Nobody's come in for the last three hours." I said slinging my purse over my shoulder. I had managed to make some money with the customers I had acquired over the last few days but since I was still building up my client base things were slow. I knew it would take time and I had to keep posting on Instagram, my website, and put myself out there physically for people to see me. It wasn't easy.

She grabbed her bag too, "Great, I'm starving."

We locked up the shop and put a *Be right back. On Lunch* sign on the door before going to find a decent restaurant to grab a bite to eat. My mind kept thinking of Lyon and how I wished he could be with us too.

"It's too bad you never got to meet him . . . " I said as we walked towards a southern restaurant.

Ru rubbed my back affectionately, "I will. When he returns you best tell me because I will hop a train, a plane or anything to get back here."

I smiled, "Thanks love."

We headed into the restaurant and sat at a booth seat as we waited to be served. I was excited to try some southern cuisine that I had longed to try before I left New York. Ru was right, and so was Lyon. I had to try my best to work on myself, to do the things I always wanted to do. Maybe this separation as they called it wasn't as bad as I had initially thought. Maybe it was a way for me to complete the things I needed and wanted to do while being an independent female. That was a blessing in itself, wasn't it?

Though the pain of missing him was often there and I tried my best to hold it together, but I knew too that if I didn't feel my feelings, I would just resent him and myself. This was a new way of being, a new way of loving and I owed it to myself and him to try.

In the days that followed, with my time with Ru, I decided to do what she suggested. To make friends. I was tired of being alone, and especially now that I was learning more about myself not only as a Divine Feminine partner, but as a witch. I researched about the things I could do: fire magick, clairvoyance and claircognizance.

I noticed that the more I learned, the more I wanted to tap in. The more I wanted to meet people like me. And not just some wannabe Wiccan, or Pagan. Cloaks and daggers just wasn't my cup-of-tea.

My phone vibrated beside me on the bed, jolting me out of my research. I looked down at the phone and smiled, Ru had safely landed back in New York. She had to go back to work, and well, the same was for me too. I had neglected so much of it because of being caught up with Lyon and all the things that came with this relationship. I knew in my heart of hearts that he'd be disappointed if I let things slip, and honestly? So was I. I had to get my head back in the game, to make my business a success and to actually make friends. Upon my research I found that there was a girls' night in the same bar I had taken Lyon. It seemed like a good idea. Drinks, food and possibly new friends!

I replied back to Ru telling her about the good news and that I was happy she landed safely. Closing my laptop and putting my phone back on the bed, I went to grab some fresh clothes and go for a shower. I was determined to not let life pass me by and to go out and mingle. Though of course my mind went to Lyon. Wishing he was here with me. My heart hurt slightly, feeling his absence. Though I knew that things would work themselves out in the end. I knew he was worth every ounce of pain and love inside of me - because I was also worth it too. This wasn't just about him anymore, it was about me, and my relationship with myself. All would be well, and I knew Spirit had my back. If my research and tarot readings didn't say it, my heart and soul definitely did. That's what I had to trust the most.

After my most invigorating shower I had changed into a beautiful deep blue dress, it hugged all my curves and came just below the knee. It was short sleeved and had a V neckline that wasn't too plunging. I did my hair up in a messy bun, my bangs going to the side as they grew out. I put on a silver necklace with a key pendant on it. Keys seemed to be symbolizing my life at the moment. I had been seeing them in visions, meditations and in tarot readings. I learned that not only was I the key to Lyon's heart, but the *key* was my symbol of new beginnings in life. Looking in the mirror I did a double take to make sure I was presentable. Once satisfied I pulled on my heels, reached for my bag to lock up the apartment and grab a cab. My heart pounded in my chest every moment that I was getting closer to the bar.

The car stopped just outside the entrance, I thanked the driver, paid and got out. I noticed right away a couple of guys outside having a smoke. They looked me up and down, but I tried my best not to pay attention. Anxiety invaded my chest as they leered at me . . . It was then I felt Lyon's hand in mine. I looked over to my right as I felt his energy. It was like he was protecting me all the way from France. Part of me wanted to believe it was a trick of my mind since I missed him. Yet, my heart was telling me this was real. Why else would I physically feel his hand in mine?

I took a deep breath.

'Don't worry, I'm with you.'

I gasped. Lyon's voice . . . he's in my head? Wait . . . we have telepathy from this distance? I remembered my research when Ru was here that twin flames indeed had telepathy with each other even across the globe. Though my logical brain couldn't keep up saying I was being so obsessive that it lead to insanity. I then heard a chuckle in my head. His chuckle.

'No. You're not going crazy. I'm here.'

I nodded my head. Okay, this *is* real. He can speak telepathically . . . All the way from France . . .

Impressive. Or creepy? Maybe both?

Another laugh chimed inside my mind. 'Sorry.'

I sighed and couldn't help but smile a little. I thought of him and directed my thoughts towards him.

'I'm glad you're here. I miss you. To be honest, I can't even be mad at you. I'm trying to make new friends like you said.'

I could see an image of him in my mind's eye (the third eye), his smirk, those beautiful blue eyes. He was standing right in front of me, his hand still in mine.

'I know - I always know where you are. I see you. It's strange, like I can imagine what you're doing.'

I laughed lightly, the two men giving me weird looks now. *Ha! Yes, go ahead, think I'm crazy. Stay away from me, weirdos.*

I could see Lyon laughing, that bright beautiful smile on his face. I smiled softly back.

'Go have fun. I'll be right beside you. Always.' He said with a loving tone.

It was really nice having him back with me in some way. To hear his laugh, see his smile in my mind. It was comforting to know someone was looking out of me. Even if I physically had to take care of myself it was still nice. I walked into the bar, the loud music playing, girls mingling and talking. I saw tables set up with different kinds of food and drinks. It was a nice vibe. No creepy weird guys here to try and pick me up. Just women like me wanting to find friends.

I found a redheaded woman, she was a few inches taller than me, slender and had a lovely face. She was beautiful and had an enchanting aura. She was setting some things up on the table.

"Hi, my name's Amelie. I came to the event you posted about online. I just moved here, looking for friends." I said with my hands clasped in front of me, I could feel the impending social anxiety.

She had turned around after putting the plates down on the table. Different types of snacks, and some even shaped into witch hats and ghosts. I was definitely in the right place. With a smile she acknowledged me and took my hand.

"Nice to meet you, so glad you could come! I'm Selene. Welcome to our Witchy Girl's Night. New Orleans is the perfect place for people like us."

I smiled wide, "Yes, it is. I actually have a shop down the street, I read tarot."

Selene gave a cute squeal of excitement. "Oh yay! Well, you are in the best place, Amelie. Let me get you a drink. Go ahead, grab some snacks, and I can introduce you to some of the other girls." I nodded with a smile.

Finally. I was in a place with the same like-minded people, I felt safe, at ease here. I turned to grab some snacks and almost burst out laughing, hiding a smirk as I saw Lyon leaning against the wall looking sexy. He was trying to get my attention in my mind.

'Stop sending me distracting thoughts Lyon.' I teased telepathically. 'I'm trying to look normal . . .'

His deep chuckle came to my mind again, 'But you're not normal.'

I sighed in response. He put his hands up in surrender and disappeared. I hope I hadn't offended him, but I think he could understand my position.

I grabbed whatever snacks I wanted: nachos, cookies, cakes, bread and dip. I was starving and I never say no to free food.

The night was pretty chill, the music was good, the food even more so, and the company was great. Selene had introduced me to the other girls, and I found out they were a part of a real magickal witches coven. Each one had different powers. We sat around the bar and got to know one another and spoke about our experiences as a witch. I was happy enough to listen to them and then there came a quiet lull. Everyone was looking at me. Selene who sat beside me gave me an encouraging smile.

"You can tell us Amelie, you're safe here. And our number one rule is that none of us talk about our experience out of the witch coven or any event."

I smirked, "Like witches anonymous?"

The other girls laughed, "Something like that." A dark-haired girl, who had Asian decent responded, a smirk on her lips. She obviously understood my humor which was great. I found out her name was Ali. I noticed how her hair tumbled down her shoulders in such an elegant way. Come to think of it, all these girls were hot. What was going on?

"Okay, so first thing I need to ask you all is, how the hell are you all so hot?"

The group giggled, "Well we are just naturally beautiful, and glamour magick allows us to become even more magnetic. So, we're glad it works." Selene answered my question and nudged me playfully.

"So, anyway." I cleared my throat and focused on them. "I'm from New York, I moved here to New Orleans to get more aquatinted with my witchy side. My family never truly understood it, so it's really nice to be a part of something bigger than me. My best friend Ru is also a witch back home. She's the one that suggested I come find my tribe."

The girls smiled and Selene took my hand in an affectionate way, "We're really glad you came here too."

Then the old clock above the bar struck midnight and the girls stood up.

"It's the Witching Hour. We need to go home, it's customary that we protect our home from malevolent spirits. Hope you have a good night, and I'll text you sometime soon. Usually we have a show-and-tell night with new witches." Selene rushed to get my number and start packing up. I could feel the tension in the air. It almost felt like a Cinderella moment of them needing to get home before turning into a pumpkin.

I looked at Selene and Ali with a quizzical look, "Show-and-Tell?"

They nodded, "It's where we show each other our abilities. We host it on the next full moon. Be prepared for the invite. It was great to meet you. Get home safely." Ali said and gave me a hug after I got out of the booth seat. I could feel my anxiety rising as I felt Lyon's anger brush past me energetically.

I grabbed my things and called a cab to get home safely. Once I was, I changed into black leggings, a tank top, I grabbed my wine bottle and a glass, heading to the rooftop garden. I wasn't ready to sleep yet. As soon as I set up the lights and sat down to pour myself a glass, I felt Lyon beside me – energetically of course.

"So, I suppose your night went well?" he asked, his tone slightly envious. I felt his hand on my thigh, and I placed my hand on the same spot feeling his phantom touch against my own.

"Lyon, yes, those girls are hot, but they're just new friends. I barely know them. But you're the only one for me. I think they put a spell on me or something. Cause honestly? Nobody compares to your beauty, or your soul. I mean that." Tears started welling up behind my eyes. I felt bad that I made him feel negatively. I heard him sigh in my mind.

"I'm sorry Amelie. I know you're making friends and I'm glad you found your kind of people. That's a good thing and I am proud of you for doing that. I think I'm just jealous because I can't be with you right now and I miss you. Things are so fucking complicated, and I am angry with myself."

I heard his monologue as I sipped my wine, feeling the warm June air on my skin. The crickets in the background, stars up above and the moon shimmering, her glow upon me. I smiled.

"I did have a great night. Of course I missed you too. I wish you could be here. You never really explained why you left . . . "

I took another gulp of wine knowing I'd need it to hear the honest truth from the one I loved.

He turned towards me; I could see him in my Mind's Eye as clearly as if he were here. "I - I was engaged to someone before I met you. It was an arranged marriage proposal by my vampiric family and Katerina's. She wanted me more than I wanted her . . . for a time, I was happy with her, or at least complacent. Then things started to change, my feelings weren't what they were before and ever since I met you, I knew I had to change things. I'd never been in love like this or have been loved like you love me. It scared me. I didn't want to fuck it up and then I did just that. I should have told you, but I was scared of you leaving me too. So, I ran."

I nodded hearing these things, feeling the weight of it in my chest. It hurt. My eyes tearing up more, I couldn't help but cry. My right hand clutched the wine glass tightly as my eyes looked downcast.

"I can feel your pain. You cry, I feel it. When you're happy, I feel it. We feel each other and please know that it is true, what I feel for you . . . no matter what it looks like, no matter what my mouth says or if I don't say what I feel, it's not because of you. It's because I'm scared and I'm trying to figure it out. I am working things out I promise."

I could feel a tingly feeling against my lips. I gasped. He kissed me. "Lyon . . . " I sobbed, "Please tell me what's going on now. I know from what Ru said in her tarot reading that you're heart-broken and . . . Well, everything you just said, she said too. I can't ignore my pain over this, but I can understand why you did it."

He sighed, "I have been running away from Katerina for a long time, *chérie*. It just blew all up in my face, and you were the start of that. It's not your fault. I'm not blaming you. It's actually what woke me up to the truth. God's miracle, if you can believe vampires get those."

I chuckled softly and wiped my nose with the back of my hand, feeling utterly disgusting. I then felt a touch on my cheek, "Amelie, you are beautiful to me no matter what you think. Even crying you're beautiful. I love you, always. Just trust me that I am doing what I can for us. There's a lot of politics involved in this arrangement, and I always hated the Vampiric Court for all this. I guess that's why I became a rock star, to rebel." He smiled softly which made me smile.

"Yeah, I can see that. So, what's happening with Katerina now?" I almost choked on her name. I hated it.

"The engagement was called off finally. Her family is trying to sue mine. I must show up at the Court at some point. It's a big political mess. Just trust me, okay? Can you do that?"

I nodded. "Yes, I can. And I always will."

I felt his energy of love surround me and then he was gone. But I knew he wasn't really gone. He was always a part of me, inside of my heart. I sighed, finishing my wine and wiping my tears. At least the truth was out. Though I knew I'd have to go through some painful challenges and heal from this. Katerina was not in my good graces, and I hated her for taking the one person in my life that changed it forever. I knew I had to forgive that, and heal, but right now, I was angry, and I hated her for it. She probably hated me too, for the same reasons, but if she attacked Lyon, I would defend him.

If anything happens to Lyon, I will come for you.

I grabbed my things, locked up my apartment, did my sage cleansing, protecting my space and headed to bed. The next days and weeks wouldn't be easy, and I had to be ready for them.

For the rest of the week, I decided to learn more about self-care. To meditate, go for nature walks and take beautiful and invigorating 'witch' baths. Which basically were baths with essential oils and herbs with different correspondences to them. Cinnamon for love and protection, orange slices for cleansing and invigoration, mint for prosperity. The more I learned about these things the more excited I was to practice magick full time. I lit my candles by magickal intention now instead of a lighter, I drank different herbal teas that were like mini potions to help with self-love or healing. It was a beautiful experience. Though I did miss Lyon . . . We hadn't talked telepathically for the last two or three days. I had begun to wonder if I hurt him. I'd get so anxious that my heart would physically hurt.

I learned throughout all my twin-flame research and experience that the Divine Feminine, which was me, was the one to heal core wounds within herself, and it was completely normal to miss him, because he was my other half (quite literally) and so it all came down to self-acknowledgement and self-care. I began journaling by the fireplace after work, meditating before bed, and opening myself up to any visions that might occur. Tonight, I had hoped that I'd see Lyon again, that we could work things out.

Sitting in my pajamas with a wrap sweater, I was about ready to meditate in bed when I heard my phone go off.

It was Selene! It was 10pm on a Wednesday and I wasn't expecting a text so late.

[SMS: Selene]: Hey Amelie! I know it's late but we're doing the show-and-tell tonight at midnight! You better get ready and get your ass over here! I'll send you the deets. - S

I frowned in confusion and shock. They really expected me to show up in two hours?? I sighed and texted back that I'd be getting ready to go over. I really didn't want to disappoint. *There better be coffee . . .*

As soon as I confirmed with Selene I ran to the closet and dresser to find some decent things to wear that wasn't overly dressy. I grabbed a pair of black high-waist leggings, and a black long-sleeved shirt that had a bit of a V-neckline. I grabbed underwear and all my essentials before hitting the shower. The warm water was so relaxing and part of me wanted to just stay home. However, if I had any chance of getting into the coven and really getting to know these girls, I had to do what they said for now. It seemed Selene was one of the nicest girls apart from Ali, so I u7 to get to know them better.

'It's not because you find them attractive now, is it?'

Lyon! I smiled hearing his voice and laughed, 'No, it's not because of that. I just want to make friends. Where have you been hiding?' I asked in my mind as I washed my hair. I could feel Lyon's energy with me, as if he was standing in the shower with me.

A chuckle sounded in my head, 'You missed me?'

I nodded, 'Uh-Huh. Sure did. I thought I did something wrong after our last . . . talk . . . ' I began to rinse my hair, grabbing conditioner to set into it as I finished up my body routine.

'No, darling. Not at all. I just wanted space to clear the air, and I needed time to think. Katerina is out of the house now, and my family is happy to see me happy. I've spoken to them about you, showed them a picture. They like you.'

I beamed with a bright smile as I finished up the shower, grabbing a towel and stepping out of the tub. I could see Lyon standing in my bathroom in my Mind's Eye. Beautiful blond in black. As usual.

'I'm glad they like me. I hope to meet them one day. I wish I could touch you, hug you, kiss you. God, I just miss you so much.' I could feel myself tear up as he hushed me in my mind,

'Shhh, it's okay. Things will go back to normal soon. Be careful with those witches, okay? They may seem great but keep your guard up. I'm not just saying that because I'm a vampire. I just want you to be safe. Take care of yourself, for I can't.'

I nodded as I dried off and wrapped my towel around my head. 'I know, I will. I love you.'

And then he was gone so I could get on with getting ready. I could understand his concern especially since he wasn't here to physically see what was going on. Only what his *remote viewing* and telepathy would show him. I learned through research of this particular power, that all that between us was remote viewing and some witches have that ability, where you can see in your mind a snapshot of what that person is doing, a form of visualization. As I finished getting dressed, I tried to somewhat style my hair. I didn't want to look like I just got out of bed. I added a little bit of mascara, eyeliner, and lip gloss before grabbing my things and pulling on my converse sneakers. No way was I wearing heels tonight.

I texted Selene to let her know I was on my way and ordered a cab to the address given. My mind ran wild with possibilities of what tonight would hold. Checking the time, I noticed it was 10:45pm, I had just over an hour to get there on time.

The cab drove through the New Orleans streets at a comfortable speed, the moon lighting up the city, I could see people partying, laughing, having fun, the neon lights were beautiful and comforting, I could practically hear the buzzing of them. For a Wednesday night it was pretty busy, almost like nightlife never stopped. I might have also seen a ghost or two among the humans. As they say, you are never alone in New Orleans.

Soon I was in front of the huge house that I was summoned to. It was a huge colonial style home with a big black gate in the front. I paid the cab driver, thanked him, and pulled out my phone, the cell service wasn't great but at least I had a couple bars. I looked towards the house, I could see the lights through the big bay window and candles flickering as well.

[SMS]: Gate is open.

My phone scared me out of my thoughts. Selene had texted me. She must have seen me coming. It was now 11:45pm. Just in time. I pushed the creaky iron gate and then latched it behind me, going up the little lane way to the stairs. As I walked towards the house and up the colonial style porch, I could see ivy wrapping its way around the impressive white columns and over the wraparound porch banister. This was definitely a New Orleans home. It was three stories high, but wide enough to house probably four or five bedrooms.

I could practically feel the magick oozing out of the home. I wouldn't be surprised if a ghost or two lurked in the area either. Laughing and soft music caught my attention before entering. Taking a deep breath, my hand turned the door handle to open it.

"Hello?" I asked, peering into the house and closing the door. Ali and Selene came over and hugged me. "You're here! Just in time girl. Here have a pick me up." Ali said with excitement and gave me a cup of tea. "Coffee will energize you too much, so tea is more appropriate especially with magick involved."

She said as she handed me the teacup, I took it gratefully. Even though the summer nights were warm, I still welcomed the warm cup in my hands, as they were always cold.

"Thanks." I said with a smile.

Selene smiled and wrapped an arm around me, "Please sit, have a snack, talk to the other girls and we'll start shortly." I nodded and sat on an antique-looking couch, very similar to the one Lyon bought me.

I wasn't sure what to expect but I definitely was nervous. Taking a sip of tea an crossing my legs I watched as the other girls had fun, laughing and chatting. A blonde girl came over to me and sat down, "Hi! You must be the newbie witch. I'm Delainey." She had a Southern accent definitely from here.

I smiled softly. "Nice to meet you, Delainey. I'm Amelie." She smiled wide and shook my hand. "I'm one of the newest members besides you, I hope we get along. It was so nice to find my soul sisters here. Where are you from?" She obviously could tell I lacked a Southern accent.

"I'm from New York but I live here in New Orleans now."

She excitedly bounced on the couch. Definitely a sorority type girl. "Oh wow, The Big Apple huh? Must be nice. I've never really been farther than Tennessee." I nodded, trying to be polite but I wasn't so sure I'd really bond with this one.

Selene smirked at me and mouthed, 'I'm sorry'. I could tell that she knew how I was feeling, and I sent a smile her way. While sipping my tea, Delainey patted my hand, "Well, do enjoy the night and we'll talk soon."

Off she went to go talk to another young girl. I sighed in relief. Delainey was nice, but too much for me. There was some kind of off vibe I was getting from her, almost like she was trying too hard to be nice to me, or to include me, I sensed a bit of envy for sure. Selene and Ali on the other hand were more chill, calm and cool.

After that energetically draining conversation I went to the snack table, perusing the assortment of sweets, and treats. I decided on a strawberry tart, grabbing a small paper plate and munching on the sweet treat in bliss. Ali came up to my right side and startled me, as I was having too much fun eating the delicious sweetness of the fresh strawberries on top of the tart, "Wow, are you gonna marry that thing or what?" She smirked over at me.

I blushed and giggled as I finished what was in my mouth "Um, no? I just really like strawberries. Also, I hadn't eaten since earlier today." I wasn't expecting to be invited to a witch party in the middle of the night.

The black-haired woman nodded, "I feel ya. It's really good and made with magick." She winked as she popped a chip into her mouth.

My eyes went wide, "Really?"

She laughed at my reaction, "Yes, most things are easily blessed with magick. Herbs, spices, and intentions of what you want all goes into food. That's why it tastes so good. You can't get *that* in a store, now, can you?" She made a fair point. I finished up eating before grabbing the tea I left on the table and finished it as well.

"Will we be able to eat afterwards?" I could sense the room was growing restless, like it was time for the festivities to really begin.

Ali nodded, "Yup, it's not goin' anywhere." She hugged me around the shoulders.

"Okay." I smiled softly, like an innocent child not knowing where to begin. This was all so new to me, even though I knew of my own abilities – but to share them with others, especially other witches, that was a new start.

Selene in all her red-headed beauty clapped her hands to get our attention, "Ladies! It is midnight, let us begin! We will be doing our show-and-tell in the basement, then a little moon-bathing ritual in the backyard, to get us all charged up again, and then we can mingle, have food and you are all welcome to stay the night or we can figure out rides home etcetera. So, let's get started!" She grinned over at me and took my hand. "Come, I will show you the ropes and don't be scared. You're in a safe place."

For some reason I believed her. Selene made me feel safe, comforted and I felt a sort of odd attraction to her. It wasn't weird because she was a woman, I was bisexual after all, but it seemed almost unnatural in the way I felt so submissive to her. Ali did say there was a glamour magick on all of them, well at least Ali and Selene who were the leaders here. There were a few others I hadn't met yet. Maybe I would later.

My chest heaved in a bit of anxiety and nerves, my hand going sweaty in Selene's soft warm palm. She squeezed my hand as she led us all down a hallway through the kitchen and down wooden steps that lead to the basement. It smelt of dust, old wood and brick. At least it was a finished basement with laminate floor-ing and not the gothic dungeon I had made up in my mind. I noticed an old black antique gothic wardrobe sitting in the right corner. Selene let my hand go to open it up with an old-fashioned key to pull out all of her magickal tools. My eyes pin-pointed on sage bundles, chalk, salt and other things that her body wasn't obscuring.

When she turned around, she had sage and chalk in her hands. Ali went to grab an assortment of candles and a lighter from the same wardrobe. They knew what they were doing and were con-fident in every action taken.

I watched around me as most of the girls were familiar with this but other than me, there may have only been one or two new girls. Delainey was one of the newer ones, but she seemed to be fitting in pretty well and not as nervous as the rest of us, if anything she was bouncing on her heels in excitement. My eyes then caught Selene and Ali who had everything laid out on the coffee table.

"So, what we're going to do, for those of you who are new, is that we will sage the space of any negative energy and influences, so all of you take a deep breath, and let go of any anxiety, nerves, stress, etcetera. And I will begin the saging process. Also, let me

know now if any one of you has allergies or a problem with sage."
Silence. I looked around and noticed nobody had a problem. I
raised my hand and Selene smiled "Yes?" I felt my face flush
feeling on the spot,

"Um, well sage doesn't bother me, but incense does.
I'm asthmatic."

Selene and Ali, both gave me sympathetic looks, "Oh no
worries. We'll be sure to keep the smoke further away from you
and we won't be using incense for this, we'll just be lighting some
candles after the chalk circle. Thank you for being honest with
us. I wouldn't want a bad reaction, especially on your first night."
Selene gave a genuine caring smile and then led us into some
breath work.

I closed my eyes, my lungs filling with air, and then exhaled
to let go of any negative energy. Surprisingly, after three breaths
and Selene's saging I felt better. Safer. Less afraid. My attention
was now on Selene's beautiful voice chanting into the room,
"Dear Spirit and Guides, protect us in this space of love and light.
Give us courage, prosperity and peace. Banish negative energy
and entities that wish to do us harm. I bring in protection to this
space and block out anything that does not serve us. Blessed be."

I opened my eyes to see her put the sage on a little plate to let
it burn out in its own time.

"Now, I will use chalk and salt to create a circle, so I need you
all to step to one side as I do this. The chalk circle is for all of us
to enter, we will do our show and tell in this sacred circle and
then we'll break it to exit and leave all that behind. Then we'll
sage and cleanse again and go outside."

We all nodded and followed her instructions. There were only
six of us. Me, Ali, Selene, Delainey and two others that I hadn't
met yet. I wondered if there were more in the Coven that didn't
show up tonight. I'd have to ask Selene later. Once she made the
circle, we all went inside of it. Selene on one side of me and Ali
on the other. I think they did that on purpose, to make me feel
more comfortable and safe. Though I found it a bit intimidating

at the same time knowing that they were powerful. I could sense it in the energy. They had a lot of magick and a lot of time to hone it.

"Don't worry, we're here to catch you if you fall." Selene whispered to me, her beautiful voice ringing in my ear. I felt my body flush again. Why did she have such an effect on me? I had to think of Lyon. He was my grounding tool. He was also the man I was in love with, regardless of the circumstances, I couldn't get distracted by beauty, for he was my sacred person and the most beautiful of all.

We stood in the circle, hands clasped in each other's hands, the energy full of magick that felt so electrifying it sent goosebumps up my spine. I focused on my breath, my lungs filling with nurturing air, and then exhaled. I looked over in the corner and saw Lyon's soft features in the moonlight that shone through the basement window, his face half covered by light and shadow. His feline figure leaning against the black wardrobe. He was here supporting me, protecting me. Then Selene broke me out of my trance, and I looked up at her with innocent doe eyes.

She smiled down at me, "Amelie. I'd like you to go first. Our newest witch. May the Goddess of the Moon give you strength and grace."

I felt a lump in my throat as I swallowed with nerves.

"It's okay, it's only a quick show for us. We just want to see what you can do." Selene said encouragingly. I nodded before leaving the girls and going into the center, Selene and Ali closing the gap where I stood. I focused my breath again, my eyes closing as I tried to slow my heart rate down. I pretended they weren't there staring at me, wondering what I could do. I focused myself on the lights above us, and my intention was to turn them off. I could feel the electricity go out, just like a light, the current was there in my body and then it was gone. I heard gasps and a slight scream from Delainey.

The girls chuckled and I felt my lips curl into a small smirk. I took another deep breath and allowed the lights to go back on,

134

however this time, the candles flickered. I could see in my mind's eye, the light of the burning flames popping, I could hear the wick's crackle. Gasps all around me. I opened my eyes and saw the flickering of all the candles and even one of the lamps in the corner by the tv was flickering. "I can light candles off and on at will now." I explained as I calmed myself.

All the girls clapped and Selene grinned, "Good job! I know we'll make use of that skill of yours. And we can build you up to more." She took my hand again as I resumed my spot.

"Alright, Delainey, you're up!" Selene smiled, but I could tell that she was rooting more for me than anyone else. I wondered why she was so into me. I could see Lyon shaking his head, arms crossed almost in a *'you gotta be kidding me'* stance, staying silent. He was observing. Nothing more.

My eyes snapped back to Delainey who nervously walked into the circle. She did a similar breathing technique but using her hands and guiding the energy where she wanted it. A couple of pieces of furniture started to levitate. I watched in awe. I'd never been able to do that, it was really cool to see how a person could use those skills.

A thought occurred then. Was Selene trying to manipulate us with having witches honing different skills on purpose? It seemed like an odd thing for her to say she'd *'use our skills'*. However, maybe I wasn't thinking clearly and with all this distracting me . . . I clapped with the rest of the group once she was done. We continued with the other witches too who had telekinetic powers, and powers of all the elements. By the time we finished it was already 1am and Selene had ordered us outside once we closed the circle.

I went up to Ali and Selene who were cleaning up with a nervous smile, hands clasped in front of me. "Hi. Thank you for doing this tonight. I just hope I don't have to do that again. I don't like being in the spotlight."

Selene turned and put her gorgeous, manicured hands on my shoulders. "It's alright. We only do it for the new girls once.

Delainey just joined a week ago and the other two have been here longer, but I wanted them to show you that you're not alone. Now that you're almost initiated, you're one of us. And you get to learn more from Ali and I - personally. We'll train you to be just like us and then one day, you can lead a group." She winked and I couldn't help but swoon in some way. Why the hell was she so damn distracting?

"She's distracting you from me."

I smiled, trying not to freak out. I heard Lyon's voice. I walked away and headed upstairs to go towards the backyard. All the girls were outside under the bright full moon. Before I could get to the back door, I felt something pull on me, a hand on my arm.

"What are you doing?" Lyon's voice again.

I turned to see his face, his beautiful, gorgeous face. It felt like he was right here, but he wasn't. I saw him in all his 6' glory in leather and black jeans. "I'm making friends, doing magick . . . Is that a problem?" I asked, narrowing my eyes. Why was he so jealous?

A slight growl mixed with a sigh rang in my head, "These women are dangerous, Amelie. They're using you; I can feel it. I feel when you use magick. I can feel everything you do; I can see through your eyes even. Amelie, please, be careful. I'm not able to protect you in the way that I want to. I *need* you to be careful."

I knew he was right in some way. I was trying to be cautious but being around these women also felt amazing. Almost as amazing as being around Lyon.

Well, you're not here . . . I said in my mind, knowing he could hear it. I felt sad because I missed him, I wished he *was* here, but he wasn't. I had to find some way to move on without him here. I couldn't just wait around for him - I needed to live my life. Of course I wanted him back, but I had to do this for me.

I could feel a silence in the energy with Lyon. I couldn't hear him or feel him. *Fuck* . . . Had I just messed this up even more with him?

With a sigh I went outside into the humid summer air of New Orleans. The moon was big, bright and beautiful. Luna (the moon) was shining all of her magnificent white light around us. I could feel her energy charging up my body like a battery already. Now, I knew how my crystals must feel. The energy of all the other women was electrifying. We were giggling, laughing and even Delainey grabbed my hands as we spun around on the grass. I hadn't felt this free in years!

My heart felt light, my body free like a child in the throes of wonder and pleasure of life. The warm air smelt sweet and fragrant. I could feel a sensuality in my body I hadn't in some time. It was if my body was able to move in a sensual, sexual, fluid way that I never experienced. Not even with Lyon. To be honest, I think I needed to be away from him to discover all of this about myself. For when he comes back physically, I could share all of this with him - when the time was right.

I then heard the door of the backyard open; Selene and Ali had come out. They were smiling wide, watching us enjoy ourselves. She clapped her hands, "Ladies! I know you are enjoying your time but let us focus on the last part of tonight before we have food and drinks. We are going to start a bonfire, do a circle around it and praise Luna for all she has given us. Part of the ritual, well you've already started it seems. We dance around the fire, giving our glory and praise to the Goddess of the Moon."

Another witch raised her hand, I didn't know her name yet, "Isn't her name Selene? Like yours?"

Selene laughed, "Why yes, in the Greek, she is Selene, which is my namesake. However, to less confuse everyone with her and me, we'll call her Luna."

The two women then started the bonfire using practical means of collecting the wood from the shed and piling it up but using magick to light it. "One main rule of magick, is always have a balance of practicality and magick. One must use both if they want to be the best at their craft. It isn't all about supernatural powers, we have to respect the earthly plane on which we live, and using those natural forces along with our own, creates the magick." Selene said as she stood up from the ground and began to lead us into another circle.

Again, we held hands, all of us staring into the bonfire, the warmth on top of the summer air creating heat and perspiration. The air blowing through my hair felt divine as I silently gave the bonfire my intentions to bring Lyon back into my life, to let go of all the trauma, drama and hurt from the past. I thanked Luna for all of her energy, all of her magick within me, and to keep aligning me into the most highest form of myself.

Selene's voice yet again broke me out of my thoughts, "Luna, give us your strength, your current of energy, vibrate through us, charge us up and allow our energy to flow to and from you. We are witches! We are the magick of all the elements! Thank you, Luna, may you Bless us!"

In unison we all shouted, "Thank you Luna!"

We broke apart and Ali used speakers to play some shamanic drum beats and music.

"Dance ladies! Be one with Luna, be one with yourselves, and live free in your magickal knowing of who you are! Welcome to the Coven!"

Selene grabbed my hands. It took me this moment to realize she changed into a loose white dress. Very goddessy. She was in her element as the leader of the coven. Ali was dressed the same with a flower crown and moved to dance with Delainey and some others. Selene spun me around the fire and pulled me close. Her hands soft, her smile beautiful. She laughed with me, and I couldn't help but blush. My heart raced being around her.

I then felt a strange feeling over me, it was like I was drunk. I didn't even drink anything other than tea. My body felt loose, limp and intoxicated. I could hear screams of pleasure and laughter. It was erotic and exciting. My eyes looking up at the moon, Selene holding me, my arms around her neck.

Next thing I knew I felt plump lips against mine. A kiss. The taste of cherry lip gloss. A gasp of surprise left me as Selene kissed me. She pulled back and grinned, grabbing my waist. "I've wanted to do that since I met you."

I chuckled nervously but I knew this wasn't right. Was I under a spell? I hadn't felt this way before and it wasn't at all the way I felt with Lyon. With him I always felt safe. This was – *dangerous.*

I cupped Selene's face and gave a small smile, "I think I want some food now." I needed to be cool, and not show that I felt something was off.

Selene nodded, "Let's go." She grabbed my hand and pulled me towards the house. Ali and the others were soon following, thank God.

I'm so sorry Lyon . . . I didn't mean to . . . I didn't mean to kiss her . . .

Guilt racked my body and all I wanted to do was be at home, in his arms, on the rooftop garden and fly above the city where I was safe with him.

9

I am not sure how I got here. This place. A ballroom. Ball gowns. 18th century men and women dancing. I looked around me, seeing how beautiful everything was. My eyes trail down to see myself wearing a red and black ball gown, sleeveless and beautiful. It was fitting for the gothic architecture. My hair had been pinned up in a stunning up-do, with some curls down over my shoulder. I wore black silk gloves that reached my elbow. A string quartet and piano man played a soft waltz. Everyone seemed to be having a wonderful time. I smiled softly. I was the observer. It felt nice to just relax and watch things unfold as I stood there. Nothing to do. No one to answer to. Just peace.

A pull on my hand made me shiver with a startle and my head snapped to see the most beautiful blond Frenchman. He wore a blue frock with white lace. Very aristocratic. I blushed at the sight of him, and then it dawned on me, as our eyes locked, that I knew this man.

"Lyon?" I asked softly.

He merely smiled and pulled me to the dance floor. He pulled me in, his soft hands moving to my waist and my right hand to guide me into a waltz. I couldn't help the smile that formed across my lips. I had felt so at peace in my own heart, here with him, in this room, with this music. It felt right. Like I was meant to be here.

Without taking my eyes off his gorgeous blue ones, I followed him, allowing him to lead the dance. I could vaguely sense every-one watching, and it seemed like it was just to the two of us in this room. He was my French Prince. We smiled and laughed as he spun me around, the air feeling electric. Soon the music had stopped, silence in the room, our breathing the only thing to be heard. I was against his chest, his lips mere inches from mine. I felt his hand cup my face and kiss me.

"I will come back to you, Amelie. You just have to keep believing in me. Believe in our love. I love you. I miss you more than words can express." I felt my own eyes well up with tears just hearing these words. I missed him more than anything. Guilt and regret coming back to me.

"Lyon, I don't want to let you go. I don't know what's happening to me. I feel safe with you here." My chest was heaving as my voice broke.

He nodded and kissed me again. The taste of his lips comforting.

"Don't be despaired, darling. I am always right there with you. Just remember me. Remember our love. If you feel lost, it will guide you." I smiled softly as tears rolled down my cheeks touching my lips, I could taste the salt.

It was then I woke up crying in my sleep. Opening my eyes to the world around me I noticed I was in a big queen-sized bed that wasn't mine. I had no idea where I was. I wasn't at home. Swallowing a lump in my throat of anxiety, I sat up. My heart palpitating in panic. I saw the moonlight coming through the arched windows; the big bed was enough to fit two people. Had I stayed over at Selene's house? I turned over to see someone in the bed with me.

"Selene?"

I heard a soft murmur of tired mumblings. I realized in that moment I hadn't felt drugged or drunk anymore. I felt normal. Was Lyon the one who saved me? It seemed like it. The last thing I remembered was feeling intoxicated and Selene kissing me. I felt a pang of pain in my heart. I couldn't have betrayed Lyon like that with a sound mind. I had to remember what he said in the dream. Or was it a memory? It felt oddly like both. I wish I could talk to him about this. All the research on Twin Flames flooded my mind; the reason Lyon couldn't remember is because as the Divine Masculine counterpart, he was purposely put into a 'sleep state' by the Divine where he cannot remember who he truly is on a soul level and the Divine Feminine's job is to awaken the Masculine, but she must do it very energetically through separation. Which is what we were currently experiencing.

With a sigh, I tried to go back to sleep so that I could be rested to get home in the morning. But something told me that Selene wouldn't give in that easily. She seemed pretty hard pressed to keep me around. I really hoped Selene was a good person, and I really enjoyed the other girls' company, especially Ali. I just hoped that I hadn't gotten myself into something I couldn't get out of . . .

The next morning, I woke up feeling a bit groggy and disoriented. I remembered waking up in the bed with Selene in the middle of the night. How much my heart hurt and ached for Lyon. I couldn't betray him like this. I knew there was only one way to not do that, and it was to get out of here. As much as I loved the girls and the freedom it gave me, I had other priorities: my business, my self-evolution, and my relationship. I needed to gain more clients and call Ru to tell her what had happened.

Getting out of bed I noticed I was wearing striped, blue pajamas - Selene must have dressed me . . . Though it felt odd, like I had been violated. I remembered when Lyon had done the same to me, but I trusted him, and even then, I questioned him. Selene . . . well I felt off about her.

Looking around for my clothes I picked each piece up and found the adjacent en suite. The beauty of this house was remarkable. A claw tub sat next to the sink and toilet where I lay the folded clothes to change into. While closing the door I peeked towards the bed, Selene wasn't there in bed this time. I wondered if she was downstairs and if the other girls had left or if they were still here. I think I was the only one intoxicated by Selene's glamour. Or whatever she used. It definitely seemed that way.

After putting on the same outfit from last night, I found some toothpaste and brushed my teeth with my finger and rinsed my mouth out with Listerine. Thank God for that! I found a brush in a bin on top of the toilet with magazines and began detangling my long locks. Once I felt more presentable, I headed down the steps to the kitchen. Each step felt like lead in my legs. The wood squeaked underneath me at each step . . . but then . . . the smell of coffee. *Ahh, heaven.* I smiled softly. I turned to see Ali sitting at the island kitchen table with a coffee and newspaper in her hand.

"Hey. Coffee smells good. Also, aren't newspapers old school?" I joked before getting a cup of Java for myself. I fixed it to my liking and heard the scrunching of the newspaper being folded up and placed on the table.

Ali smiled at me as I went to sit with her. "Good morning. I like the old school ways. Technology is literally sucking the life out of the post-millennial age."

I laughed as I sipped the delicious life force that is coffee.

"Where's Selene?" I asked looking around to find her. The house was eerily quiet.

"Oh, she went to drive Delainey and some others home."

Oh, good. I thought. "Cool. Well, after coffee I need to head home, shower, change and get to work." I replied trying to be as nonchalant as possible.

Ali nodded, "Well you can always shower here, and I have spare clothes."

The energy suddenly felt very different. It was almost like she didn't want me to go home. "Thanks, but I really need to go. I have other things to take care of." I said as my eyes looked around the kitchen to see the calendar on the fridge. *Holy shit! Lyon!* I remembered his concert was coming up. He did say before he left me that he would come back to New Orleans when the time was right.

My heart skipped a beat, butterflies in my stomach. I needed to go to that concert. I took out my phone and googled *The Devil and Desire USA Tour*. I scanned the information and saw he was coming in a couple days for an outdoor event in the park. It was perfect weather for it too, and in the famous Lafayette Square! I hadn't been yet, and it was often used for concerts. This would be perfect, to see something I haven't before, and to reunite with him.

Pocketing my phone, I took a few more sips of coffee before moving to rinse out the mug and place it in the sink. "Well Ali, please let Selene know I had a good time getting to know the girls. Let me know if you need anything or if you are in the area. We should grab a drink or coffee." I smiled politely before grabbing my purse and keys that I left where we had tea and snacks before the ritual.

I took a deep breath and headed towards the door. My heart racing from the caffeine boost and my excitement. I turned the doorknob stepping onto the front porch, my eyes squinting in the sun. I couldn't be happier to see the cab I discreetly ordered on my phone. I almost bolted towards it.

I had to admit that the energy in that house felt almost sinister. Or at least some kind of trickery. As soon as the cab dropped me off, I pulled out my phone to call Ru once I had some privacy.

"Amelie! How are you? How are you settling into New Orleans?"

I all but gasped and almost cried, "Ru! I need to tell you everything that's happened. Something fucked up happened to me last night." I continued to explain the whole story with the ritual, Selene and the end of the night.

Ru's voice of concern wasn't unnoticed, "Girl! You need to watch out. It sounds like they did some kind of magick on you. They may be witches, but not all are on our level, as in, not all are good. It sounds like Selene might be using Black Magick to seduce you. Seems like she's got it out for you for some reason. I'm not trying to judge anyone, but I know dark magick when I see it. Please be careful."

I nodded, wiping my eyes as I walked through my apartment. "Yeah, I will. At least I got out of there alive. I plan on going to Lyon's concert. I need to talk to him, get his advice. I know we're in separation, and in Divine standards I'm not supposed to reach out and just wait it out till Lyon is fully awakened, but I need to see him. Maybe we can clear things up."

Ru encouraged me and also again reiterated to be careful. As soon as we hung up, I went in straight to the shower. I felt safe in my place. The water cleansed me of the night before. *Protect me, Spirit and Angels.* I silently prayed.

Once cleaned up and changed I went to the kitchen, grabbed some wine and a snack before heading to the rooftop. It was a beautiful night, and the moon was high above me again.

"Luna, please protect me from any negative energy and anyone who wishes to hurt me. Protect Lyon too. Help us be together again." A cleansing sigh of relief left my lungs before I sipped my wine. The couch underneath me was soft and comforting. I could almost feel Lyon with me.

"You're safe, I see." He said telepathically. I smiled.

"Oh Lyon, I've never been more happy to hear you. I'm sorry for last night. You were so right. There's something off about Selene and Ali. I appreciate them taking me in, but I feel weird about it. The fact I felt so not myself last night around Selene was a huge red flag. I was so scared." I felt warmth around me energetically. Like he was hugging me. "Forgive me?" I asked him tears welling up again.

"Of course I forgive you. I'm sorry for being an asshole. Forgive me?" He said.

I laughed lightly and nodded, "Of course." I responded. At least for now all was well, I was safe. Or so I thought. "Also, I saw your concert posters. I'm really excited! You're gonna rock it! I am gonna come down as soon as I can. I've never been to Lafayette Square before either, so this will be fun. I need to see you."

I heard his laugh in my mind, and I could see his smile, "I'm happy to hear that, darling. I've been dying to see you too. There's so much to say."

We left it at that, and I felt at peace for the first time in a little while where I could actually rest easy.

The night of Lyon's concert arrived. I had been busy cleaning, organizing my things at home and responding to emails. I hadn't even gone to the shop yet. My plan was to reopen after the concert and be able to go through all the new shipments I received. I could imagine the amount of dust that was sitting there over the last few days. Part of me felt guilty, I wasn't the best shopkeeper, and I hadn't even really focused on my own business that I invested so much time and money into. All this drama with Lyon and Selene was making me incredibly aware that I was slipping.

I distracted myself from all my internal conflict by changing my look for the concert. I put a punk, gothic, rocker look together, very 90's with a plaid dress, combat boots, and crosses. It reminded me of one of Lyon's photos on his profile. I had screenshot it into my phone and whenever I felt sad or lonely I would look at it. Oftentimes the nostalgia made me cry.

Tonight, I would not cry. I needed to be strong for him, for us, for myself. I painted my nails black and on each ring finger I had white crosses on it. Oh not to mention, I dyed my hair a deep red. I had always wanted to change my look, and tonight seemed like a good night to do it. It was sexy, edgy and it made me feel good. Sometimes a girl just needed to change her look. Admittedly, the look was inspired by a character from the movie *Queen of the Damned*. As much as it was . . . not the best movie, I loved the character outfits.

I gave myself a once over in the mirror, my deep red lipstick matched my hair, and I was satisfied with the overall result. I looked good! A wide grin cracked open on my face and a giggle left my lips. *Time to go get your man, Amelie.*

Grabbing my purse and leather jacket to go along with the outfit, my phone vibrated. Ali had texted me. *Oh no.* What did she want? I had been home for less than 24 hours and now I was being summoned. On Lyon's concert night!

As I shrugged my jacket on, I looked at my phone and it seemed like it was an emergency. Ali wanted me to meet her downtown.

At least it was on the way to the concert. I replied that I'd be there shortly and that I had something else to do so I couldn't stay long.

Anxiously I took a cab to the meet up spot on St. Charles Ave. When I got there I noticed it was a really swanky looking Southern restaurant and bar. It was beautiful inside with wood, brick and modern fixtures. With a sigh I walked in to see Ali waiting for a table.

"Hey!" She smiled and gave me a hug. It felt genuine.

"Hey, wow this is . . . nice." I took in the view very impressed. My eyes found the clock on the wall, and it was 7pm already. The concert started at 9pm. I had some time to have dinner and a drink, I guess. Well, that's what I justified anyway. We sat down once the waiter greeted us and gave us some menus. I ordered a glass of red wine, as did Ali.

I perused the menu trying to figure out what I wanted. I absolutely loved Southern food, but I had my limits on oysters, which of course was very popular in Southern cuisine. I peeked up to see Ali looking at me.

"What's up?" I asked with amusement.

Ali closed her menu and leaned into me. "I need to tell you something."

I put my menu down and grabbed my wine glass taking a sip as soon as the waiter put it on the table. "Okay." My voice came out shakier than I expected. I leaned in a bit closer to hear her over the noise and music.

"So, I know where you are going tonight. I couldn't help but notice the other day what you were looking at on your phone."

My stomach lurched and I felt a heat of panic rise up my spine, my cheeks flushing with worry. Ali moved to take her hand in mine. "I know that whoever he is must mean a lot to you. I can tell from your get-up alone that you follow his band. I've heard him around before. I don't know if you know Amelie. I know you're new to the whole witchy thing and I want to protect you." She took a pause, and I sipped my wine nervously with my free hand. "He's a vampire, Amelie."

I gulped my wine down fast and started to cough, grabbing my napkin to cover my mouth, wine dribbling down my chin. A look of worry on Ali's face was evident. "I'm sorry to shock you, but I needed you to know. He's dangerous to our kind. I had to tell Selene." Another wave of panic. Fuck! Ali moved to give me a hug and pat my back.

"We've got you girl. We're here for you. You need to come home with us. You can't see him. Selene is pissed. Not with you, but with the situation. If he finds out about our Coven, it could be over for us - you understand? We witches gotta stick together."

This was exactly what I was worried about. "I love him. Please Ali, let me go to him." I whispered, eyes filling with tears.

Ali nodded sympathetically. "I know. But you can't see him. As a member of our Coven, you must respect and follow our rules. Selene and I put those rules in place for a reason. No matter what you think Amelie, this is for your own good. So we're going to have dinner, Selene will pick us up and you'll be moving in with us." It was so matter of fact I had no time to argue. My brain couldn't even comprehend the control they had over me. I felt my body relax suddenly, almost as if I wasn't controlling it.

"Okay." I nodded and wiped my eyes.

Ali smiled and hugged me again. "I promise it will get better. We love you." She kissed my cheek and all I could think about was how I'd never see Lyon again. I was being ripped from him all over again. My heart broke, guilt and shame wracked me again.

Lyon, I love you. Lyon, please help me . . .

I prayed to him in my own telepathic way. I had a feeling that if I were to stay with them they'd make me forget about him. I had no choice. They were more powerful than me and now I was stuck in a Coven I couldn't get out of.

Fate really had a sick sense of humor. At least before all this happened, I had one more moment with him on my rooftop, and I slept in my own bed, cleaned my place, I had one more day living my own life. I just hoped I could get out of this before it was too late. Not just for Lyon, but for my own safety. I couldn't even tell Ru. Ali would know. It was now I realized these weren't just witches, but dark witches. Why else would they compel me, intoxicate me with their powers, seduce me with glamour? I wouldn't do that to a person, it was wrong. I was being magickally manipulated.

I sat through dinner and drank more wine (might as well if I'm going against my will back to live with the Coven), and then I sneakily texted Ru in the bathroom with what little free will I had (I told Ali that I needed to use the restroom after all that wine). All I wrote was SOS. She'd know what that was. It was a code we used to use with each other if we needed help in emergencies. I then deleted the text messages and turned off my phone. I didn't want them to know anything. Witches could do many things but one thing they couldn't do was manipulate technology. That was reserved for ghosts.

I left the bathroom and saw Ali was paying for the bill.

"It's on me." She said and took my hand to lead me outside. Selene was standing in front of her black Mercedes Benz.

"Have a nice dinner?" She asked, her eyes on me. I could feel the attraction for her again. Damn it! I hated it. I only had eyes for Lyon, and she knew that. They were trying to stop me from having any sort of attraction and love for him.

"Yup, the wine was excellent." I smiled. Which it was! I knew that I had to play along, it was the only way to get out of this. Lyon and Ru were right! I should have been more careful. If I didn't pick up the phone, I could have been on the way to the concert in the Warehouse District to be with the man I loved. I just hoped that he would know something was wrong. I hoped that my telepathy worked.

I dutifully got into the car; Ali went into the backseat with me to keep me company. I often wondered if Ali was friend or foe. I knew she didn't want to hurt me, maybe she really wanted to protect me, but she also was following Selene's orders. As much as I liked Selene and Ali, I knew in my heart I couldn't trust them. I couldn't trust anyone. I was on my own.

Once we arrived at the Coven House, Selene escorted me upstairs. I had my own room with a beautiful queen-sized bed, a wardrobe for all my things, a vanity for make-up and doing my hair, I even had a little balconette to go outside, which faced beautiful Magnolia trees.

"I wanted the best view for you. I want you to feel comfortable and at home here. I know that it's not an easy transition, but this would have happened anyway. It's what we do when we are a part of a Coven. We co-mingle and live as one." She placed her hands on my shoulders, her breath hot on my neck.

"What about my apartment, my job?" I moved out of her grasp and took a few feet of space, crossing my arms. I wasn't happy to be here.

She smiled softly, patiently. "We'll take care of all of that. Your duty now is to practice with the other girls, soon Amelie you'll be helping Ali and I run the Coven. You're truly powerful, I felt that when we met, and I want you at our side. It's an honor. You won't be taking as many orders as you are now. You'll have more freedom. I come from a long line of wealthy witches – I can take care of you financially. It's not a problem. However, as for your phone you will have to give it up."

I scoffed, my heel digging into the carpet beneath me. "So what? I don't get to leave the house grounds or something? Like a prisoner?"

She chuckled, "No silly. Of course, you get to go out into the city and everything! We're not medieval! I will give you a new phone with my contact information and the other girls. We just can't have any outside distractions; it affects how we work together."

Pfft. Yeah, like having a boyfriend or best friend who worries about me.

She seemed to sense my energy and moved towards me again, her hands on my arms, and moving to take her hands in mine. "I promise you'll fit right in. We have parties, meals together, it's like sharing a dorm. Plus, free rent." She winked. "Now, I'll let you get settled; we'll go shopping tomorrow to get you new stuff.

151

Also, we have a routine list for chores, so nobody is off the hook from doing the house maintenance. I'll show you that later and let you adjust. Come downstairs for some tea after."

She left and I moved to sit on the bed defeated. How was this happening? Was I really here? I looked outside, my feet moving again to the balconette, and I saw the full moon bright and beautiful. The smell of the magnolias was comforting and sweet. I wondered if Lyon was looking at the same moon as me, if he was thinking about me too in this moment. I hoped he didn't think I was flaking on him. I would never do that. These past three weeks felt like an eternity away from him and now I was being delayed even further without my consent. *What the fuck Spirit?!* I swore at the universe. *You think this is a game?! What am I to learn of this??*

My internal dialogue raging against my belief in a Higher Power. I went to check my phone but realized it was gone. Selene must have grabbed it from me when we were talking. Smart. A liar, manipulator and a thief. Great.

A sigh of frustration and acceptance of the situation left me. I was emotionally exhausted, a mix of sadness, anger, confusion and guilt filled my body. I felt like I could explode at any minute with all this inside me.

"Lyon, I hope you know I'm here. I miss you, and I need your help. You were right this whole time. I should have listened to you. I'm sorry."

I knew I was talking to myself but if there was any hope that he'd hear me, that was enough for me.

I went back inside and headed downstairs to where I heard Selene talking to a couple of other girls in the sitting room. They were having tea. The old antique furniture always reminded me of Lyon. If I wore an 18th century dress, I could pretend that I was in his sitting room waiting for him to keep me company, the image in my mind made me smile, but I hadn't realized people were looking at me.

"Amelie!" Selene smiled, putting down her teacup and standing to give me a hug. "Welcome. I'll fetch you some tea, come sit." I nodded and sat down in the empty spot on the couch beside her. Two other witches were here as well, I remembered their faces in the rituals we did. A young woman of Creole descent, her hair short and she wore a t-shirt and shorts. I didn't blame her; it was damn hot in New Orleans.

"Hi." I smiled and she took my hand. "Hey, how are you? My name's Raquel. I'm one of the newer girls. Been here a few weeks . . . I know it's weird living with a whole bunch of girls you don't know. Took me a while to get used to it, but honestly, it was nice to get away from my family."

Hmm, another girl who was from a broken home. I smiled politely and shook hands with her, "I'm Amelie. I understand. I moved here due to a lot of drama too."

Raquel smiled sipping her tea, "Well, at least I'm not the only one with drama."

I laughed, "Yeah, well, we're witches after all. I think we're allowed to have some drama." Oh, it was so nice to meet a decent human being. Raquel's energy seemed sincere. I didn't know yet if I could trust her, but she seemed solid, for now at least.

Selene came back with a cup of tea and a biscuit. "So, you two are getting along nicely." She smiled happily and sat back down inching over towards me. It seemed that Selene was obsessed with me. She was always touching me or trying to get close. I didn't know if that was because she knew about Lyon and I, or if she really liked me. She was gorgeous, funny, kind, charismatic but I knew deep down in there she had a lot of darkness to. I couldn't be fooled by her seductive nature. She reminded me of a Siren. Beautiful and dangerous. They could be words to describe Lyon too, but he was genuine, he didn't use his powers on me, he was just himself.

Now I could understand to a degree what Lyon was going through with Katerina, from what he telepathically expressed to me. That wasn't a true relationship or a real life. I took another sip of tea and realized I hadn't introduced myself to the other girl, she was younger and also had red hair like Selene.

"Oh, I'm sorry for being rude, I'm Amelie."

Selene turned to me, "Hey, I just noticed you dyed your hair red. It looks good on you. Now we're twins and with Beth we'll be triplets." She joked. I smiled at the young girl named Beth.

"It's nice to meet you, Beth." She smiled meekly and drank her tea. Selene chuckled, "Beth is our youngest besides Delainey. And she's very shy, but we'll work on that." I could see Beth seem to stiffen and nod. I looked between the two girls and Selene, trying to take the attention off of Beth.

"So, are any of the other girls coming?" I asked.

Selene nodded, "Ali should be back with Delainey. I'm hoping that over the next week or so we can recruit more girls. Our Coven is small."

I hummed in thought, "Well, I don't mind that we're small. We don't need an army of witches." I joked.

Selene cupped my face in her hand, asserting dominance gently. "Oh, darling girl, you have no idea what's out there. We women need to stick together. Besides, it's not like I'm going to recruit a hundred. That's too much, too suspicious. Just enough to protect ourselves and to keep it low-key."

Regardless of her explanations and intentions it seemed very odd to me. Was she planning on rising up against the vampires? She leaned in to kiss me, I gasped into her mouth, feeling my body lean into hers seemingly naturally, yet my heart felt guilty. I hated that Selene had this effect on me. Beth moved to leave. I could feel her nervous energy bounce around the room. Raquel coughed awkwardly, "Uh, we're gonna head upstairs." She ushered Beth out of the room, my ears picking up on their hushed whispered and footsteps.

Selene pulled away and smirked, "Now I have you all to myself."

I blushed and took another sip of tea. "I actually had a question."

She nodded, "Mhm, anything." Her demeanor changed to a more maternal figure. "What is it?"

I ran a hand in my hair and rested my elbow against the couch backing. "Are there werewolves out there? I mean, I know there are vampires, and we're witches. Are there other creatures out there?"

She contemplated this question for a moment, "To be honest? I don't know. I sure hope not. I know ghosts exist. I mean, New Orleans is full of them. I know all the new fantasy books talk about all that, but I'm not one hundred percent sure if that's accurate at all. I think that if we did have werewolves, it would complicate matters so much more. To be honest the war between witches and vampires is enough. Even ghosts get fed up, they're kind of the middleman in the situation. It's not their fault their souls are tethered and we're the only ones who can see them – unless you're a bona-fide medium and New Orleans does have them, but there are many that are fake." She gave a sarcastic smile and a roll of her eyes at that notion.

I couldn't help but laugh. "You're beautiful when you smile Amelie." she said admiringly. I blushed again and moved to finish my tea.

As I finished, I reached over to put the cup down on the table and became more serious, "Selene, I know that you have an attraction to me, that much is clear, but my heart is with someone else." I gave her my most assertive tone.

She smirked again and moved to take my hand and help me stand up, "I know. But he's not here, and you cannot deny you like me too. And as your Coven leader, I cannot have you stalk-ing vampires in the night. Hence, you will have to just endure my crazy flirtations." She grinned. My theory was confirmed. Ali showed Selene the posters for Lyon's concert, and they knew what he was to me. Selene *was* trying to keep me away from him.

Right on cue the door opened. Ali and Delainey walked in.

"AMELIE!"

I winced at the high-pitched squeal of the bubbly blonde. "Hi Delainey."

She hugged me and hopped up and down. "I am so happy you're here! I heard you got the best room in the house, so jelly." She pouted and took my hands in hers.

What was it with these girls and being so touchy? Though I knew I had to get away from Selene. "Hey, why don't I show it to you?" I slyly asked.

Delainey grinned, "Please!" She pulled me so fast upstairs. I was so happy to get away.

As I ascended the stairs, I saw Raquel peeking through her candle lit door, "Psst." She passed me a note and I grabbed it before Delainey dragged me upstairs like the Sorority girl she was.

"It's so cute! Oh my God! Amelie, you're so lucky! I wish I had a little balcony too."

I smiled and closed my door behind us. "Well, you're welcome to come visit my room sometime. Where do you stay?"

She pointed above us, "I'm on the third floor, on the last door of the left. I have a cute little hovel. It's like an attic room sorta thing. I like it, but this is so much nicer. Though it suits you. I can see why Selene saved it for you."

I nodded and scratched the back of my neck, feeling the heat well up at the base of it.

Delainey sat on my bed, crossing her legs at the ankles. I took off my leather jacket and moved to sit beside her, the moonlight coming through the French doors. It reminded me of my home. My heart ached for Lyon. I felt incredibly guilty, like I was cheating on him. I felt eyes on me and realized I had been in my head.

"Oh, sorry Delainey, I'm just thinking a lot."

She gave a soft smile, "It's okay. It's not easy living with girls. It's like the Sorority but different." She giggled. "Just know though, I'm here if you need anything. I used to take care of the girls back at the University."

It was nice to have someone care about me, even for a moment. "Thanks Delainey."

I looked around the dimly lit room, Delainey had turned on the light before I entered and I noticed the sheets were blood red, and the furniture was dark wood. Like home. Yet this *wasn't* home. I felt like Selene was trying to mimic my style.

"Hey, Delainey?"

She turned to look at me curiously, "Yeah?"

"What do you think of Selene? Like, do you think she's different than the other girls?"

The blonde chuckled, "Well duh, she's hot and the leader. She has to have a certain authoritative vibe, right? As someone who did something similar, if you're not, then nobody respects you. I think she wants to be adored and respected."

I nodded. Of course, Delainey didn't seem to see what I saw. My eyes looked over to the leather jacket I put on the chair of the vanity and remembered Raquel's note. My intuition telling me not to open it with anyone else in the room.

"Delainey, I'm sorry to cut this short, but I'm really tired. Can we maybe talk tomorrow?"

She nodded and jumped off the bed, "Sure. No problem! I'm glad you're here though. I'll see you tomorrow at breakfast."

I smiled and nodded, "Okay, goodnight." I watched as Delainey closed the door behind her.

Once I knew she was out of the area I grabbed the note and read it, my eyes going wide as I read the words: *I know. Selene is dangerous. Be careful.*

I knew it! I knew that all my instincts were correct. I had to play this safe. If Raquel knew the truth, then maybe I would have an ally. Tomorrow at breakfast I would try my best to align with her. If I was to stay here against my will, I needed someone to have my back. As much as I hoped I could trust Delainey it seemed she sympathized with Selene, and I couldn't risk that she'd flip on me.

I moved to go to the bathroom, realizing I had an ensuite, I had to walk through my closet to get to it. Well at least I didn't have to share a bathroom with anyone. I found fresh face cloths, towels and toiletries. I looked in the mirror back at myself. "You got this Amelie." I said before washing up and removing my make-up.

When I looked up after splashing water on my face I gasped. My eyes looked into the mirror and saw Lyon. It was as if he was my reflection.

"Lyon?" I whispered.

All I heard him say was "I hear you."

My eyes fluttered trying to make sense of everything I just saw. I knew that we were Mirrored Souls as they say, but to see his reflection in the mirror back at me wasn't what I expected. Taking a deep breath, I finished cleaning up and slipped off my boots, dress, and socks. I neatly placed them on the vanity chair before changing into a white tank top and pajama pants that were neatly folded on the vanity. Selene or someone must have put them there while I was in the bathroom. Once changed I slipped into bed, praying to the Universe that nothing bad happened while I slept, that I was protected, and the same too for Lyon. I wanted out of this mess, out of separation from Lyon and to go back to the way things were.

Yet, something inside of me knew that things wouldn't be the way they were. I had to keep going forward with faith that we would be together again, against all odds. We'd make it through this. With that thought, my eyes fell closed and I drifted off to sleep.

Images in my mind flashed before me, I was tied to a tree or a pyre, Selene was standing in front of me, all her gorgeous beauty adorned in black. She smirked at me and laughed a menacing laugh before lighting the pyre up. I was engulfed in flames.

My screams tore through my throat when I saw Lyon running towards me. "Amelie!" He shouted. His beautiful face torn in an expression of undeniable pain.

Selene turned to him and said, "This is what you get for falling for a vampire, Amelie." It was absolute torture to be burned alive while my lover watched. I could see Lyon trying to reach me but then I woke up gasping for breath, sitting up in shock, my hands going to my throat as if I had inhaled smoke.

Whoa. What the hell?

I shivered against the blankets and my eyes peered to the window, the moonlight still shining through the French doors. I gulped down my fear and then realized in my hazy dream-like state that Lyon was standing in front of the window, his side profile so glorious to behold. He was wearing his leather jacket, his arms crossed, but his right hand turned upward, his fingers daintily relaxed as he was in pensive thought. It was then I saw the 1700s Frenchman - the demeanor of a thoughtful Prince. *Wait, was Lyon a French Prince?* I'd have to ask him next time. I couldn't help the smile on my face though, watching him, my heart leapt for him.

I had no idea if this was real, if he was really here, or if this was just a in between from dream and reality. Either way, I was happy to see him.

Lyon was the one I loved with my whole being. I couldn't allow Selene to continue keeping me away from him. With a deep cleansing breath, I relaxed and laid against the pillows.

"Goodnight, Lyon." I whispered going back to sleep.

10

Days turned into weeks. I had no idea how long I was there for. Especially since I didn't have my phone to keep track of everything. After my horrible nightmare with Selene and Lyon, I was forced to endure her company for shopping. I got all the kinds of clothes I liked, which I have to admit I enjoyed. As soon as I came home, I ran up to Raquel's room, knocking on her door before entering the small, cramped space. "Hey, I just survived my shopping spree." Raquel smiled and patted her bed to allow me to sit.

"So, I just found out a few things while you guys were gone. I did some snooping, and you are right. Selene is practicing Black Magick and has some sort of notebook with our names in them and other witches she plans to bring forward. She's obsessed it seems with not only you being by her side, but wanting to create some sort of witch coven so grand that it could go to war against the vampires. And another thing . . . " She peered over to her door to make sure nobody was listening, "Beth is her youngest cousin, and she keeps Beth quiet and subdued in order to take over the inheritance so that Beth can't ever receive anything if something happens to Selene herself. She wants all the power, money, and control." I couldn't believe what I was hearing but it made so much sense. I knew now that I had my confirmation on everything my intuition ever told me about Selene.

I planned an outdoor picnic in the backyard of the house. Raquel, Beth and Delainey had joined, while Ali and Selene went out to grab some magickal supplies in the Warehouse District.

"So, I was thinking . . . Maybe we could all do a girls' day in the Garden District . . . " I said as I had sat on the fuzzy purple blanket and set out our spread of cheese, crackers, fruit and charcuterie. Beth sat beside me, her hair in cute little braids that made me think of *Anne of Green Gables* - one of my favorite stories.

"Where would we go?" Her meek little voice asked.

I smiled over at her as Raquel sat down and dug into some strawberries. I fixed my sunhat over my head as I answered Beth, "Well, I would like to sight see. Look into more witch lore. This can't be the only Coven in town . . . I feel like we're prisoners here in this house. We hardly go out. I went out shopping with Selene once and that was . . . kinda unbearable. I haven't been able to contact anyone. It's the middle of summer, we should at least go out and do something fun! I moved to New Orleans to immerse in Southern and witch culture. This . . . " I said pointing to the house, "Wasn't what I had in mind. It'll be just the four of us. No, Ali or Selene. Besides, I'm almost at their level, they have respect for me, I can definitely get them to agree." I went along with everything Selene and Ali said just to keep my place of power in line, it was the only way I could survive in this house. If you can't beat em', join em'.

Raquel grinned as she pushed her Ray Ban sunglasses over her eyes, "That sounds like a riot to me." She nudged me playfully. We got on really well and she reminded me of Ru. How I wish they could meet. "Yes, exactly." I grinned right back at her.

I hadn't told the girls about Lyon yet. I wanted to but I had to be sure I could trust her and Beth.

Delainey smiled silently, "Yeah sounds great. Just make sure to follow the rules, yeah?" I inwardly rolled my eyes; Delainey was definitely not on our side. She wanted to make sure we followed everything correctly. Maybe she was trying to get in close with the other two powerful witches. She definitely was competing against me as I was now the third most powerful witch, I just had to bide my time before taking action. I had learned how to harness my powers even more. My psychic ability was outstanding, I could predict things like never before, or just know things about a person, which to be fair I had before but now my gifts were more developed over the time that I stayed here.

I could honestly light a whole field on fire, not that I would actually do that unless in dire circumstances. I shivered at the memory of my dream . . . Being burned at the stake *sucked*.

I also could communicate with small animals. I was a huge animal lover anyway, but I could talk with them, command them sometimes. The crows were my messengers and I always asked them to talk to Ru, to get her to help me, or at the very least to tell Lyon how to find me. I knew he had good tracking skills as a vampire, but the problem was that Selene had enchanted the house so that no other supernatural being could enter or find our location.

I think she did that on purpose, knowing how much I loved Lyon, and I am sure she wouldn't put it past me or him to try to get back to each other. Just another reason to get the fuck out of this Coven.

Raquel had a look like she was planning something. Delainey moved "I'm gonna go get some lemonade. Anyone want some?" We shook our heads. The three of us didn't trust Delainey to try to poison us or something. I always felt that Delainey had a darker side the more she stuck around Selene. She did everything Selene asked, kissed her ass, and just seemed more like a watchdog for Selene the more I was around her. People could always put on fake masks, but energy never lied.

Raquel leaned into Beth and I, picking up a piece of cheese, "Listen, we can't have her come with us. She can't be trusted . . . so I thought I could make up a tea for her, like a sleeping draught. She won't know what hit her and bam! She's out like a light."

I couldn't help the smile and laugh that came from me. "You're so dramatic."

She pushed me lightly, "Shut up, you know it'll work."

I nodded and turned to Beth, "What do you think?"

Beth smiled and took a strawberry in her fingers placing it to her lips eating it, "Do it!"

Raquel hummed in an impressed tone, "Girl, who knew you little one would be a rebel! Goin' against Big Cuz like that."

Beth giggled, "I want freedom too, so whatever it takes." Beth was the kindest and the youngest, she also didn't speak much or talk about her powers. Whatever she could do I was pretty sure was powerful, she was someone with such a longing for freedom just like the rest of us. She was the most entrapped because she was related to Selene, and everything about Beth depended on Selene's authority. I wanted to help her too.

"Amelie? What if you took over the Coven? Wouldn't it be better?" She asked.

I coughed not expecting that question, "Oh, I'm not sure Beth. I never thought of it.. Maybe? I just don't think I want that responsibility."

Beth nodded, "Well, think about it. I think you'd be a good Coven leader. You're smart, funny, kind, fair, and you think of others. Not just yourself."

I placed my hands on my heart and smiled, "You're the sweetest to say that, thank you."

"I'm back!!" Delainey said in her Southern twang. At least we had a plan of action, one that hopefully none of them would see coming. I was determined to get some kind of word out to Ru. She was the closest and lately Lyon had gone radio silent. I didn't hear him or feel him. I was beginning to get a little worried, but maybe this had to happen . . . I couldn't sit and worry about it too much for I had to get out of this place and take Beth and Raquel with me. I knew that Ru and Lyon would be proud - at least I was trying.

In the week that followed we were having record breaking heat, but luckily, the day of the outing with Raquel and Beth we were able to find a day that was cool enough to go explore. The midsummer heat of July was absolutely sweltering, my hair felt like a rat's nest with all the humidity. Today I asked Raquel to braid my hair in an elegant loose braid, with a few loose strands falling around my face.

"Beautiful." Raquel said with friendly affection. At least I knew she wasn't trying to seduce me like Selene. "Red looks good on ya, Amelie. I think that's what I'll call you, Red. Like a code name."

I laughed at the sentiment as she complimented my red hair.

"Okay, what do I call you?" Raquel thought for a moment,

"Ooo, what about Ra? Like the Egyptian God of the Sun? I mean, I do love the heat in New Orleans." Her subtle New Orleans accent flowing through my ears. It was beautiful and less annoying like Delainey's accent.

"I like it! Fuck gender roles!" I grinned, giving her a high five with a giggle. I looked in the floor length mirror Raquel had in her room. Her space had Egyptian meets Roman decor. It suited her. I wore blue shorts that frayed at the hem, not too short, ankle boots, and a white peasant top. I put on a little bit of mascara and lip gloss and finished off with sunscreen. "I like this look, it's fun and perfect for the day out."

Raquel nodded, "Yup!" She wore a cute, patterned dress that was black and gold. It screamed Egyptian Goddess. Her hair in a beautiful hair wrap and some black eyeliner and mascara.

"You look amazing too!" I complimented back.

She blushed and smiled, "Awe shucks, thanks."

"Now, what about Delainey?" I asked.

Raquel smiled, "Oh, I didn't even have to drug her. I convinced her that it was too damn humid that her hair would balloon out. She was horrified at the idea and decided to stay here. Apparently, Selene is going to have a pool party later."

I rolled my eyes, "Of course she is. Ogling all the bikini clad women to choose her next target."

Raquel laughed and hugged me, "I gotchu girl. I won't let her harm you."

My body relaxed into Raquel's arms. It was so nice to have a good friend here, she was just like Ru.

"Thanks, Ra." I chuckled.

I pulled away to see her smile down at me, "You're welcome, Red."

I sighed changing to a more serious tone, "I need to talk to you about something, but it's highly sensitive, kinda taboo and I can't talk about it here."

She nodded in understanding, "Hey, no worries, I've got your back. I want outta here as much as you do. We don't have time for nonsense drama. You can tell me anything. And if I can do anything to help, let me know."

It was ironic that Raquel liked being here in the beginning but after seeing all the shit Selene was doing, she realized the grass wasn't greener on the other side.

After a moment of comfortable silence, a knock came at the door before it opened, and Beth entered. She looked adorable in her new sun hat she got when she went shopping with Selene. She was ready for the day, wearing a romper, a white T-shirt underneath and converse sneakers.

"Hey! You look good!" I said with a smile, wrapping my arms around her in a hug.

She giggled, "Thanks. I am so excited to go explore! Also, Selene said we're having a pool party and attendance is a must." She rolled her eyes in contempt, just like I did.

I groaned. "Can't she just like . . . fuck off?"

Both women stared at me for a moment before laughing. I blushed and chuckled too looking at the floor.

"Let's get goin' before you set fire to the whole damn place." Raquel said gently pushing us out the door. I quickly went to my room to get my purse and sunglasses. I bought aviators, they reminded me of Lyon's that he had. It made me smile to think I had a piece of something that kept me tethered to him in some way.

We headed out of the house and to my car (which I convinced Selene to let me have back). I was so excited to fucking drive again! Freedom felt so good. We laughed getting into the car, rolling down the windows and turning the AC on to cool it down. Beth sat in the back and Raquel sat beside me.

"Oh my God, it's so nice to get the hell outta that house!" Raquel said as she got buckled up. I had never seen these two so happy. I turned on some tunes and drove towards the laneway that led to the main road.

"Downtown NOLA here we come!" I said, putting my hand out the window, the girls following suit.

"WOO!" We all exclaimed. Oh man it was so nice to do this, it reminded me of the road trips with Ru.

As we drove, I felt my heart beat with joy, the freedom and absolute pleasure of being around good people had me almost crying. We danced in our seats to the beat of the music; it was then on the radio they mentioned *The Devil and Desire.* One of *his* songs came on the radio.

"OH MY GOD!" I screamed and turned it up.

Raquel and Beth gasped, "Whoa, girl. You a fan of them or something?"

I nodded, "Y-Yeah, you can say that."

I didn't mean to freak out, but to hear Lyon's voice over the speaker had my heart and mind running wild. I could tell it was a new hit from his USA Tour (the one I missed), and it was about me. His love for me, his loneliness.

Don't forget about me baby,
I'll be waiting all my life for you.
I'm trapped in a cage I can't get out of,
You're the key to end this misery.

All of a sudden, I broke down crying. Raquel turned the volume down slightly and put a hand on my shoulder, "Whoa, Amelie. Girl, you, okay?" I nodded, wiping my tears as we sat at a red light.

"Yeah, sorry. That was just . . . beautiful." I felt Beth's hand touch the back of my shoulder from where she sat.

"You love him, don't you?"

I gasped at Beth's gentle honest question. I felt flustered. I didn't know how to respond and then the light turned green.

167

"Can we talk about something else?"

Raquel nodded and changed the station to some pop music. "There. We're not gonna let some dramatic rockstar ruin our girl's day."

A laugh left my lips as I cleaned myself up, "No, we're not."

We drove for another thirty minutes before finding a parking spot in downtown NOLA. I wanted to also go to the Garden District after. For now, we all agreed to go get some food on Notre Dame St in the Warehouse District, it was a perfect area for cafes and restaurants. I was absolutely in love here. As much as I loved New York, the city of New Orleans was just so different, much more cultured (in a way I couldn't begin to explain), and open to witches and other spiritual beings.

The three of us spent the day getting to know each other more deeply and laughing like we haven't since I arrived at the Coven. I learned that Beth is really good at knowing things about a person by touching them, or an item that belonged to the person in question. I never had that gift, or knew anyone that did, until now.

"It's not something that I talk about. Mostly because Selene doesn't allow me to. She keeps me quiet because I know too much." She explained as we had drinks and lunch. "That's how I know, Amelie. About . . . what happened in the car."

I got a little scared to open up, but I knew I had to.

"I'll tell you guys about it, once we go to the Garden District. I want to walk around there, and maybe grab a coffee."

They both nodded in agreement, both smiling supportively. It had been at least two months since I spoke to anyone about Lyon, and I couldn't help the feeling of a lump in my throat. I knew I had to tell them, it was the only way to get them to trust me too, to get out of this mess together.

After finishing lunch, we walked back to the car and drove towards the Garden District. I found a parking spot not far from Lafayette Cemetery. Many tourists were exploring, visiting shops, and eating at restaurants, not many were coming to the Cemetery, which was good. I could have privacy with the girls.

Once I parked the car, we got out and headed towards a coffee shop nearby. Each one had a different vibe, some more modern and elegant and others more historic and rustic. I chose one that had a mix of both and ordered a cappuccino. Beth ordered an iced coffee, and Raquel got the same as me. I didn't care if it was hot, I still drank hot coffee in hot weather.

"Let's go find a quiet place to sit." I said as we took our drinks to go and found a park bench near the cemetery. The smell of summer was in the air as the warm breeze blew past us. I smiled contentedly with the freedom of being outside. I wished that I could do this with Lyon. Though it would have to be at night. I had faith that we'd have our time together again soon, but for now I was enjoying time with my new friends.

"I have to tell you guys; I don't know what I'd do if it weren't for you. You both have kept me sane, grounded and headstrong to get out of this Coven. I think everyone glamorizes Covens and I'm sure for others it's great, but having complete control over one's will is not okay."

Beth nodded, sipping her coffee, "I know. I wish Selene would stop, but she's got that old heritage power, and the mindset that we need to be the best."

Raquel scoffed. "Yeah, some bullshit that is. What's her fuckin deal?"

My shoulders shrugged in response, "I think she wants to recruit more girls. I made a joke about an army way back in my first days here, and I know she despises vampires . . . I don't think it's a joke to her."

Both girls looked at me with wide eyes, "So, that's why she's keeping us in line? To separate the two races." Raquel was stunned.

I nodded. "Yeah, I think so."

Beth nudged me to say more with a kind smile. "It's okay Amelie, tell us, I mean I already know."

I sighed, taking a sip of my coffee, savoring the espresso mixed with chocolate, cinnamon and oat milk.

"So, the band we heard today, the one that made me cry. Well, the lead singer is my boyfriend. That song was about me, about us. He's a vampire."

Raquel looked at me with a stunned look, blinking a few times to process what she just heard.

"GIRL, WHAT?!" She yelled, but she wasn't angry.

I shushed her, index finger on my lips. "I wasn't expecting to fall in love with a vampire, okay? I didn't even know the whole witches hate vampires thing till he told me. That's why Selene is constantly trying to seduce me, to make me forget about him, she wants me to fall in line with her. As tempting, beautiful and seductive as she is, I love Lyon. That's his name. He's from France, and we met online. We started our physical relationship literally after a week."

Both girls laughed, "Man, that fast?"

I giggled too with a blush looking down, "Shut up." I joked before continuing, "He's amazing. I know the whole political shit is a factor, but he's really a good person. He takes care of the people he loves. But due to some fucked up shit in his life . . . We had to break up, sort of. My best friend Ru, who is a lot like you Ra, helped me understand what we have is special, spiritual and unlike any other kind of relationship."

Beth nodded with a smile, "You're Twin Flames. It's a rare kind of relationship, but it happens. I know about it."

I turned to look at her kind, small face, her innocent eyes showing kindness, "Yes, that's what I was told."

Raquel nodded in contemplation, "So, you guys had to like break up because of destiny or some shit? Then you met Selene I'm guessing?"

I nodded. "It's more complicated I think but that's the gist of it yeah. I miss him so much guys, I cry all the time, I just want him to know I'm okay. We telepathically talk, I see him sometimes, like energetically."

Ra gasped, "Like remote viewing? I heard people can do that. That's one of your powers?"

I gave a shrug, "I think so. I'm still figuring it all out."

I felt Raquel shift beside me to sit facing me, her one leg crossed on the bench, her drink in her hand. "So, what's stoppin' him from coming to you?"

I chuckled darkly, "Well, turns out he has or had another woman."

Beth and Raquel both gasped, "What an asshole!"

I put my hand up in defense, "He was in an arranged marriage type of situation. He didn't want to be, and he didn't expect to fall in love with me either. We didn't even talk about this in person, only telepathically because well . . . You know. I'm here now and stuck."

Raquel's hand touched my shoulder, squeezing it gently, "You won't be stuck for much longer. We're gonna get out of this mess, or at least try too! Is there any way you can get a hold of him or your friend?"

"I did send Ru an SOS, maybe she's planning on how to get here? Since the house is enchanted to be protected, we'll have to find a way to dispel it. Also, I need to figure a counter spell for Selene's seduction glamour. That's the next step." I could hear the confidence in my voice knowing I had some sort of action plan.

It felt so good to release myself from the pain I had been carrying on my own. And to finally start getting a way out of the Coven.

"What will you do once we get out?" Beth asked. Her eyes were worried, and I could tell she didn't want us to part.

"Well, you both can stay at my place until we figure something out, I'll probably go to France to find Lyon. I mean I don't really know. I'm just going by the seat of my pants at this point." We all broke out in laugher.

"One thing you never told us Amelie, was really how you came to be here. You said your family was messed up, kinda like mine, but what really happened?" Raquel questioned gently.

I took a deep breath, "Well that's a story for another day. How about I tell you on the next bonfire night. Should be coming up soon, right?"

Beth nodded, "Yeah, maybe write down some things that are burdening you and put it into the fire. I will give Selene credit that it does work."

I took Beth's hand and squeezed it, "Thank you Beth, for helping me open up and to trust you both." I finished my coffee, getting up to put it into the trashcan.

"Okay! So, the drama is over for the day. Let's go hunt some ghosts in the cemetery." I pointed dramatically, one hand on my hip the other pointing at the mausoleums. The girls both laughed, following my actions of discarding their drinks and following me into Lafayette Cemetery, both of their hands in mine, we were Soul Sisters now, a witch coven of three. Soon to be four, once I could reunite with Ru.

After a few hours we finally made it back to the house just in time for the pool party. It was roughly 6pm by the time the girls and I had entered the house. We agreed to put our swimsuits on and join the girls. However, Raquel and I decided that in order to figure out more about Selene's magick usage and her plans we had to dig deeper. I was going to go into Selene's room to look for any evidence of what she was doing, and Ra would keep a look out. Beth planned on staying outside, keeping an eye on Selene, and she would give a signal if Selene was on her way into the house.

It was risky but worth it.

I changed into a cute white and black striped bikini. The top was a halter piece, and the bottoms were high waisted, a pin-up vintage style, it even had cute little side pockets. I took my hair out of the braid allowing the curls to frame my face and shoulders naturally. Grabbing my flip flops I headed towards Selene's room. Hers was down the hall on the other side of the mezzanine, across from Raquel and I.

As I opened the door, I was happy to see the door wasn't locked. I swiftly moved around her room, which was spotless and tidy. I had to admit I liked her style, and I remembered thinking that exact thing when I woke up in her bed months ago. A shiver went up my spine as I thought about how long I'd been here. Two going on three months felt like an eternity. I looked through her closet and found nothing, searched her bedside table, nothing. With a frown, tapping my foot impatiently, I tried to figure out what she'd keep around here that nobody would suspect.

I thought back to the first days I got here and when I was around Selene. I noticed her scent! *Her perfume!* That's what she must be using. I walked over to her vanity and saw a little purple perfume bottle. Taking the cork off of it I noticed the bottle was a mini potion bottle. I inhaled the scent briefly and immediately felt that similar sensation of feeling intoxicated. *This is it!* She's using glamoured perfume, that's how she keeps it up! I smiled to myself, putting the bottle back and ran to Raquel.

"Hey, I found something . . . " I kept my voice low as I exited Selene's room and pulled Raquel into my room. "Selene is using perfume, a homemade version to glamour herself. She wears it daily and whoever smells it immediately goes under her spell. So now I just need to find some kind of spell to keep me from getting affected." As much as I knew about tarot, my fire gift and telepathy, this was out of my league. I sat on the bed, fingers in my hair.

Raquel grinned, "Oh this is where you need me! I know all about protection spells. I dabbled in Voodoo, especially with my family as it was passed down . . . I thought this Coven would be good for me to branch out . . . I was dead wrong. Though there are some good Hoodoo and Voodoo spells I can try out for you. It's harmless, I promise. Southern magick tends to get misconstrued as "devilish" but a lot of it is just down to cultural practices and is now even considered an individual practice. It'll be just a simple protection spell, and maybe a charm to keep on you. It should stop Selene's effects on you, until we can at least figure out a way to dispel the house."

I exhaled a sigh of relief, "Oh thank you, Raquel. This makes me so happy to know someone's on my side. You and Beth are literal life savers."

Raquel gave me a small smile and took my hand, "Like I said before, I got your back. You were so brave to tell us the truth today, thank you for trusting us. Just before we go downstairs, let me get you some protection."

She pulled me towards her room and did a quick cleanse with some sage, chanted some words of protection and gave me a protection amulet, a simple crystal on a chain. "Wear this or keep it in your pocket at all times, never take it off. Unless in the shower or bath." She warned me with a stern look, "I am just doing this quickly, but I'll do a more in-depth job later. I'll need a lock of your hair. It's to help bind the magick to you so that you're always protected, until we release the spell. Now, let's get downstairs before Selene gets angry, we're not down there. And I could go for a good hot dog."

I laughed, pocketing the crystal, and headed downstairs to try to enjoy the barbeque and the pool on such a hot day.

Pop music blared in my ears as I went outside and soaked in the sun, laying on a towel on the ground near the apple tree we had in the back. The summer heat was almost unbearable, however the shade from the tree protected my sensitive skin. Raquel brought me a delicious hot dog, while Beth grabbed another blanket to sit with me and passing me her sun hat.

"Here, you should wear it for a little bit." She was so sweet and thoughtful.

I felt a kinship to her. "Thank you." I said softly with a smile.

The hairs on my neck standing up as I glanced over to see Selene staring at us. I don't think she was happy Beth was giving me attention - then again, she didn't like it when anyone gave me any attention. A frustrated sigh left my lips as I braced myself on my elbows.

Raquel groaned, "Here she comes . . . "

Selene all of a sudden was in front of me.

"Amelie." She said gracefully with a smile, "I'm glad you all came back, I trust your little trip was fun. Now we can all be together for some fun. Come in the pool!" Next thing I knew I was being pulled up and the hat taken off my head to go towards the pool.

"Selene, I don't really like water . . . " I tried to protest.

Selene laughed and tugged my hand, "I won't let you drown silly. I just want you to myself!"

Of course you do.

Looking over my shoulder I gave Beth and Raquel a look that said 'save me' before I stepped into the water. Delainey was on a floatable lounge chair enjoying the water and the sun.

"We missed you Amelie! You're never around to hang out anymore." The blonde protested with a pout.

Selene nodded in agreement, "Yeah, the other girls have been hogging you an awful lot."

I looked around to notice Ali wasn't there, "Where's Ali? Is she not joining us?" My brows furrowed in concern as Selene smiled softly,

"Oh no she's fine. She's coming, she just had to do something."

Uh huh - sure. I thanked God for Raquel's crystal of protection, it seemed that it was working. I didn't feel the usual sense of being intoxicated. Shit! I realized that crystals weren't supposed to go in the water!

Oh fuck . . . I need to get out of the pool.

"Why don't I go get everyone some fresh lemonade?" I offered. "I just really hate water and plus I burn so badly. I don't want to look like a cooked lobster."

Selene rolled her eyes and laughed, "You're such a drama Queen. But whatever, sure I could use some."

Getting out of the pool to grab the lemonade pitcher, finding my way around the kitchen I filled up the pitcher and used a towel to sneakily dry off my crystal. The hair on my neck stood up as I felt eyes on me turning to see Ali watching me.

Coming up behind me she said, "Let me help you." while taking the pitcher from me. Her dark eyes landed on the crystal and then me. "I know what you're doing Amelie."

My eyes looking into hers, I was sure my fear was showing. The lump in my throat not allowing me to speak, my stomach dropped, fear became my companion in this moment.

Ali placed a hand on my shoulder, "It's okay. I won't tell anyone. I - I want to help too."

"Amelie, where's my lemonade?!" Delainey called which made me jump.

Ali squeezed my shoulder, "Go to them. We'll talk later, but whatever it is you're doing, I'm in."

I nodded silently, grabbing more cups as Ali took the pitcher outside.

"I bumped into Ali and spilt some lemonade on myself. I also realized we needed new cups!" I said with a smile, putting the cups on the table then casually went to Raquel and Beth. I took the hot dog that Raquel got me, munching on it while trying not to throw up.

"So, Ali caught me, she saw the crystal. Fuck Ra I am so sorry, I didn't think Selene would pull me in the water." I looked to Raquel, my heart feeling like I just betrayed someone. Raquel and Beth both squeezed my arms supportively.

"You didn't know, I shoulda said somethin', besides you did great. What did Ali want?"

I finished what was in my mouth, and spoke again after swallowing, "She wants to help. She was onto us, but she said whatever we're doing, she's in. She'll come talk to me later."

The three of us stayed together throughout the party until it was time to head inside. The sun started to set, and nighttime was upon us. I headed to my room and was just about to get ready for bed when I heard someone knock at the door and enter. I thought it was Ali, when I turned around to greet her, I realized it was Selene.

"Selene! What are you doing here?"

I wasn't expecting her at all. The ambient lighting of the candles burning in my room casted shadows on the walls. The moonlight shone through the sheer white curtains of my balcony accompanying the candlelight.

"Didn't see me coming, did ya?" She laughed and closed the door. "We gotta work on your psychic skills more."

I chuckled, "Yeah, probably." I looked up at her as she moved closer. She was still wearing the same perfume, I could smell it, yet I didn't feel her affects. I knew it wouldn't work forever, which is why I tried to keep my distance from her. Now she was in my room again and I knew what she wanted. I could sense it in her energy. She wanted to seduce me entirely. I gulped.

She wrapped her arms around my waist, her lips very close to mine. "Now, I truly can have you to myself. I kept staring at you all day in that bikini, teasing me." She smirked, her hands moving up my body, caressing my curves as she kissed me. I gasped, almost paralyzed to move with shock. What the fuck was happening?

"Amelie!"

I heard Lyon's voice, angry and jealous.

Oh my God! Lyon!

I pushed Selene off me, "Stop! Selene, you've been trying this with me for months, I'm not going to sleep with you so just stop! I have a boyfriend, and you may not like that he's a vampire, but he's the love of my life! Stop trying to tear us apart! Stop trying to hurt me!" My eyes scrunched in rage, my heart beating wildly like it was going to jump out of my chest, fists balled up in anger.

Before Selene could answer my door burst open to see Ali standing there. "Selene! You may be the coven leader, but this takes it too far! Get out of Amelie's room!"

Selene glared between the two of us, "Fuck you, both of you!" She stormed out, the lights in the house going haywire with both our magickal energy.

Ali rushed to me as the other girls came to the room. "Are you okay?"

I nodded, shaking. "I - I feel like I cheated on him . . . " my hands in my face as tears streaked down my cheeks. I felt awful.

Ali hugged me, "No, no you didn't - she's been forcing herself on you for months, but this time you were able to stop it. We better prepare for a damn battle because it's coming." Ali looked to Raquel and Beth who were sitting on my bed.

I nodded, "Well, that's what she's gonna get. Wait, what happened to your glamour?"

Ali laughed, "Glamour? I never needed one, you just thought I was hot. Besides, it's not to change appearance, it's more to attract people to you to get what you want. I only ever used it in the beginning while working with Selene. Until I met you, I didn't realize the manipulation she was doing and had me go along with it . . . I'm so sorry. After tonight there's no doubt in my mind that we're ending this now. The next full moon we'll be prepared. It's the best time for our powers to hopefully overtake hers. For now, I'll go along with Selene, I'll apologize to her and get her good graces back, then we'll strike."

It was crazy to think I had been away from Lyon for almost four months. The next full moon was in August. I had to endure two more weeks. I really hoped that Ru would come find me. I hadn't lost hope but any extra magick would be appreciated right now. We had to protect ourselves, de-spell the house and take down Selene all on the full moon. No pressure, right? I just hoped that Lyon and Ru would make their appearance soon. And if they didn't, well then, I was on my own.

In the days that passed the pool party, Raquel had done her proper protection spell using her old rituals from home, she did it for me, herself, Beth and Ali, as well as our bedrooms. So that if Selene ever decided to go inside it, we would be completely protected from her trying anything.

Ali had smoothed things over with Selene as well, pretending to go along with her again as the second in command. We were to set up a full moon ritual with Selene. The Coven had to be present and that was the night we would strike. I found out that Ali discovered some old spell book in the basement on the day of the pool party that belonged to Selene's family which had been passed down to each woman in the family. Beth was to be the next in line as there weren't any other siblings or cousins to pass it down to, however, with Selene's love of power she was trying to keep the legacy with herself. She locked Beth away or kept her from anything to do with magick so that she wouldn't have access to the family secrets and inheritance. Which is why Beth was so quiet and meek when I first met her. It all started to make sense!

It really was sad to see a family ripped apart by dark forces and power. I never wished to have that much power, or what I did possess I only wanted to help others with it.

I kept to myself, being as quiet as possible, reading in the tearoom. I made myself a cup of Earl Grey and sat in the armchair by the fireplace. It was a chillier night and I had noticed that as August came the nights were shorter and the air was becoming cooler. Wearing a long-sleeved blouse and leggings, along with slippers and my hair tied back in a side braid (which became my new favorite hairstyle, and I also dyed my hair back to my natural auburn) I focused on the pages in front of me. I then smelt something . . . familiar. Stopping what I was doing, my brows furrowed in concentration, and I sniffed the air. Cologne? It was the same one Lyon wore. I looked up to see his essence sitting by the fire. I knew he wasn't really here in the flesh, but our telepathy and remote viewing was getting stronger.

"Lyon . . . " I whispered. Luckily, the house was quiet. I was alone down here.

"I am so sorry about what happened a few nights ago . . . please believe me I'd never cheat on you."

My eyes tearing up from the pain I might have caused him. I felt him closer to me, crouched down at my feet. I could feel a tingling sensation of his hands on my thighs.

"I know. It's not your fault. This Coven . . . The house, it's consumed you. It's trying to tear us apart. I know you're fighting, and the fight isn't over. I'm trying to get to you, but we can't find you. Are you hiding from me?" His brows furrowed with concern.

I placed my hands over where I knew his to be. "No. I am trying to get this house out of its enchantment. I have a plan. I just have to wait till the next full moon. Trust me. It's not you. You're the one keeping me sane. Some of the girls . . . My new friends . . . they're helping."

He nodded, "Keep them close, Amelie. This might be the start of a war if this doesn't get resolved. I'm looking to you for strength as well but know I'm always here. I love you, you're not alone."

I felt my heart open wide, like a weight had been lifted.

A sigh of relief left me as I smiled, "Thank you Lyon."

I moved to sip my tea and turned to see Raquel. "Hey, sweetcheeks. What ya doin?"

I smiled back at her, "Hey, just reading, having tea. Keeping my distance with everyone." Raquel also had some tea and moved to sit with me.

"Yeah, I noticed that. I'm just glad you're safe. By the way, I heard you talking . . . "

My face flushed in embarrassment as I looked down, "I was talking to Lyon. I see him sometimes, hear him. Tonight, I smelt his cologne!"

Raquel gasped, her eyes wide, "Damn, that's pretty intense. Not many people have that ability. Must be new. Is he like a ghost?"

I laughed, "No, he's in my mind, we telepathically talk, and I feel him, his touch. It's like he's actually here but I know that he's not."

I sipped my tea with a moment of silence before speaking again, "I miss him."

I saw her face go from shock to empathy, "I know you do; we'll get him back. We'll get out of this place. By the way, what Beth said weeks ago, I think she's right. About you being our new leader."

I pressed my finger to my lips, "Shh, don't say that too loudly," pointing to the hallway and then my ears. Raquel nodded, "Right. Well, it's just a thought."

I squeezed her hand reassuringly "Thanks for your support, and not thinking I'm totally nuts when I tell you these things between Lyon and I."

She smiled back, "Girl, it's your love life, your man, your experience. Who am I to tell you anything? I just hope it works out, and I want to help in any way I can. We're bonded for life now."

I laughed joyously and so did Raquel.

"The Sun Queen and The Empress." I joked, it was a play on the Egyptian Sun God Ra and the tarot card The Empress.

Raquel grinned, "Oh I love that. I can't wait till we have more adventures and I want to meet your best friend Ru! She seems cool and I bet we'd get along."

I nodded and grinned back, "You definitely would."

I was so grateful for the friendships I had forged.

Maybe it wasn't all bad. Maybe this was meant to happen to free these girls and step into my power. Maybe this was the path back to Lyon.

THE ROAD TO REUNION: LYON

II

I had been lying in bed in misery for weeks on end. With everything going on between Katerina and Amelie I felt like a fool. How did I allow this to happen? How did I go so far as to fuck everything up? A frustrated sigh left my lips as my forehead dug into the pillow.

I was either depressed, unable to go hunting, or I was out binge drinking with Alex and Gabrielle. We went as far as to go to some rave in downtown Paris and . . . Well . . . I lost it. It got so bad they had to drag me back home and lock me in the basement so I wouldn't go out . . . I remember laying on the cold floor, chained up against the wall, my bare back against the cement.

When a vampire overdoes it, it becomes an addiction, like any drug addict - they'll do anything for the blood. I was ashamed. What would Amelie think of me? She always said no matter what she loved me, but would she if she could see me now? I had gone cold on her telepathically too. I could imagine she was probably frightened, especially since we had no idea where she was. We had been telepathically speaking prior to this happening and there were times she sounded distressed or angry. I promised to look out for her, to protect her, and what was I doing? Being a coward.

"Amelie, please forgive me . . . " I whispered as I pulled out my phone to look at pictures of her. I felt the need to see her face. I wondered where she was. Her phone didn't seem to be picking up any of my text messages, and telepathy seemed radio silent.

My mother had tried to find Amelie through her friend and ally, but no tracking of any kind was working. It was like she disappeared. I was growing more despaired by the minute.

A knock on the door whipped me out of my thoughts, rolling over to sit up, running a hand in my hair to make it less messy, I hoarsely called, "Come in."

Alex and Gabrielle opened the door, their faces looking sad and worrisome. I moved to sit on the edge of the bed beckoning with my hand for them to come in. They knew the drill. Enter. Close the door. Alex leaned against the wardrobe as Gabrielle came to sit right beside me, taking my hand, her eyes that looked just like mine, were filled with tears.

"Lyon, I'm scared for you. Please, come out of your room, please be good. We want to help." I smiled softly in reply to her worry. My family really did care about me.

"Where is Maman?" I then questioned looking between the two of them.

Alex crossed his arms and shrugged, "We don't know. Last we heard she was looking for Ru and Amelie. It would seem that Amelie has no trace, not even electronically. Though she might have found Ru through social media, so that's a good thing."

Gabrielle squeezed my hand, "Brother, we need to find Amelie. Not only for you, but I am worried something is happening to her. Have you had any weird dreams, visions, anything you can tell us?"

I looked over to my siblings questioningly, "Well . . . I did have past life dreams before of her and I. Like she was reincarnated. She was a French woman before, but now she's American. Oh! And I have telepathy with her . . . But I've gone radio silent on her since . . . You know . . . " I said referring to being locked up.

It was coming back to me a bit more now. Over the last weeks my brain was so clouded with pain and anger that I hardly remembered my benders.

"The night I binged . . . " I couldn't look at them. The shame I felt was unbearable. "I did it because I was jealous. Amelie was flirting with someone, at least it looked that way in my head. I remembered feeling all these sexual feelings inside of me that weren't mine. I felt jealous, possessive. I remember us having a telepathic argument. I remember seeing her in a house full of women. It was like I was there, but I wasn't."

Gabrielle shared a glance with Alex. "We need you to describe that house. It must be in New Orleans; Amelie wouldn't have left that city unless it was with you."

Another thought crossed my mind.

"The weird thing is too, the night of my concert in New Orleans, I went to her place, it was clean, but nobody there. It was as if she had been there recently. Her workplace had new boxes of deliveries she hadn't yet opened. I know Amelie, she wouldn't shrug off her work like that. I have a feeling that she meant to work that night or the next day, and something took her away. She hasn't been home since as far as mother found out."

I let go of my sister's hand and folded them in my lap. I heard footsteps and then Alex's hand on my shoulder. I dared to look up at him.

"We'll find her, brother. You need to be strong Lyon. Remember, she needs you as much as you need her. You're in this together. You are one. Think about how much she'll need your strength in that house. You said a bunch of women. We need to figure out whose house that is, because my gut is telling me, she's in some kind of cult or coven." His tone meant business and I knew that I needed to get my act together.

Gabrielle nodded, "Yeah, you did say she's a witch, right? Maybe she joined a witch coven?"

I gasped, "Oh, I didn't see it before! It makes sense. I mean - her actions, her emotions, her attitude towards me. It was as if she was being changed in front of my eyes at times, just before I got jealous. I could sense some sort of spell-work being done on her. They hate vampires after all, it would make sense they'd try to manipulate Amelie's opinion of our kind." My eyes scrunched in pain, and I couldn't keep the tears in any longer. "I don't want her to hate me." I sobbed. Everything was happening so fast that I couldn't seem to keep up with all of it.

The soft hand of my sister rubbed my back, "Shh, no she doesn't. She wouldn't! This isn't your fault or her fault. It's whoever manipulated and took her. Amelie is like you. She's strong. Never forget your strength, Lyon. Remember who you are. You are a Prince; you are next in line for father's throne. You are a rock star rebel with a gentle loving heart. She loves you for all that you are, brother."

I felt myself leaning towards my sweet sister's shoulder. "You're right." I sniffled. "So, what do we do?" My words muffled into her shirt.

I felt her fingers in my hair. It always soothed me.

"Well, firstly, you need a bath, and fresh clothes." Gabrielle said with a teasing voice.

Alex laughed, "Yeah, you stink!"

I scoffed, "Shut up, Alex." Letting go of my sister and smiling softly, I gave them my thanks.

They both nodded, "We're with you Lyon. We'll protect you and her. She's family too." Alex said before helping me up and Gabrielle went to run my bath for me. It was so nice to be taken care of by family.

A few moments later they both left me to my thoughts in the tub. My memories flooding back to me as I soaked in the warm water. Being down in the basement was awful. It was an old dungeon that was used only for emergencies in case one of us did something we'd regret. Which in this case, was me.

All I could do was think of Amelie. Telepathy was all we had. Her beautiful image and voice would keep me company. I wasn't down there for long, maybe three days. Yet, those three days felt like eternity. I felt my body craving human blood like a drug-addict, my body shaking. I remember the growling cries that left me as I craved more and more. I knew that the family was just protecting me and protecting humans from me.

I almost devoured an entire bar! That was monstrous! That wasn't who I was, or who I wanted to be. After a while of withdrawal, I went silent. I stayed in my room sleeping, crying, or just lying there looking up at the ceiling depressed. I didn't speak to Amelie (through telepathy of course), or anyone. Alex had to bring me bagged blood just to keep me fed, afraid if I had a live human, I'd go crazy all over again.

With a sigh I splashed water on my face and let go of the negative thoughts. Grabbing a white towel, I got out of the tub, dried off and changed into my black jeans, a black quarter length shirt, and tied my hair in a low ponytail. Looking in the mirror I saw how horrible I looked; more pale than usual, dark under-eyes, blue eyes turned into a steely gray color and the rims going red. I wasn't myself. I wasn't the man Amelie fell in love with. I had to make this right.

Giving myself a few moments to myself, I sat on the freshly changed bed sheets, Gabrielle must have done it while I was bathing. Closing my eyes, focusing on my breath and then on Amelie. I could see her sitting in a room with a cup of tea reading a book. A smile broke on my face. She looked so beautiful, more herself, her energy radiating power and a feminine energy that shone so brightly like an angel. My angel. I was so proud of who she was and who she became despite the circumstances. I hoped that she could be proud of me too.

In the vision or what I thought was a vision, I moved towards her. A gasp left her beautiful lips, her eyes looking right at me. I reached my hands out to touch her thighs where she held her cup of tea and book in her lap.

It felt like I was in the room with her. I suppose this was the remote viewing gift psychics spoke about. I'd have to ask my family more about this. I could practically smell Amelie's perfume. We spoke for only moments, forgiving each other, saying how much we loved each other, when someone came into the room, and I felt my eyes snap open. A gasp left my lips. That was incredible and yet so surreal!

This felt more powerful than any visualization I had done with her in the past. I often doubted my conversations with her in my head, especially through withdrawals. Though I remembered I could read her mind in person so hearing her from far away wasn't that farfetched, right? I wondered if she could feel it too.

Either way, I found a way to get to her, to the other half of me. A new sense of purpose and empowerment filled me. A new determination. I was going to get Amelie back, no matter the cost.

Lifting myself off the bed I went to go find my siblings. I searched the house, my eyes looking at everything from a new perspective. I hadn't left my room in weeks; I didn't know the concept of time. I checked my phone to see it was 1am Paris time, and it was mid-July. August was only two weeks away. The summer was almost over! I couldn't believe how much time I had wasted in my own downhill demise. With a sigh I pocketed my phone and entered the library. Alex and Gabrielle were reading and drinking blood from wine glasses.

Alex looked up to see me enter and put his book down. I watched him move to the bar cart, picked up another glass of wine and handed it to me. "How do you feel?" He asked with genuine concern, his tone gentle.

I took the glass gratefully and sipped it, "Better. I feel more myself. I don't ever want to be the person I was again. I'm so sorry for what I put you all through. You must be all ashamed of me." I looked down at my feet not being able to look at them. Gabrielle moved at lightning speed to hug me.

I chuckled and looked down at her small frame. Like Amelie's. Her big blue eyes peering up at me, "We could never be ashamed of you. We were concerned and scared. Mother had to leave us after it happened to go find Ru, in hopes of finding Amelie. She was just as scared."

I felt a sense of guilt for that too. "What about the Court? The trial and everything?"

Alex put a hand up with a confident look, "Mother's taken care of it for now. It's on pause. I think she paid the judge or something for an extra amount of time. It was to get you back on your feet as you were in no condition to stand trial."

I nodded, "Good, because I don't plan on doing it without Amelie present."

The tone of my words came out way more confident than I had expected. A gasp left both my siblings and my signature smirk came back on my face. "I want her to be with me when that happens. I want to prove to them that our love cannot be broken. I want to marry her. I want her at my side as my Queen. I am next in line, right?" I jokingly side-eyed my brother, who had stepped down from his royal duties to pursue his business career. Alex and I laughed as his hand clapped my shoulder. It was the first time in months since I laughed.

Gabrielle started to cry, "Oh I am so happy to hear that sweet sound!"

It was happy tears at least. I hugged both of them, grateful to have them in my life.

"Let's figure this all out together." I said letting them go and moving towards a Queen Anne's armchair, it was a forest green, like the color of the couch I bought Amelie for her garden. I missed those moments with her terribly. It was then I noticed the fireplace roaring. Even in the middle of summer the mansion got cold, and it was more for aesthetics than anything else. Amelie would love it here.

I quietly sat and looked around the room, for the first time really sinking into the feeling of gratitude. I was alive, my siblings were loving and supportive, and my mother was trying her hardest to help fight for my happiness. Amelie was alive and well so far. I had nothing to truly complain about. Of course, my heart ached for her, her touch, her lips, her loving soul. I knew in my heart we'd make this work; we'd be together. No matter the separation or the hardships. No matter of any old karmic cycles. This was my fresh start with her and with myself. My body sunk into the chair, feeling relaxed, no tightness in my jaw, or hands. I was free. Within my own body. I had run from myself for so long I forgot what it was I really wanted out of life - then I met Amelie, and she awakened something that was lying dormant for centuries. Pure love. I wanted to tell her in person that I was so grateful for her, that I loved her, and that she meant the world to me.

Looking now towards my brother I leaned onto my knees with my elbows, hand clutching the wine glass. I sipped it thoughtfully before speaking. "So," breaking the silence, my brother and sister snapping up to look at me from their seated positions across from me.

"I know you asked me to tell you all about the things I saw in my dreams and visions while I had been going through some of the most horrific times as of late." They nodded silently.

"I want to tell you everything, it's just very emotional and hard for me to express . . ."

Gabrielle rushed over to crouch at my side, her hands on my knee, "You can count on us to listen, always. Please, take your time. Do you want to go outside to a cafe or something to tell us? We can -"

I cupped her cheek lovingly, "I don't think that's wise considering what I have just gone through. I wouldn't mind some fresh air, though. Why don't we go to the garden? I'll bring my blood with me, and there's more right?"

Alex nodded "Yes, in the fridge in the kitchen. We kept it for you for your recovery."

Recovery.

It seemed such like a taboo word, that of an alcoholic. Did I have a drinking problem? Was this going to affect my relationship with Amelie? I pondered this before speaking aloud, "I need to ask you both. Do I pose a danger to people? To Amelie?"

They both looked at me, Gabrielle now standing to grab her jacket. I stood up as well, not liking the height difference of my seated position. They looked unsure on how to answer that.

"Maman is the better person to ask. Apparently, she's seen the worst in all of us. She'd have the better answer to that question." Gabrielle answered while putting on her jacket.

I nodded and walked with them to the gardens. It reminded me of Versailles' Garden; the roses in the garden gave off such a lovely smell and it always reminded me of Amelie. She loved roses.

"Everything reminds me of her." I whispered more to myself than anyone.

Alex wrapped a brotherly arm around me, "I know . . . We'll get her back for you. We won't give up. Just keep your strength up, you need to be at your best for her. And for yourself. Otherwise, you'll only drag her down. We don't want to see that happen."

Turning my head to look at him properly I nodded, "You're right."

My legs carried me onwards towards the centre of the garden. The moon at its highest peak, looking up I saw how radiantly beautiful and bright it was. I could feel every ounce of energy in my body vibrate. I loved this feeling. I wondered if Amelie felt this way too. Or if we looked at the moon at the same time, it gave me comfort knowing that maybe we were, even on opposite sides of the world.

The grass was soft underneath me as we all lay down, side by side, the moonlight shining upon us. A sigh of relief left my lips. I kept staring at the moon, but I felt the eyes of my siblings on me.

"Firstly, I just want to say that I didn't know I possessed this gift until I met Amelie. I've always been very intuitive and could connect with other forms of the supernatural, but this wasn't a thing that occurred before. From what Maman's books said it's called 'remote viewing' you can see the person from wherever they are. Usually through meditation. I'll tell you what I saw. But after, I'll explain what happened before . . . before I lost it . . . "

Taking a deep breath and exhaling, I began to tell my story.

"Well tonight after we spoke and after my bath, I went to try to connect with Amelie. I wanted to see if I could see the house and her. I managed to go into a meditative state, and I saw her sitting in an armchair, similar to what we have here at home. She was so beautiful, simply sitting in the quiet space, reading, and drinking her favorite Earl Grey tea. I sensed that she was more herself, less aggressive or trying to change for anyone. I noticed her energy was all her own. I could see everything as if I was there. She could see me too with her psychic gifts. I crouched in front of her, my hands on her knee, she felt me. She placed her hands on her knee where my hands were. We spoke and apologized for things. I knew that my jealousy had hurt her, and whatever was happening between her, and Selene wasn't her fault. She was being manipulated by dark magick. She apologized to me for what she said too and for allowing it to happen for so long. Then someone came into the room, and I came out of my trance."

I sat up, one leg crossed, the other knee bent up towards the sky, my elbow resting upon it. Alex sat up too. "Well, do you know who it was?"

I shook my head. "No, it was a woman of course, but I didn't sense a threat. The house was definitely old. New Orleans style. Hardwood flooring, white baseboards, the old Victorian doors and furniture. I didn't see any symbols or anything that depicted witchcraft though. Although I could smell it on them."

Each supernatural being had their own scent depending on what the creature was or who was smelling them. Vampires have a very seductive and alluring smell to humans. While witches (depending on the witch) smelt either very bitter or very sweet. Amelie always smelt sweet because her essence was kind and soft and certain smells, I attributed to her like coffee and roses. Everyone's scent was based on one's personality as well.

Gabrielle sat up and frowned, "Keeping it in plain sight. That's smart if they are indeed a witch coven not wanting to be found. Next time, see if you can look at anything that looks suspicious."

I shrugged, "I'll try but I only see where Amelie is, I can't roam the whole house. Besides, if she can see me or feel me, then maybe they can too. I don't want to risk it." My sister gave a nod in understanding, and I continued, "All I know, is that she's safe for now. She misses me. That's all I need for now."

"So, what's the rest of it? What you had to tell us?" Alex asked.

"Well, the night I went mad . . . I had seen Amelie with Selene. The coven leader, a red head. She had been seducing Amelie from the start. Except I didn't realize it was manipulation. Maybe Amelie did feel some sort of attraction, I don't blame her. Selene is beautiful. However, I could feel Selene's dark energy, she uses her beauty to get what she wants. She's dangerous. I was trying to tell Amelie and she didn't want to listen. We got into an argument and well . . . when we went out that night I just got so consumed by anger and jealousy that I saw red. I wanted to drown my sorrows in alcohol and blood. I wanted to not feel anything. To distract myself. I never want her to see me like that. I had already scared her when we met, I don't want to do that again."

I sat in the feeling of guilt and shame as I retold the story, "I just remember thinking that Amelie had replaced me. That she was happier with the witches and maybe she was choosing them over me. I was scared to lose her."

Alex patted my back, "Fear of abandonment, jealousy, it can make anyone do crazy things."

I nodded sniffling, realizing that my eyes were wet, and I was crying. "I don't ever want to lose her, Alexandre. I can't."

"You won't!"

I gasped, my eyes snapping open to look to see my radiant mother. She wore a beautiful long gown, with a flowing sash around her arms. She definitely looked like a Queen. She was smiling and stretched out her arms to me. I ran to her and hugged her like my life depended on it.

"Mother." I cried in her chest.

She held me like a mother would any child. "Shhh, darling boy. I'm home. I am glad to see you are better."

I peeked up at her and moved to stand properly, my legs felt like jelly, but I braced myself on the white pillars of the house.

"Where did you go? What do you mean I won't lose Amelie? Did you find her?" She shushed me with a shake of her head and put her hands up, now realizing they were covered in fine silk white gloves. Just like she wore back in the 18th century.

"I have something for you." She said and took my hand.

Alex and Gabrielle ran towards us confused as much as I. I followed willingly, allowing my mother to lead the way. Walking through the long hallways of the house, chandeliers lit the way and the sound of our shoes on the hardwood flooring could be heard. I tuned into my vampiric hearing and heard a heart beat. A human. It wasn't Amelie of course but I was shocked to see who was standing in one of our parlor rooms. The room was decorated very neatly with white furniture, a fireplace against the wall and a big HDTV hung above it. Classic and modern.

A woman a few inches taller than Amelie with darker skin, gorgeous curly long hair, a pretty heart-shaped face and big expressive eyes, one dark and one blue was staring at me. Could it be?

My mother dropped my arm as I stood there gaping, shocked to see this woman, here, in France. In my home! "Lyon, this is Amelie's best friend, Ru. She's come to help."

I could feel powerful magick within her. Yes, this was the same Ru Amelie always talked about, her scent told me the same. I blinked a few times before moving to greet her, taking her hand in mine, she smiled gently shaking my hand.

We both stared silently. It was as if we were meant to meet this way. I could sense a bond of friendship with her. We both loved the same person in different ways. I sensed I could trust her.

"I'm here to help get Amelie back. I've been trying to reach her for months! She sent me one text before her disappearance. Plus, I've always wanted to come to Paris. I figured I might as well come here to meet you all and figure out a plan." Ru let go of my hand as I put mine in my pockets. She dug out her phone to show me. "That was in early June. Just that, *SOS*. Nothing else. I know she's in trouble and for her to not answer any of my texts or calls is not like her."

My mother smiled softly, "Well, good thing that Lyon acquired a new skill it would seem. Why don't we get you settled Ru, and we'll all talk about how we can save Amelie."

Gabrielle grinned, "Oh! She can stay with me, non? I never have girlfriends over." She pouted.

I laughed at my sister's antics, "Ru, meet my obnoxious sister, Gabrielle." I smirked.

The petite blonde stuck out her tongue and scoffed. "Leave my asshole brother to his insults."

Ru laughed. "I can see why Amelie likes you." She patted my shoulder and smirked. "Don't worry, we'll get her back. I wanna beat these bitches up myself for takin' my sister."

"Oh, sorry. I'm very honest."

We all laughed, "Honesty is great. The French love being blunt." I winked and squeezed her arm gently before Gabrielle went to show her upstairs.

"Well, now we gotta feed a human. Another witch." Alex observed.

I nodded. "I have a feeling we're in for something dark Alex. Not because of Amelie or Ru. I trust them implicitly. But I think something between the races might start if we don't intervene now."

Alex nodded, his arms crossed, same stance as me. "I agree. We need to find Amelie soon."

The three of us: Alex, Maman and I dispersed shortly after Ru went upstairs. Alex went to speak with our mother, catch her up to speed as to what had happened with me, while I went to Gabrielle's room. I wanted to get to know Ru, and at the same time, get to know more about Amelie. We had only knew each other for such a short amount of time, but it felt so much longer. With the dreams and the stories that my mother told me, it all pointed to a past life relationship and getting to know this Twin Flame relationship was confusing but the more I discovered about us and about myself the more it was making sense.

Even though I had been alive for a long time, Amelie had been reincarnated into this lifetime. I had been with so many others, and then Katerina which took over my mind. Only now was I truly awakening to the truth and understanding the connection between Amelie and I.

Taking a deep breath, I raised my hand to knock on Gabrielle's door which opened just as quickly.

"Hi, I wanted to speak with Ru on her own if that's okay? Considering she should be going to bed soon and well . . . we'll be asleep in a few hours. I wanted to take this time now before we figure out a plan."

My voice sounding so foreign to me now, the shame, guilt, regret of everything ebbing and flowing like waves of the ocean, each crash was worse than the last.

My petite sister smiled and left the room without question. I walked over to Ru, my legs feeling stiff all of a sudden. Meeting Amelie's best friend this way wasn't what I had hoped for. Closing the door, I sat on the vanity chair while crossing my legs in a gentlemanly manner.

"I'm glad you came. We tried so hard to find Amelie. I always heard about you from her, I wanted to meet you, under much better circumstances." I chuckled, hearing her chuckling along with me. She turned her body towards me. A symbol of trust.

"She absolutely loves you Lyon. I think I'm the only one who truly understands your guys' situation. I told her all about the Twin Flame aspects, and how you both had to heal. It would seem that you went through something awful. I can feel it." She motioned her hands to me.

I nodded. A lump in my throat appeared, tears in my eyes, "I didn't want her to see me like this. I don't know what came over me, Ru. I just lost it. I think my past, all the emotions of running away from pain, from true love, from vulnerability caught up to me that night. Did my sister tell you what happened?"

I watched as Ru shrugged her shoulders, cocking her head to the side a little, "She told me enough. Mostly, I can see it on your face. You look exhausted, scared, lonely." Her voice was soft, gentle and not at all forceful. Compassionate. Just like Amelie.

"Thank you for not hating me . . . It was never my intention to hurt Amelie . . . God, I never wanted that. I know I fucked up."

My body shuddering, sobs leaving my throat releasing the lump that was once there. It was as if a floodgate opened, and I couldn't stop myself. My hands reached up to cover my face as I cried. I didn't like being vulnerable around people but something in Ru opened me up wider than I thought possible.

What was it with witches doing this to me?

Ru moved to sit across from me in a lounge chair. She grabbed my hands and pulled them from my face. Her eyes warm and concerned as she looked into mine. Tears pouring down my face. I always wondered how we vampires were able to cry. It was a bodily function that stayed with us even in death.

"I am ashamed of all of it, Ru. Of lying, hiding from myself, not being honest sooner, for leaving Amelie out of fear. Now she's in that place and I'm scared I will lose her. I know we telepathically speak; we even remote view each other somehow. That's how we planned on figuring out where she is."

I watched as Ru's face went from worry to impressed.

I tilted my head to the side frowning slightly, "What is it?"

Ru smiled softly, "You both have spiritually grown then. Not everyone can do this, and Amelie didn't have that gift before. I agree that it is useful for locating someone that you can't otherwise locate in a spell. Lyon, we need you to do this for us, it's the only way. I can help with magickal support, protection, but this, this is on you. Do you think you can do it?"

I wiped my tears and nodded, "Yes. Though the only thing is, I can only see parts of what is around her." My eyes never left Ru's sweet face to gauge her reactions, her heartbeat telling me that she was calm, confident and trusted me.

"Don't worry, we can work on getting you better range. It takes concentration, deep meditation and practice. If you can do it, then we can figure out where she is. Maybe . . . Hmmm . . . I have an idea. Since we know she's in New Orleans, it might be best to go there. We can get a room and do it from the hotel. Then we drive our asses over there. Or . . . you fly I guess?"

I laughed at her question, "Amelie told you that?"

She nodded with a blush, "Yes, she tells me everything Lyon. I know more about you than you do."

I barked another laugh and hugged her. "Oh, thank you Ru. I needed this. I think I needed you most of all in this moment. I can see why Amelie is your best friend."

Pulling back to see her face I saw her smile a soft genuine smile that was full of love and friendship. I could tell that we'd be good friends.

"Well, I am sure you are hungry. Let me take you to get something to eat and I want to hear more about you and Amelie."

Ru grinned as her stomach growled and we laughed. "Yes, sir! Besides, I need to know more about the man my girl is in love with."

I smiled softly, she deeply cared about Amelie, and I could see the trust she held for her. I drove us over to a late-night café and as we sat down and ordered our coffees we began to chat and get to know one another.

Ru spoke first, "I meant to ask are you like royalty? I got that feeling with your mom back there. Does Amelie know?"

I nodded, holding the coffee cup in my hands, enjoying its warmth, "Yes. I am a Prince. I'm supposed to take the throne once my mother stands down. It was supposed to be Alex's turn, but he stepped down to work on his business career and he didn't want the responsibility and because I didn't want it, Mother was forced to stay on. I think she wants me to take it soon though. Originally, I was supposed to marry another vampire Katerina. She was my betrothed . . . That was when I met Amelie." I snuck a glance at her to see her reaction, but she was so intent on listening instead of reacting. "So, that's why I left New Orleans to come back home to deal with it all. I didn't do the best job of that. And no, Amelie doesn't know. I have yet to tell her."

I went silent, allowing Ru to say anything she deemed necessary. "Lyon, while I don't agree with how you went about things, you were doing what you could at the time. You also weren't awakened yet until you met Amelie. Usually, the Divine Masculine, which is you in this case, wakes up to things later. This was meant to happen. Katerina wasn't your forever; she was just a karmic partner who was in the way of you and Amelie. She was also your teacher, to show you who you truly were. Karmics are meant to show you pain, the side of yourself you hide away from. It looks like you started healing some of that. By choosing freedom that's a huge start. I know right now it seems like a set back from your hard work, but this is just the beginning for you. Have compassion for yourself. I know Amelie would."

It was my turn to scoff. "Wouldn't she think me a monster? Ru, I drank a whole bar full of people, that's not something I am just going to bounce back from. And it certainly doesn't grant me any merit of forgiveness from Amelie, on top of my previous mistake."

Ru took my hand gently, like Gabrielle would. "I know you're not perfect, nobody is. Amelie thinks you are because she sees the utmost best in you. She sees the *real* you. The you that you were always running away from. I'll bet there are things she knows about you that you don't realize. Witches are very perceptive and depending on their gifts can have claircognizance where you just know things. She has always had that gift. Now, all you need to do is work on you. Forgive yourself, for she will forgive you. She always will. You won't ever lose her. If anything, she's afraid of *losing* you. You are both one in the same. You are the Divine Masculine to her Divine Feminine counterpart as Twin Flames."

I sat in silence as I processed all that Ru said before I asked my next question.

"So, Ru. I wanted to ask more about you and Amelie. I know that she moved away from where she grew up, she left you behind, what happened? She never really said."

Ru finished what was in her mouth before speaking, "That's up to her to tell you, but what I can say, is that her family is highly dysfunctional. The person she was dating before you were not up to par with her at all. I think she longed for love, that she was hoping it would work out, but I told her to come here. I taught her how to do tarot readings and other spiritual practices like saging her home from spirits or evil entities. I grew up with witchcraft in my family, even some voodoo stuff, but I don't do that. It's not something just anyone can do. However, I do have Creole in my background and always wanted to go to New Orleans myself. I just didn't have the courage to go. Amelie did and I encouraged her. Now that she's there, and I know what's going on, I think I might stay there too. I don't want this, what's happening to Amelie, to happen to anyone else. Besides, I'd love to learn more about my culture and my family. My mom is psychic too, like me, but she keeps quiet about it. Amelie's mom was the same I think, and that's something we had in common. However, my mom always accepted my witchy side, Amelie's mom didn't entirely. But it's really up to Amelie to tell you." She finished taking a sip of her coffee.

I nodded in respect, keeping the mug close to me. The warmth giving me strength and comfort. It felt like Amelie was with us in this room. "I understand, thank you for telling me that much. I think we were so swept away with our passion that we didn't get to know each other in that way yet. I want to though. I want to start over. I feel this need to do it, to see her, talk to her, to give her everything I couldn't before."

Ru smiled again, "Well, now's the time to be the King. I mean, like metaphorically. In tarot, the King energy is one of empower-ment, strength and courage. But knowing you're an actual French Prince . . . well that might be a little more literal." She teased.

I rolled my eyes playfully and grasped her wrist lightly, "Thank you, Ru. I don't think I can say that enough. I'm so glad my mother found you. How did you end up going with her? It would probably seem odd to see some vampire coming up to you and asking you to go to France with her."

"Yeah, it was a bit awkward, I found messages on my Instagram account, at first, I thought it was a hacker, but as soon as she told me who she was, that she was your mother, and you all needed help with Amelie, that's all I needed to know. I knew she was in trouble, but I couldn't track her, not even with a locator spell. It's like her location is blocked."

My brows furrowed slightly, "Yes, even my mother couldn't find her. She's very good at finding people. It would seem some kind of dark magick is keeping her location hidden."

Ru nodded, "Which is why we need your power to help us." Taking another piece of her croissant eating it slowly.

A sigh left my lips again, "Yes. I will do it; I just hope it's enough. I do agree that going to New Orleans is the best. I wonder though, are you sure you want to room with me? You don't feel unsafe? Given the history between our two races . . . "

Ru shook her head, swallowing and sipping coffee before answering. "You love Amelie, and I can see she loves you more than anything. I also think you're super fucking cool. Besides, I was gettin' ready to come over here to find you pretty soon, until your mom found me. Regardless of the past, I believe in you two. I believe in your love. So no, I don't feel threatened."

I smiled and let her arm go before looking out the window. "Well then, tomorrow night we plan with my family and go from there. Hopefully I can do what you need me to."

It was Ru's turn to take my hand, my eyes meeting hers, "Hey, even if you need extra time to get it right, I'll be there. Whatever it takes. Amelie is safe for now. You'd feel it if that weren't the case. Twin Flames can feel everything. You'd know in your heart if she wasn't okay."

I nodded silently. Looking towards the window again I could see the pavement wet with rain. "Amelie made me see a whole new way of life. I don't want to stop until we find her, until I'm with her again. This time I won't ever let her go."

I looked back at Ru who had finished her croissants. "Wow, you were hungry." I teased and smiled, resting my hand on my chin, elbow on the table. "So, I guess you'll want to know more about me, huh?"

Ru nodded, wrapping her hands around her mug, "If you're plannin' on marryin' my best friend, then yeah."

My body jolted upright so fast I hardly knew what to do. "You know??"

She grinned this time, "You can't fool me. Pretty fast though don'tcha think? At least take her on a date first."

We both laughed. "Oh, I plan on doing everything with her. But of course, we'll take it slow, I don't want to lose her in any way. I want people to know she's mine." Looking down at my hands I braced myself for telling Ru more about me.

"Not even Amelie knows this about me. I wish I had told her before. I was a French Prince back in the 1700s. I had always been one as a human. My immortal mother and father adopted me into their family, I would be the youngest of three. Well Gabrielle looks young, and acts it, but she's a couple hundred years older than me. Alex is the eldest. My human family were killed in the French Revolution, that's when I was turned. My mother turned me when she saw me dying and bloody in the streets of Paris where the Bastille fell. I was 39 years old, and I was supposed to reign over my village in Tours, France. That didn't happen, so the vampire family I have now, decided that I would be a Prince in their household as they were royalty. We all looked alike, so it made sense. I met a woman not long after the turn, she looked just like Amelie, was from a middle-class gentry family, I absolutely loved her, we met at one of my parent's balls. They told me I was absolutely smitten when I first saw her. Though because of our differences in status, culture, and lineage we couldn't ever be. I don't remember a lot about that time. My mother says that I went through a big depression and despair, I blocked it from my mind. Until I met Amelie. It turns out, she's that same woman, reincarnated . . . That's why I feel so strongly towards her. It's why we have this special bond I have never had with anyone else. It all makes sense now. Though I ended up with Katerina due to politics. My mother had tried to keep the peace with the Vampire Court - it's our society's law maker. Even royalty has to listen to them. I always wanted to rebel against it. Katerina was only meant to help bring our families together to reign, like a

Renaissance arranged marriage. I thought it was so stupid . . . For a time, I think I did care for Katerina but not like I love Amelie. She woke me up to the truth."

Ru listened deeply, but her quizzical look made me pause. "Wait, why did this occur anyway, the arranged marriage? What happened to bring that about?"

I nodded in understanding, "Oh right, well my father died. He was potentially killed by a vampire hunter, or a witch. It's unknown how it happened, but he died, and Alex didn't want the throne, my mother being Queen took over until I was ready. I was supposed to marry Katerina to secure the crown. I never wanted to be with Katerina, but it was my political obligation to marry to become King, which is what my family originally wanted. Now, all I want is Amelie at my side. It wasn't easy to tell my mother the truth of who I fell for. Apparently, our races used to be quite close, we co-existed, until the Revolution. We turned on each other for protection of our people. Witches blamed us for hunting humans and thought we were the ones who brought this on them. And the war ensued. That's why the Vampire Court was created. To keep the races apart, to restore the vampire race and society."

I stopped then. It was so much history in one night to explain.

"Ru, I think I am done explaining for one night. It's emotional. Just know that Amelie is the sole reason I want to break free from all of this political nonsense. She's the one who gave me strength to fight back. I want her with me when I go up against Katerina's family and the Court. I can't think about all of that though until we rescue her out of that coven. And whoever else might be a victim there."

Silence filled the space now. She finished her coffee before we cleaned up and closed the cafe. It was nearing sunrise and we both had to get to bed.

Once we got back to my house the rain was pelting down on the roof of the car. I looked over at Ru. "Thank you for not judging me, for being a friend and ally, and for being Amelie's best friend.

You were there when I couldn't. I admire that. I respect you. You're always welcome in my home."

Ru looked over at me and we gave each other a hug, "Of course. Always. Also, I guess I don't need to ask your driver for any help today, I'll be sleeping like you guys at this rate." Her eyes looked to the clock on the radio it was 3am.

We laughed and I smiled over at her, fangs showing, "Get some rest."

I helped her out of the car and lead her towards the house. Gabrielle decided to sleep in my room with me and give Ru her bedroom.

As I lay in my bed, the cushions and pillows all around me, I smiled as my eyes closed to rest for the night. My soul sang with happiness and hope. This is what family was all about. Protecting, supporting and loving one another in hard times and in good. This is what I was fighting for. I wanted a good home for Amelie, and that's what I was going to give her.

As I slept, I dreamt of being in a ballroom, Amelie in her past form, my undead heart beating with pure love and happiness. We were the star of our own show, laughing and smiling as we danced, the people watching us. It feels so real. I can't believe these memories were locked away in the recesses of my mind for so long. I often wondered what happened between us. Was it the war between witches and vampires? Or was it something else?

"Because you are a Prince, it is your duty." I heard. A hand on my shoulder, my father. He looked between us and gave me a stern look. "Excuse us, mademoiselle." He spoke to her in English. Amelie gave me a sad look, holding my hand a second longer than was appropriate and moved along. I saw Katerina in the corner smirking.

I glared at my father, "How dare you do this to me. Do I not get any say?"

He moved me to the hallway; I looked behind me to see my mother watching us as I left. I looked at my father who was shorter than me, darker hair, we didn't look alike at all.

He gave me a look between sympathy and distain, "Son, you are a Prince of France, you need to act like it. When I am gone, Alexandre and you will be the next ones after me, should you take the crown. I don't make the laws. Don't make this complicated. You need to marry Katerina sooner rather than later. At least spend time with her, dance with her. Her father wants her to marry you, so you both can keep the vampire traditions going, to make the Court happy. I know I'm asking a lot, but to keep this family in its current position, you cannot see that other woman again."

I watched my father's face in horror. My heart breaking. No . . . "No! I won't do what you say!" I yelled defiantly.

He gripped my shoulders and angrily came close, "You will, or that girl is as good as dead if Katerina's family have their way. If you love her, protect her, stay away from her." He backed up, fixing my frock and lace. "I am sorry, Lyon." He gave me one last glance of apology, patting my shoulder, "You're a good boy."

He then went back to my mother. I couldn't believe this. I ran out of the ball outside into the garden as fast as I could. I looked up to see the moon was high and bright, it was the only comforting thing in this nightmare of my life.

I heard footsteps and a heart beat, turning around to see my lovely Amelie. "You heard all that didn't you?" I asked, turning my head back to the moon. I was angry - no enraged. My hands involuntarily clenching. I felt her small hand around mine. I relaxed immediately.

"I did. I know it's hard, I hate this too. If I am to die, I would die for you, Lyon." Her sweet French-British voice calming me. I looked down at her, my heart breaking. I was sure it was evident on my face.

"My darling girl, I am so sorry for all of this. If I had a choice, I would run from all of this. I want to keep you safe, and I know how powerful Katerina's family is . . . they would stop at nothing to make sure I was theirs."

Her head leaned on my shoulder, "We could be like Louis and Marie Antoinnette. Beheaded in love together."

I scoffed, "How romantic."

She giggled, "As long as I was by your side, I could do anything. Remember that. I will always love you."

We looked at each other and I leaned in to kiss her, her lips were the softest and sweetest I would ever know.

"Come back to me." I whispered. She nodded as tears rolled down her face. I tried not to break down, wanting to be strong for her. I put all my feeling, all my love into the next kiss.

"My heart is always with you." I said to her before sensing Katerina coming to find me, the neck hairs standing up a sign of my intuition and vampiric senses kicking me. "Leave now, be safe. We'll meet again soon."

She nodded silently crying. "I'll never forget you, Lyon."

It was then I was being shook awake, "Lyon! Are you alright?!" My sister's voice came booming into my ears.

"W-What?" I asked sniffling. Realizing then I had been crying.

"Oh, sorry. I had a dream . . . No, a memory. The night I lost Amelie back in the 1700s. You weren't in the family yet."

I sat up wiping my tears. Gabrielle moved to hug me. "Oh Lyon, don't worry, this won't be the end for you two. I won't let that happen. I'm here now, you have an extra person by your side. And now there's Ru. You didn't have us before. Now you do."

She cupped my face affectionately and kissed my forehead, "My brother, you are stronger than anyone I have ever met in my life. You can do anything."

I wanted to weep at her words, "Amelie said almost the same thing. She said she could do anything with me around."

My sister nodded and hugged me tight, my arms wrapping around her small body. "Thank you, Gabrielle. How is Ru?" I then asked pulling away. The petite blonde chuckled,

"She's fine. Alex is making her dinner right now. He learned how to cook apparently."

I sniffed the air and smiled, "It certainly smells good. I'll need to learn from him to cook for Amelie. Though I did manage a breakfast and coffee for her." Gabrielle let out a little giggle again, "Of course you did. I can't wait to meet her. She already feels like a sister to me."

My family was so damn supportive it drew me to tears. My father wasn't here to see it, but because of his passing this allowed me to be free. Then again, maybe he would have seen the truth as my mother did. My father loved me, he wanted to protect me. I see that now.

"Okay, so let Ru know I'll be down soon. I'm going to clean up and pack. And I need a drink." I replied coming out of my thoughts.

Gabrielle smiled again, "Blood cocktail?"

I laughed at how she knew me when I was stressed, "Please."

She nodded and went out the door to let me clean up and get myself together.

After much needed TLC I headed down the staircase with my luggage bag. Just a small carry on. Being a vampire had many perks in that I could pack light and didn't need many things. I could hear laughter and light jazz music in the kitchen.

Setting my jacket and bag at the door I sauntered down the hallway and smiled, "Well you all seem cheery." I teased. Gabrielle handed me the drink I asked for as I sat down across from Ru.

"How did you sleep? And how is - whatever Alex made you?" I motioned towards her plate full of food.

Ru giggled, "Oh he's a great cook. Didn't know vampires were so handy in the kitchen."

Alex beamed with pride as he stood near the wall, resting his back against it, arms crossed. Always adorned in his business waistcoat and grey pants. It would seem the 18th century never left him.

"As for sleeping, dude, that was the best bed I've ever slept in!" Ru exclaimed with food in her mouth. We all conjoined in laughter at her excitement.

"Well, come see us anytime." Gabrielle said. "Right boys?"

We nodded with a smile, "Of course. You're part of the family now I think." I said as Alex nodded in agreement. Ru blushed and silently ate.

For vampires who had eternity, sometimes we took up our human relationships faster knowing they were on borrowed time unlike us. It made me think about Amelie. How within one week we fell in love, separated, and now on the road to coming back together within the span of four months. Past life love was everlasting and ever moving. Not everyone understood that, but who cares? Nobody other than Amelie and myself needed to understand.

Fuck what others thought.

A new sense of duty lit up within me. I was determined not only to get her back, but to protect what was mine, to be the Prince I was meant to be, with her by my side.

Hours later Ru and I had taken a red-eye flight to New Orleans. Considering the time difference, I had to make sure that I wasn't landing in direct sunlight. We talked, joked, watched movies on the airplane and eventually she fell asleep. I let my thoughts wander to Amelie as I sat in my seat, looking out the window seeing all the little lights of the city coming into view as we made our descent.

I wondered if she was okay, which was something that never left my mind. My heart fluttered in nervousness now, a little anxiety thinking about how this astral trip would work in the hotel room. I had a sense of dread in my heart, like something terrible was going to happen and I could only hope that I could stop it.

I knew Amelie was strong, I had to believe that she could handle things on her own, but the masculine part of me wanted to protect her and felt that if I couldn't, I had failed her.

I was shaken out of my thoughts when Ru woke up and shook my shoulder. "Hey, where did ya go?"

My eyes averted down to her and smiled softly, "I was just thinking about Amelie, about what we're about to do."

She stretched and sat up, blinking blearily as she looked out the window to see we were about to land. The seatbelt light came on and the announcement came that we were landing onto the tarmac very soon.

"Don't worry, everything will be okay. She's tough like you, I'm sure we'll find her." she said with a yawn.

I nodded, sighing out the anxiety in my chest.

A little while later, we were out of the airport, the night air humid, sticky and warm. A huge difference from France, but I loved the sweet air of magnolias, lilacs and jasmine. Taking a deep breath for a moment I closed my eyes and smiled. I felt at home here. Maybe because I knew I was closer to Amelie and no matter where we were, she was my home.

Ru giggled which got my attention to her, my eyes opening. "I missed being here." I said shyly scratching the back of my head before getting into the cab she called for us. It was so wild and intense to be back. My heart panged at the thought of Amelie's apartment empty without her in it, her scent, her laugh . . . I needed to bring her home. An intense sadness came over me at the thoughts that played out in my mind. I looked out the window, watching the streetlights and people go by. Music playing in the streets, the jazz tones making me nostalgic.

Ru took my hand and squeezed it. We silently looked at each other, I knew that I wasn't alone. Ru quickly became a very good friend to me, and we had only met 24 hours ago. Yet, those 24 hours made me feel so much closer to Amelie and to the life we could share – the life we *would* share together.

Once we got to the hotel, Ru checked us in, and we headed to our room. The hotel was modest, not expensive, but not a rat trap either. We walked up the carpet adorned spiral staircase as this was an older building (of course everything in NOLA was heritage or vintage). When we got to our assigned room I put my bags down on the double bed. We had two beds in the room. We organized our sleeping arrangements for when I had to sleep during the day, Ru would go out to explore New Orleans on her own for the time I was asleep and try to get any information on Amelie or anyone she was associated with. Someone *had* to have seen her.

I lay on the bed with an exhausted sigh. I was emotionally drained and hungry. I had to compel the security at the airport to allow the blood bags through (Alex had put them into my carry on) as I wasn't ready to go back to drinking from live humans yet. Ru sat beside me on the edge of the bed where I lay, "Hey, I am the human here, you shouldn't be sleeping." She teased shaking my leg.

I laughed lightly, "Oh, c'mon you slept on the plane. Besides, this is more emotional exhaustion. Are you hungry?" The answer to my question was her rumbling stomach.

I immediately sat up. "Okay, so let's go explore. Find a nice Cajun restaurant for you to try." A smile broke on my face, excitement flooding me, "I love it here! It's my favorite city besides Paris. Probably because New Orleans came from France's colony and culture. I can speak both languages here fluently and people understand me, which is nice. Anyway," I clapped my hands to get us going, "let's get you food and we'll figure out what we're gonna do." I said while getting up to change, I needed to take off this leather jacket for one, it was extremely humid, even for me.

Vampires can feel temperature similar to humans as we can tolerate more cold and more heat. I preferred to be comfortable however, with fall and spring weather, though the summer heat radiated within me, and I felt more human. I personally just had a thing with wanting to feel a certain temperature on my skin. Ru and I took turns changing in the bathroom. I pulled my hair back into a small ponytail, keeping the front pieces framing my face. I grabbed one of my cross necklaces and wore that to go along with the look. I smirked at myself in the mirror. An elegant rock star. I always looked good. I couldn't wait to see Amelie, to see the way she looked at me, with such adoration, respect, and love in her eyes.

While we walked down Bourbon St finding a place for Ru to eat, I realized how close we were to Amelie's old apartment, she was in the French Quarter so close to everything and not very far from the Garden District. I wondered if her scent lingered in the city . . . stopping myself I stood in the middle of the sidewalk, closing my eyes and focusing. I sniffed the air. Inhaling and exhaling. I focused my mind on Amelie, remembering her familiar sweet floral scent mixed with vanilla. Her perfume. I could smell a miniscule whiff of it in the air. She had been here recently, but it wasn't that recent. Maybe two weeks ago? She must have been down here for some reason . . .

I heard footsteps and Ru's scent coming towards me. Snapping my eyes open I moved towards her. "Sorry, I had to try something . . . Amelie was down here. Briefly. About two weeks ago. I don't know why, but the important thing is, is that she was here. She's okay."

Ru looked up at me in surprise, "Wait, how do you know that?"

"I can smell her perfume, it's very faint, not picked up by the human nose." I explained as we then continued our journey to a Louisiana pop-up restaurant. It had outdoor tables, and an awning, we could enjoy our time outdoors, listen to the jazz music around us, and enjoy the atmosphere in an authentic way.

"Order whatever you like, my treat." I told her as she stood in line to order. Of course I didn't get any food, but I ordered myself a traditional Bourbon Sour.

We sat underneath the moon and stars at the picnic area, Ru had ordered a basket of fries, gravy, and Cajun chicken strips with a glass of red wine. I sipped on my drink thoughtfully taking in couples, families and friends gathering together for the weekend and enjoying themselves. This city has so much mystery and zest for life and the macabre that I couldn't help but fall in love more and more every time I came here. I knew that once we found Amelie I would bask in moments like this with her more and not take anything for granted again.

Ru munched on her food and took a sip of wine while she waved a hand in my face, "Earth to gothic rock star."

I blinked looking over at her with a side smile and chuckled, "That nickname is gonna stick, isn't it?"

Ru nodded, "Mhm, yup. It's your new name now."

We both smiled and I couldn't help but feel utterly content in this moment. Ru gave me another reason to fight for what I believed in, and she gave me a deeper sense of family. Knowing that she and Amelie were witches, and they didn't hate me or my kind, spoke volumes. As the Prince of France, I wanted to show the world, particularly the supernatural world that this was possible. The races could co-exist again. That was becoming my next main goal apart from getting Amelie back. It was my duty and purpose to do so. I couldn't hide from responsibility anymore.

As we enjoyed each other's company my mind flittered back and forth to Amelie. I was trying my best to be present and enjoy the city, but it wasn't the same without her. Ru took my hand as we walked down Bourbon Street down to Canal Street. She could sense my unease and pulled me to a stop. "Hey, we'll get her, don't worry."

It seemed that was a mantra she often told me, and it was meant to be comforting but I was getting on edge. I needed to drink.

"Ru, I know you mean well, but I'm getting kind of . . . edgy . . . do you think we could go back to the hotel room? I have my supply there and maybe we can see if I can do that remote viewing thing."

Her eyes looked up into mine, soft brown into my grey-blue ones. I felt bad for being a bit of a buzz kill but at the same time we were also here for the sole mission to get Amelie back, the three of us could celebrate later.

"Of course, Lyon. Let's get you fed and secured. I brought all my protection spell stuff too." She linked arms with me then as we walked back to the hotel.

Some people stared at us like we were a couple. If I was in a better mood I would have laughed, but my heart only had Amelie in mind.

As soon as we reached the hotel we prepared for the ritual. I locked the door and grabbed my bagged blood out of the hotel fridge, putting it into a mug and microwaving it. Nobody liked cold blood.

I sat on the bed drinking my meal when it was ready, while I watched as Ru prepared the circle, she placed salt around my bed and told me to stay where I was. I swiftly removed my boots and sat cross-legged on the bed. I didn't want to take the chance of accidentally ruining the salt circle. She closed the drapes as well and lit some candles to invoke protection. Her voice was soft yet commanding and then she chanted something in a language I didn't understand, before she took oil and rubbed it over my forehead, like a Catholic would at sacrament. I took a deep breath to relax my muscles. I realized that I had built up so much tension over the last few days. Finishing the last drop of blood, I put the mug on the bedside table and focused on Ru's voice. She looked down acknowledging me,

"Okay, for this next part, I need you close your eyes and allow your mind to be still. I will help you open up your Third Eye more so that you have better visibility."

I nodded, "Okay, I'm ready." I whispered.

She nodded and spoke the same words in the same chant as before but with more force as I inhaled closing my eyes and exhaling. I repeated it once more allowing my body to relax, allowing my mind to be at ease. I thought of Amelie and where she could be. Eventually Ru's voice became distant and then quiet.

As I was in this meditative trance I looked (inwardly) around me, my mind focusing on a big white house. It was a mansion, up on a small hill, it was definitely a New Orleans' style Victorian home. A black metal gate met me as I stepped closer. My eyes taking in the style of the home. The windows were old. The porch was a beautiful wrap-around with white columns to support it.

I noticed a black Mercedes in the driveway.

That's Amelie's car!

Shrubs and plants adorned the front of the house too, I could smell the magnolia trees. Leaning into my sense of smell I sensed Amelie. In my astral body, I felt my legs walk towards her as if on command. I floated around the back of house, the big magnolia tree surrounding a black iron balconette. Something that was decorative and practical. The moon was at it's highest. Amelie's perfume hit me like a brick wall. I felt so at peace and yet so emotional simultaneously. How much I have missed her. Landing on the balcony silently, I watched for any intrusion of someone other than Amelie – nothing. Taking another breath I stepped into her room.

My vampire eyes taking in everything, her bed, the wardrobe and vanity. I could see a walk-in closet and another room adjacent to that, probably a bathroom. I had to give it to the Coven leader to least give Amelie the best room. Though I knew that this wasn't what Amelie wanted. She wanted to be at home with me and Ru, watching movies, eating popcorn, or going dancing and having a fun time.

Don't worry, baby. I am going to bring you home.

I heard a gasp, my eyes looking around and finding Amelie entering her room from downstairs. A teacup and a candle in her hands. I blinked in realization that she opened the door with her mind.

My word.

She was getting incredibly stronger with her powers, her will was extraordinary. I was totally impressed. She entered, closed the door with her foot, and put the items in her hands down on the vanity.

"Lyon? W-What are you doing here?" Her voice was surprised but also a little sad. I knew she missed me too since our last talk which was a while ago.

"I came to see you, to make sure you were okay." Stepping closer to her, my right hand moving to caress her cheek. I felt the energy in my fingertips from the astral projection. I knew she had to have felt it too. A small smile on her lips told me she did. The moon and candle lights flickered on her beautiful face.

"I miss you. Ru is with me. I plan on getting you back home. I don't have much time, but please tell me where you are. We can't physically track you . . . " I spoke fast, I knew in my astral body that I was coming out of the meditative state.

Amelie sat on the vanity looking up at me. God she was gorgeous. Even more than I remembered her being. Her power gave her more beauty than I had expected. I could sense a confidence within her that wasn't there before.

"Ru is with you?? Oh God, I am so glad she's okay! I tried getting to her on my phone before they took it away. I'm glad you guys are safe. I'm sorry this is how you met her; I wasn't expecting it to go this way . . . "

She fell silent and I knew that I had to get the information soon. I crouched down and touched her knee, just like I did the night she was in the sitting room.

"Darling, I don't have much time. Please tell me your location." My words were anxious and rushed.

She looked down at me, covering my incorporeal hand with hers. "Selene, the leader, put an enchantment on the house. Nobody can find it if they are supernatural. That's why you and Ru couldn't find me. I know we're in the countryside . . . I had to drive at least an hour to get into the city."

I nodded with a smile, "I smelt you. Your perfume told me you were there a couple weeks ago."

She nodded with the same smile. "I'll have to explain everything later. Honestly Lyon, I don't even know the address of the house. It's like she charmed that too . . . I never see any mail. She either hides it, or she isn't registered to get mail here. It's so fucked up . . . Lyon, I am sorry I couldn't help more. Know I'm doing all I can to fight her, to get out of here . . . "

I nodded frantically my eyes pleading with hers. "I will get you home. I promise. Stay strong, stay safe. I love you." I then felt myself waking up.

No, no no! Fuck!

My eyes snapped open back to the room around me. Ru looked at me with concerned eyes as she sat on the opposite bed. Anger filled me. "Fuck!" I growled. Ru watched with wary eyes.

"Sorry. I was so close to figuring it out! I got to talk to her." I explained angrily while Ru quickly moved to give me more blood.

"Here. You did a lot tonight. More than I expected. What happened? What did you see? What did she say?"

Ru had so many questions it was only natural. Taking a deep breath to relax, I took the blood and a Kleenex from her dabbing my forehead to clean off the anointing oil and took a small sip of blood. Ru got more comfortable once I calmed down.

I patted her knee, "Sorry." I didn't mean any harm and wanted to show her that she could trust me before continuing to tell Ru everything I saw in the vision.

I took another sip of blood before continuing making sure to tell Ru every detail so we could hopefully get a location, "She said that she doesn't know the address, no mail ever goes there, and she doesn't even see an address on the house. Though I know that she drove there, her car was there too in the driveway. They must have enchanted it once she got into the Coven."

Ru nodded, "They lured her there and then once they got her they must have done an illusion spell to keep things hidden."

I told her everything that transpired between Amelie and myself before an illuminating thought came to me, "Tomorrow night we should ask around to see if anyone saw her. We have pictures on our phones we can show them, and maybe see if they recognized her or anyone she was with."

Ru nodded in agreement, "Yes, good idea. For now, you should rest. That takes a lot out of a person. I'll clean up the room and we'll pick it back up tomorrow. At least now we know she's an hour away from us, in the country and you know what the house looks like. That's more than we started with. Good job, Lyon." She hugged me gently before getting up to clean up the mess.

It felt good to see my darling girl. To interact and to see where she was. She didn't look hurt physically, but I could tell that her mental health was waning. Her determination was at full throttle. I needed to help her get out of there soon. Though I wasn't so sure she needed me in that way, she was pretty strong on her own now. I was so proud of her. Pride and ego wouldn't stand in my way this time. I was going to help her even if it was to hold her hand or pick her back up if she fell. I will always support her.

The next night, Ru and I were sitting in a cafe on Basin Street, not far from Amelie's apartment. Along the way there we asked the locals if anyone had seen Amelie or the people she was with. Not many people had, but one person did say they had seen two redheaded girls and a young Black woman get into a Mercedes Benz and drive towards the Garden District. They said Amelie's hair had changed from the photo I showed them, but the same face, same eyes, same girl.

We decided to go to the Garden District and see if I could pick up on her scent more there. New Orleans was known for the supernatural and the spiritual – odd things often happened in this city.

Lost in my thoughts again, wondering why Amelie would have dyed her hair and then dye it back again to the beautiful auburn that it was. Was she changing for someone else at the time, was Selene coercing her into doing it? Or was it something she wanted, but then changed her mind? My mind rattled with questions; it was almost unbearable.

Ru snapped her fingers in front of my face, I looked over at her and smiled, "Sorry," I apologized, "I was far away in my mind."

She nodded, "I can see that."

We were sitting by the electric fireplace, more for ambience and comfort than anything. It was still too hot to even have the heat on, even as the nights drew cooler as the summer passed by. I saw Ru get up and order another coffee to go and as she grabbed her coffee, I walked with her towards the door that led outside. The night air was refreshing. Inhaling the scent of peonies, jasmine and fresh lilacs comforted me in ways I can't explain. The scent made me feel like I was meant to be here. Home. Yet, it wasn't truly a home without Amelie here. I could still see myself here more than in Paris. I knew Amelie and I would have to talk about our future together and I wondered if I could live half in Paris and half in New Orleans.

"Hey! Earth to Lyon!" I turned to see Ru looking a little annoyed.

"Oh, *merde*, I'm doing it again. I'm so sorry Ru, I'm not trying to ignore you, I just have so many thoughts in my mind." I admitted as we walked down from Basin to Bourbon Street.

The crowds were getting bigger, the sound of the old jazz music filling my ears as we walked by. Walking towards the streetcar stop that would take us to the Garden District, my eyes looked at Ru's face more clearly.

"I know you're concerned for me and Amelie. I am too. I've been thinking about our future together, what to say, all of that. I'm nervous, anxious and scared all at once and then the other half is excited. However, from this moment forward I'll be more present." I said giving her a small bow of gentlemanly conduct.

A smile lifted on the corners of her mouth as she hugged me, "I understand, and I know she'll feel the same way as you. First things first is to get her out of that horrid place. And we don't want to waste any more time. Between your sleeping, and me having to take human breaks at night, it's narrowing down our timeline here." I nodded stoically. I understood the weight of our actions and that we were on borrowed time.

"I am sorry. I forget sometimes. What it's like to be human." I said as I pulled away from her embrace.

The streetcar got here just in time for us to board, Ru sipping her coffee beside me. "I wonder if we'll find anything there." I said to her thinking out loud.

She turned to look at me and gave a reassuring smile, "I'm sure we will, and if we don't then we stick to the plan, go back to the hotel, you do your remote viewing thing, and we get more details that way. Either way, things are speeding up and we can't afford to keep waiting. We need answers as soon as possible. I can feel that something is gonna go down, and I don't want to lose Amelie because of it."

I could feel the sense of dread and anxiety not only within her but within myself. As much as I wished my family was with me in this moment, I knew this was my cross to bear, my responsibility and I had to become the Prince and the man I said I was going to become. No excuses.

Upon our arrival in the Garden District, my legs carried me straight to Lafeyette Cemetery. Ru trailing behind me with quick strides to keep up with my long-legged steps. I could smell the perfume Amelie wore. It was calling to me. Even if it was too faint for humans to detect, I could still smell the faint whiff of it. Had I let this opportunity go before coming here, I might have missed it entirely.

Finally, my feet stopped at the entrance. I could feel my heart palpitating beneath my chest, my palms becoming a little uncomfortable. If I could sweat – well they'd be a sweaty mess, like when humans get anxious. For me, it feels like an uncomfortable tingling sensation. I rubbed my fingers together as one does when anxious. Ru caught up to me, breathless. "Lyon . . . Jesus dude . . . Could ya have waited??"

I looked down at the girl before me, my eyes stern, my purpose finally welling up inside of me. "No. I need to get in there. I just – I know what could happen in that cemetery. Ghosts tend to not be so fond of vampires. Some even play tricks on our minds – unless we are trained or gifted at blocking them out."

Ru snorted, "Um, hello, you have me! I can protect you."

She rolled her eyes before pulling out a necklace and putting it around my neck. It had some sort of stone in it. I think it was Amethyst.

"Do I do anything with it?" I asked humbly.

"No, you just wear it. I've done all the spell work on it. I have one too, just in case. Nothing should touch you."

I smiled gratefully at her and took her hand squeezing it affectionately, "Thank you."

As we made our way into the cemetery my vampire eyes took in all the sights, the moon high and illuminating the flowers left behind by loved ones, I could pick up on the faint scent of roses. I saw bats flying high into the moonlight, other animals roaming around the graves looking for food. It was quiet. Not a human in here other than Ru. It was us and the dead.

As we kept walking, I followed the scent of Amelie. Mausoleums and old gravestones were weather worn as I walked deeper into the heart of the cemetery, looking to the left I saw a statue of an Angel holding flowers in her hands. It reminded me of Amelie. *My Angel.* This reminded me of our rooftop time together when I held her in my arms and flew up into the sky. She called me a Devil and an Angel. A pang of remorse and sadness was felt in my shallow beating heart. Ru squeezed my hand. She could probably sense this in me. Witches and vampires were very perceptive to energy and emotions.

"Do you sense anything? See anything?" She asked. I could hear the anxiousness in her voice.

"I smell her perfume, it's much more potent here than in the French Quarter . . . "

I was about to say something else when I saw a ghost. An apparition. One moment she was there and the next she was gone. I turned my head, brows furrowing as I tried to make logical sense before I heard a voice coming on the left side of me.

"Why are you here?"

I stopped dead in my tracks, pulling Ru's arm slightly as she took a step to move ahead and was being pulled back like a yo-yo.

I looked down at the young woman in front of me. She was about Amelie's height, wearing a white gown. Her face was small, beautiful. She looked like she was from the 1800s, a ghost from the long past.

"I am searching for someone. Someone I love very much." I explained.

The woman smiled and pulled me close. I could feel her! It was if she was here right now in the flesh.

"Someone you love? A woman?" She asked.

I nodded. My voice leaving me for a moment. I had never experienced this type of spirit before.

"Are you playing games with me?" I growled. I knew of their trickery. Yet, the protection amulet Ru gave me seemed to work. It wasn't like this woman was invading my mind. She was just as perceptive as the rest of us. She cupped my face gently.

"No. I think I might have seen her . . . I see many people. Even in the day. Yet, most of us are slumbering, just like you vampire."

I felt Ru drop my hand and take out her phone, my eyes on Ru as to not be captivated by this spirit, "This is her. Except apparently, she had red hair, she was with another younger redhead and a Black woman. Have you seen them?" She asked the ghostly woman.

I saw the ghost frown as she focused on the cell phone. "Hmmm, I think so! I hadn't felt such power in this cemetery in centuries. Except for you, dear vampire."

I glared in annoyance, "Please, stop calling me that. My name is Lyon."

The ghost gasped. "Oh, so you are him! Yes, yes, I heard her talking about you . . . She misses you. She longs for you. She wishes to be away from those evil women in which she resides. Except, the two she was with didn't seem so evil. I think they wanted to help her?"

Ru smiled at the ghost, "Well, thank you, miss. We appreciate it. But if you slumber during the day, how come you saw her?"

The beautiful ghost smiled and looked as if she was blushing, "Oh, I wanted to see what was going on. I haven't been around very many women my age in so long. I was 24 when I died. My name is Cassandra." She did a curtsy and I smiled gently, feeling no harm from her at all now. I felt myself soften towards her.

"It's a pleasure to meet you, Cassandra." I said, giving a soft bow of respect. Old habits die hard.

She giggled, "Well, it seems we are from the same or similar time period. Oh, I haven't had friends in so long. I only ever wanted to make friends . . . Or at least enjoy my afterlife in some way. Listen," She beckoned us closer and whispered, "You need to go find those girls. I can sense something brewing in the wind. Do you feel it too?" We nodded. "I'll help if I can. I haven't left this cemetery in so long, and now that you can see me, I feel more alive than I ever did!"

She clapped her hands giddily and smiled, "Oh, despite the circumstances I am delighted. Should you ever need my help, call upon me by name. I'll come to you." She cupped my face again, "Gentle Lyon. Go to her." She turned to Ru, "And you . . . young witch. You will find what you are looking for in the women you seek. Companions, family, it's all there. What is your name?"

I could sense Ru's blush from a mile away, "I'm Ru. I'm a Creole descendant witch."

Cassandra grinned. "Well, you are here among your people now. Once you find what you are after come see me sometime. All the other ghosts will be so envious I have new friends! But don't worry, I won't let them hurt you. Besides, you both seem well prepared. Now go! Time is of the essence. I can confirm that your lovely lady is waiting for you." She patted both our shoulders.

"Wait!" I reached out to Cassandra before she could vanish again. "Where is Amelie?" I needed a location, a concreate answer.

Cassandra gave me a forlorn look, "I cannot say. Other than she is most hidden by people of supernatural kind. Most likely in an area not many people travel in New Orleans. Away from all the tourists. I am sorry, I cannot be of more help to you. I truly wish you the best. Call upon me if I can be of more assistance later in your journey. Goodnight to you both. She smiled at both of us and vanished.

A sigh left my lips, eyes blinking rapidly to try to process what just happened.

"Well, we have confirmation. And extra help! Let's go back to the hotel. Maybe I can use my laptop to scout places that Cassandra talked about." Ru said with a small smile. I nodded silently as we exited Lafayette Cemetery, now with more information than we started.

Later that night, Ru set up the laptop on the hotel desk scouting for places that Amelie might be. I sat on the bed as I allowed her to do her thing, drinking the bagged blood my brother provided for me.

An excited gasp left Ru which had my attention. "Aha! Okay, so there are two possible options where she could be. Prairieville or Baton Rouge. My gut is saying Baton Rouge."

I licked my lips before responding, "Well, what makes you think of that?"

She spun around on the chair to face me, "Well, it's Selene were talking about. As much as I know she wants her privacy, I can't imagine her in some boonie town like Prairieville. Baton Rouge at least has amenities. For someone as glamourous as her she'd want Amelie to feel . . . *special* . . . taken care of."

A lump in my throat started and my heart began to race with a fiery passion. "She won't ever take care of Amelie like I do. Though she's not wrong about one thing, Amelie is special."

Ru moved to take my hand in hers supportively. "We're almost there Lyon. We've almost got her." She then looked out the window, "The sun's coming up. Let's rest up. I think we should rent a car and see if we can drive towards Baton Rouge tomorrow night. Maybe you'll pick up her scent?"

I nodded agreeably. "Yes, I agree. Good plan. I'm going to take a shower and relax before sleeping. Thank you for all your help," patting her shoulder gratefully before putting my mug of blood into the sink to wash it and head into the bathroom.

As I closed the door a breath of relief left me. Moving to turn on the shower and let it warm up, once under the water I closed the curtain and sighed. All these months of pent-up stress starting to release a little. I had been wondering about Amelie and waiting to find the right time to get back to her and with Ru's help and devotion it was bringing me that much closer to the woman I love.

I couldn't help the emotional release as I stood under the cleansing, comforting water. Tears starting to well up from inside of me, sobs leaving my chest. I hadn't cried this much in a while. I just wanted her back in my arms. We could figure the rest out together later. For now, all I wanted was her. I didn't care about the Court or Katerina, or any of the political bullshit. I didn't care what others thought anymore. All I wanted was my girl in my arms tomorrow night.

Once I released what I needed, I started to clean myself up. Not that I really needed it but it made me feel better. Within five minutes I was out of the shower, dried off and wrapped in a towel. I went to go grab my clothes and opened the door. I trusted Ru to at least be modest with me. It seemed she was still glued to the computer screen when I moved to put my dirty clothes into my bag and grabbed new ones. She turned around and grinned, "Damn, Leo! No wonder Amelie is obsessed with you!" She teased.

If I could blush, I would have. "Stop it." I chided. "At least pretend to not see me in a towel . . . *Mon dieu!*"

I shook my head, hearing her laugh though made me smile. "And I'm Leo now?"

Ru smiled as she closed the laptop and got up to get ready for bed as well. "Amelie, I think mentioned it once. It's cute! Do you hate it?"

I chuckled softly, "No, I don't hate it."

Of course, leave it to Amelie to give me a sweet nickname. A pang of sadness hit me in my heart then. We looked at each other with a knowing glance and I then gave her a curt nod before heading into the bathroom to change into sweatpants and a white tank top. I felt positively American, but it was comfortable.

Once the two of us were finally finished for bedtime, we got into our separate double sized beds, facing each other, with only one lamp illuminating our faces. She snuggled into the bed, covers around her like a burrito. I lay with my head on my hand, the blanket only around my waist.

"Lyon?" She asked softly.

"*Oui?*" I responded in kind, a small smile on my face.

"Once we get Amelie back . . . Can I stay with you guys?"

My heart melted in an instant. She was the sweetest friend, and I could see why Ru and Amelie were best friends.

"Oh of course you can! Don't worry, we'll figure it all out. Do you plan on leaving America?" I was honestly curious.

She nodded. "I want to be with you and Amelie. Whether that's here in New Orleans or France, or half-and-half . . . Whatever. I just have never felt so connected to people like me like I do with you and Amelie."

I gave her another soft smile, my heart feeling so warm with love.

"No matter how it turns out to be, you're always welcome in my family Ru. No questions asked. And like I promised you; we'll look into your family heritage once we save Amelie."

She smiled and nodded before moving to turn off the lamp and go to sleep. I turned onto my back looking up at the ceiling praying to God that we'd get Amelie out of the Coven tomorrow. With the thought of her in my arms, lulling me into dark oblivion.

The following night, Ru and I rented a car to drive towards Baton Rouge like we planned. It was a silver sedan, nothing special, but something good on gas and I didn't want to get a flashy car and make it obvious. I wanted to be as inconspicuous as possible.

As soon as dusk hit, we drove out, I made sure to get her some take out as well and I fed before we left. If we were going to rescue Amelie, we both had to be fully energized. We sat comfortably with music low in the background so we could talk.

"Let me know if you need anything or a bathroom break, yeah?" I asked glancing over at her briefly. She had a soda container in her hand slurping on the drink she ordered.

"Yup, will do, sir." She smiled giggling softly before looking out the window. I rolled the windows down as it wasn't too hot or humid, the breeze was refreshing and made me think of when I'd ride my motorcycle or when I'd fly high into the clouds, the wind in my hair. I smiled at the thought.

Then one of my songs came onto the radio. I smirked while turning up the volume to let Ru hear it.

Her eyes went wide as she looked at me, "Yooo! This is you??"

I nodded, "Yup, this is the song I wrote for Amelie. I had to try to reach her in any way that I could so I figured my song would be heard and she'd know how much I loved and missed her." How I had the time to write between Katerina, coming back and forth the New Orleans and dealing with my own shit I had no idea. Either way, I was glad I did it.

Ru bopped her head to the song, I grinned and started to sing it in real time, going along with every word that I wrote.

She laughed, "You're good! I can't wait till you do a live concert again. A proper one."

I nodded, "Me too. It will come, once we figure everything out."

She nodded eating her fries while sipping her soda. It was around 7pm local time and because it was late August I was lucky that the sun was starting to set earlier, which for me was great, not so much for humans who loved the light.

Dusk had quickly turned into the deep blue almost black night sky. Stars above the city lights, only seen by vampiric eyes. Ru had just finished her dinner and threw the garbage into the back-seat of the car as I looked to the GPS on my phone which stated that we were almost to the location in question. My song died out on the radio turning to some pop song which I turned off.

I felt Ru look at me, turning to her I shrugged. "I don't feel like pop music considering all of the tension of getting Amelie safe and sound. I just can't be bothered with having fun at the moment."

She nodded in understanding. The mood went from carefree fun to anxious and serious. We sat in silence the rest of the way.

Once in Baton Rouge I stopped into a gas station needing to fill up the tank. As Ru went to use the restroom and buy another snack, I used my vampiric senses to scope out where Amelie might be, using her scent as my go-to.

As I finished filling up the car, I felt a jolt in my body. My heart stuttered as my head felt lightheaded like I was about to faint. Vampires didn't faint . . . I clutched the car with a gasp.

What the hell was that?

I saw Ru coming towards me worried. It felt like some kind of force field was lifted and I could feel Amelie's presence much more strongly.

"Lyon! What the hell happened?" I looked to see her panic-stricken face.

"I-I'm okay." I stuttered.

Inhaling slowly and exhaling I slowly opened up the car door, silently motioning for Ru to get in. As we got in I started it up driving towards the open road as fast as I could.

"What is it?" Ru asked.

"I know where Amelie is. She's not far."

I heard Ru's questioning mind before she voiced her questions.

"I think Amelie somehow lifted the spell – the one that stopped us from finding her. It's like a barrier was broken. I could feel it into my own body. Like . . . like something opened inside me. I can't explain it in words, it's just . . . a feeling." I tried to explain as my brain was on rapid-fire.

She put her seatbelt on as I sped at 160 clicks with the car in the open country road. My heart felt like it was speeding up as fast as the car was going, my anxiety, excitement and anticipation hitting me all at once. I was so close now. With nothing to stop Ru and I on the open road I knew that this was it. This was our road to reunion.

THE ROAD TO REUNION: AMELIE

12

The night has finally come. The night I will leave this place. I will leave this house and Selene behind. Ali stood behind Selene's every order, command, and wish – until tonight. It was mid-August. The end of Summer. I was ready to get back to New Orleans and be in my own apartment, to Lyon, to be in his arms again.

Never again would I ever allow anyone to manipulate me, undermine me, or make me feel small. I was the Divine Feminine and I was one of the most powerful witches in this house – no, in New Orleans! How dare Selene or anyone take me away from what is rightfully mine and away from my new home!

The plan was set in motion. Raquel had done a protection spell on Beth, herself and I. It was an extra measure to make sure this went as smoothly, or as victoriously as possible.

Everything was happening so fast, but if it wasn't now, it would only take longer, and I wasn't going to stay in this house a day longer. I didn't even care about the stuff in this house, except for my phone. Selene was distracted by a new recruit "show and tell" event tonight which gave me the advantage. She was good on her word for bringing in four new girls to make a total of ten. Yet, this would be their first and their last night in this place. I wasn't going to let them stay in this bullshit house, in this bullshit Coven.

As I got ready for the day, I fixed my curly hair in the mirror, satisfied with my outfit of black jeans and a green quarter length sleeve shirt. I made sure to wear my labradorite crystal for protection against Selene's glamour, which allowed me to see past her illusions. As I was pulling on my black combat boots, I heard a knock on my bedroom door. Beth had entered.

"We found where Selene keeps the phones, all the ones collected upon arrival. I wanted to help you find yours." She said with a small smile.

"Oh, thank you! That's perfect, I'll come down to get it. I can't wait to get out of this place . . . are Raquel and Ali ready?" She nodded.

After the events of the pool party Ali kept up the façade of co-coven leader but would give us tidbits of information of what Selene's plans which were to bring about a new reign of witches, to take out the vampires of New Orleans, and then across the globe. It was going to be a vampire genocide! I would not allow her to hurt Lyon, or any other creature that I deemed important. This whole race war between the vampires and witches was disgusting and I was not tolerating it.

As soon as I laced up my shoes I got up and grabbed Beth's hand with a smile, "Let's go."

We headed downstairs sneakily, Raquel was behind us too, slipping out of her room as she saw us on the mezzanine. I could hear Selene and Ali talking amongst themselves in the basement (noise carries in this old house) about how to get the new girls started tonight. I looked at the time – 8pm. In about three hours they would arrive and start the rituals, the same ones I did when I got here. I scoffed inwardly.

I was ending this. *Now.*

Beth snuck down the hallway and motioned for us to follow her. The hardwood flooring creaking as we tiptoed across to Selene's office.

Raquel whispered "I'll keep watch. Get my phone, it's purple."

I nodded, following Beth to a door down the hall, the office. I found the desk that had standard office supplies on top. I tried pulling open the drawer on the right side, but it wouldn't budge.

Of course it was locked.

Stepping away from the desk in frustration I searched the bookshelves. I remembered in old Victorian movies; many people would hide things in books. My gut instincts led me to a beautiful green colored book, with a matching green ribbon inside the pages, the book was about Green Witches or alternatively called Kitchen Witches, the gardening, herbal kind.

I opened the book to find a small old fashioned gold key inside. Perfect! I grabbed it, hastily putting the book back and passing the key to Beth. My heart racing so fast I thought it might beat out of my chest. I hoped we wouldn't get caught. She opened the desk drawer, and we found our phones. I grabbed Raquel's purple one and my own. Beth grabbed hers too. With a grin I looked at Beth smiled before Raquel told us to hurry up. The two of us put the key back, pocketing our phones and heading out of the office before Selene found out. Raquel ushered us upstairs before we could be caught. As soon as we were in her room, she locked the door as I passed her the purple phone and sat on her bed.

"That was *awesome*, but scary."

We all giggled. It was *absolutely* terrifying! My heart was still racing.

"At least that part is over with. Once we dispel the house, we can finally turn our locations on and get help! I can call Lyon or Ru. I know they're looking for me."

Raquel and Beth shared an uncertain look.

"Do you think they'll take us with ya'll? At least just as far as Downtown New Orleans?"

I nodded without hesitation. "Of course! Whatever you girls need, I'm here to help. I'm sure we can figure something out."

A sigh of relief left Raquel lips. "Ah, thanks girl. Makes me feel a little better. I don't wanna be left here . . . "

I gave them both a reassuring look, "Of course you won't be left behind. I wouldn't do that to you girls."

They both smiled. Silence fell upon us for a few moments.

My mind wandered to how we could end this enchantment of the house. However, my magickal research (I found some old

books about spell work) showed that since the house was technically a physical item, a simple magick spell wouldn't work. No
magick can dispell an item attached to a person, unless it was
physically destroyed.

"Guys . . . " Raquel and Beth looked towards me knowingly.
"We need to burn this house down . . . before those girls get
here . . . We need to bring Ali with us too. No magick can stop this
spell. One of my late-night tarot sessions told me as much . . . I
thought it would be easier than this – apparently not." I explained.

Raquel moved to light her sage. She didn't have to say anything.
I was with her. Beth moved to light some candles. I stood up and
watched as they did this. Raquel dropped her burning sage on
the wooden floor, Beth knocking over the candelabras and ran
out of the room. With my Fire gift I focused on the fire that had
sparked, the flames growing bigger, climbing higher.

We then rushed down the stairs, our footsteps sounded like a
heard of elephants. I turned on my phone hoping for signal. Ali
and Selene rushed up the steps. Ali came to the top with Selene
behind her, she boldly, and silently turned around to elbow Selene
in the ribs, then kicked her down the stairs. An ear-piercing
shocked scream left Selene's lips. Ali closed the basement door.

"Let's get out of here." She said as the flames were dancing
across the top floor mezzanine. Delainey rushed down the stairs
to the second floor from her room.

"What the hell is goin' on??" she screamed, looking absolutely bewildered.

"Amelie, did you set the damn house on fire with your
Fire Magick?!"

I nodded. "I did. I'm getting the fuck out of this house, away
from all of this. I'm going home and back to the love of my life.
I don't care what you or Selene say. I'm over this fucking Coven.
This wasn't a true Coven – this was tyranny and abuse."

Delainey rushed down the stairs before the flames could get
to her. The thick black smoke billowing, consuming the second
floor, rising towards Delainey's floor up towards the attic.

"We gotta go!" Ali said grabbing my hand as Selene was pounding on the basement door.

Beth, Raquel and I followed Ali outside of the house, my feet just landing on the porch when I felt my hair being yanked from behind. My scalp burning in pain. A scream left my lips as my hands clutched the person who grabbed me. I looked up to see Selene's red hair in my face.

"After all I've done for you, this is how you repay me!"

She dragged me back inside the house. *No!* My gut lurching into my stomach, my heart racing. As fear gripped me. I didn't want to die in a burning house. Beth, Ali and Raquel were already at my car, they turned around to see me being pulled back in the house. I moved my hands to grip the threshold of the door, my scalp hurting, I felt my hair starting to rip out of my head. Tears pricking my eyes from the pain. The flames engulfing the whole house now.

Ali rushed towards me. "Selene, enough! Your reign of terror is over! Let her go, let us go!"

Selene pulled me closer to her chest, spitting venom at Ali. "You ungrateful bitches! I gave you power, a home, a place to belong. Amelie is the one that I always wanted. That vampire leech doesn't deserve her. He's a player, a user. He just wants to drain you dry, and then what Amelie? You'll be dead . . . I can't let you die to that fiend!"

I sensed fear in Selene. She genuinely believed in what she was saying. She obsessed over me for months. This was an unrequited love gone wrong, the kind you hear about in movies – except this was real. This *was* happening.

"Please . . . Just let me go." I wheezed. The smoke choking my lungs. Selene's fingers gripped me tighter, her one arm wrapped around my chest. She was desperate. Delainey was right by her side. She was just as warped and seeking approval like Selene.

Ali put her hands up in defense. "Please, Selene. You don't need to do this. You'll have other girls, but this is not the way. You can't force people into this. Just because you have family inheritance and power doesn't mean you can abuse it! I believed in the Coven when we first started. Giving women a place they belong, to use their powers for good, to start something new. This . . . This is not it . . . Killing Amelie won't make this better."

She turned to Delainey. "Is this really what you want? Straight out of university, to become a killer? To go along with whoever tells you to? That's not what this was about. This was about female empowerment. Not tyranny. Not murder!" Her voice was frantic now yelling over the roar of the flames. The house creaking and groaning as it was starting to fall apart.

"Ali . . . Move." I choked out.

I looked up at the beam above us, concentrating all my energy, the electricity building within me, I could feel the heat within my spinal column, my fingertips electrified. The beam crashed down, making Selene let go and setting me free from her grip. As this happened Ali jumped back with a scream. She grabbed my hand. We coughed, the black smoke almost blinding us.

"Get to the door . . . " I groaned, my lungs not being able to take much more. Ali grabbed my wrist helping me to the door but as soon as she touched the door handle, she pulled back. It was too hot.

"The door must have shut on its own or Selene did it with magick." Her voice was scared and shocked at the same time. I was too busy being strangled to pay attention.

Delainey and Selene were down at the end of the hallway, slowly moving towards us. Delainey used her Levitation Gift to move the beam out of the way. "You think that's goin' to stop us?" She smirked; her blonde hair covered in ashes looking like a corpse bride in her white dress.

Ali put her hands up making a barrier to protect us. She turned to me, "Find a window to break or something!"

I moved to the side entrance towards the kitchen, trying to find anything to break the glass. Everything was on fire. The flames were too thick, too high . . .

I looked out the bay window and what I saw shook me to my core.

Lyon and Ru came out of the car. They were here. Lyon was here?! My chest automatically wracked with sobs. I couldn't die in here.

"Lyon!" I screamed as loud as I could, even as my throat and lungs burned. My hands pounding on the glass. I saw the two of them rush to Raquel and Beth trying to figure out what happened.

"Hurry!" Ali cried out in fear. Her strength was weakening due to the fire as well. The house groaned and creaked again, another beam fell behind me making me jump and scream. Lyon knocked on the window.

"Amelie!" I heard his voice muffled by the fire and glass. "Stand back!"

I coughed into my sleeve and nodded turning away from the window to shield my eyes. I heard breaking glass, the pieces falling everywhere, the front of the house shook, falling apart. I screamed falling to the hot floor. The beams that held up the porch and front end of the house were now falling apart.

"Hang on." He said moving to hold that part of the house up. My eyes adjusting to the light and the air of outside. The smoke billowing out.

"What about Ali?" Delainey was now throwing objects like a poltergeist to break down Ali's shield.

"Don't worry, I'll get her out once I get you out. You're my top priority now. Please, darling, get outside." I watched his face fall into fear and so many more complex emotions. Fear, regret, sadness, love, relief for finding me.

I looked between Lyon and Ali. I couldn't leave her. Even if Lyon said he'd get her out, which I believed, I still couldn't leave her behind. Witches had a code too.

"I can't leave her." I whispered before moving to help Ali.

'AMELIE!" He yelled. Almost a growl.

I helped by giving Ali my energy to hold up the shield.

"We do this together." She gave me a look of pure determination. I held her hand in mine, my right hand up like hers and focused on the shield. Delainey and Selene laughed manically.

"You think you're more powerful than me??" Selene grinned, "Wow, that's so cute. But I'm going to kill you both and your little boyfriend."

Delainey was still throwing objects and it was getting to the point the house was going to collapse on both of us. I then saw a flash of movement from the corner of my eye, then Lyon was there. I don't know how the front of the house was being held up but I had a feeling the girls outside were helping. Lyon was behind Delainey. He picked her up and threw her to the ground, knocking her out.

I watched in subtle horror and shock as he grabbed Selene, his fangs bared, eyes wild, his tone angry and low.

"You won't get the chance." He sunk his fangs into her as she screamed. Ali and I were then able to bring the shield down.

"Amelie!" Ru shouted from the window. "Come on!"

I saw the window was held up by vines. Beth was standing beside Ru using a new power I never had seen before. She was finally free of her delusional cousin, her full tapped potential now available. She held her hands out to her sides, her magick manipulating the tree roots, vines and plants. They were holding up the house so we could climb out. Selene's screams stopped. The house starting to crumble. Ali climbed out with the help of Ru.

"Okay Amelie your turn." Ru said motioning for me to start next. As soon as I went to take a step out, the house shook. I fell back with a gasp. I looked up at the ceiling. One last piece of the roof was collapsing right on top of me. If I was to die right this second, at least I knew I fought till the end, that I got to see Lyon and Ru. They came for me. The love of my life never stopped loving me, never stopped trying to find me. Tears left my eyes at the thought. As soon as the last piece fell I closed my eyes scared for the impact. But it never came.

I opened my eyes to see Lyon standing above me, holding the ceiling piece in his hands like Superman. His face slightly straining from the weight.

"Amelie . . . Go . . . " He groaned. "Go . . . "

I coughed, my lungs at their full capacity of smoke. I knew I had to do as he said. I always could trust him. I slowly moved my body to sit up, and crawl towards the open window. Once I was out of the way, Lyon threw the ceiling towards the kitchen and rushed to help me out. Just as he helped me get onto the porch, the boiler in the basement blew up shaking all of us to the core.

I held onto Lyon for dear life.

"I've got you." He said softly and held me close, carrying me in his arms bridal style. He then spoke to Ru, "Get the girls out of here, go to the nearest hospital. I'm going to take her myself. I'll be faster, but I can't take everybody."

Ru nodded and helped Ali, Beth, and Raquel into the car.

"Come on, let's go. I'm not letting you go this time." He said to me pulling me closer to his chest before ascending to the sky. My eyes focusing on his beautiful face. My Angel. My Devil. My savior.

I woke up days later in the hospital in New Orleans. Lyon had stayed with Ru in my apartment once they got their things from the hotel. They set up the girls from the Coven into a hotel for a few days until I recovered. I had bad smoke inhalation, as did Ali and we had to be monitored for any lasting side effects.

Delainey and Selene were pronounced dead, their charred remains were found in the house, and the house fire was ruled an accident from a candle falling over. The reports on the news stated that the girls who were supposed to go to that house ended up calling the police once they saw the destruction. I was happy that no criminal charges were laid against any one of us, and now that Selene was gone, Beth had been told that her inheritance from Selene would be passed down and with that money she would be free to do whatever she wanted.

All of this was translated to me from Lyon and Ru who visited me in the hospital. It was so nice to be back in New Orleans and with the people I loved the most. Once the doctor gave the go ahead, I was allowed to go back home. There was so much I needed to catch up on. I missed four months of my life and I wanted to start over – *again.*

Lyon held my hand as he sat beautifully in the chair beside my bed.

"I'm so glad you're awake, that you're alive. I was so scared. I never will leave you again." He kissed my hand.

I leaned in to kiss his sweet lips. "I've missed your kisses."

He chuckled, "I've missed yours too."

I coughed slightly. He frowned and put a hand on my forehead. "I'm okay, love. Just still recovering."

He nodded, "I know. I told my mother I'd be staying a while here. My family understands, and when we're ready, they want to meet you."

I nodded silently. I wanted to meet his family but in this state I definitely wasn't ready. We still needed to get to know each other again, to take things slow and I knew he understood that.

Ru then came into the room. "Hey girl, I got you coffee."

I grinned, "Oh man, I am so excited for coffee."

Lyon playfully rolled his eyes. "My competition."

His dry French humor shining through. I laughed and then winced at the sharp pains in my throat and lungs still.

"Don't make me laugh! It hurts . . . " I pouted before taking the coffee and thanking Ru.

"But I missed your humor. I've point blank just missed you."

He smiled softly again, his blue eyes shining with love back at me. "Me too." He pressed his forehead against mine affectionately before I sipped my first coffee in a week. The flavors of bitter and sweet blending together perfectly on my tongue. I moaned with a smile, eyes closed briefly before opening them, seeing my beloved staring back at me with such adoration. "It's good?" He asked.

I giggled, "Yes, but not as good as you."

He leaned forward to kiss my lips once more before visiting hours ended. "I'll be back tomorrow. I love you."

He whispered as I leaned into him, inhaling his beautiful scent of pine, cinnamon, cloves and leather.

"Okay, hurry back. I love you too."

The nurse came back in the room to usher my best friend and beloved out the door. She smiled looking at my adoring family as they left, then at me. I took a few more sips of coffee and placed the Styrofoam cup on the bedside table. The nurse then walked towards my bed, looking at my chart and took my vitals.

"You have an incredible support team I see." She said.

"Yes, I do. They're my family. Not by blood, but by choice."

She nodded as she moved to put a light sedative in my IV to help me sleep. "Oh, when can I leave?" I asked.

The nurse looked down at me softly, "Hopefully tomorrow. Once the Doctor is satisfied with your results you should be able to leave in no time. I'm sure you're eager to be with him, huh? He's a handsome man."

I giggled, feeling my eyes become heavy. "He's the best . . . " As soon as the words left my mouth I was out like a light, with thoughts of my Lyon.

The next evening the Doctor said everything seemed normal. My lungs were smoke free, and I was on inhalers to offset any asthma symptoms I may have. I had to take them twice a day until I was clear.

Ru came to get me as Lyon was still hiding from the setting sun. I was told that we were to meet back at my apartment.

Oh, how I missed my place.

The nurse helped me get dressed and wheeled me in a wheelchair towards the registration desk. Ru was standing by with a coffee in her hand. "Hey babe! So glad to see you up and outta here."

"Yeah, they took good care of me." I looked up at my nurse who had the kindest disposition. "Thank you." I said to her.

The nurse smiled, "You're welcome, be well."

She handed me the discharge papers that had the Doctor's signature that I was allowed to leave and was handed the medications they had prescribed me. We said goodbye to her before Ru took the wheelchair, handing me her coffee to hold in my lap as she pushed me.

"Oh, this is such a tease! I want coffee . . . " I pouted.

I heard Ru laugh behind me, "Oh hush. I'll get you one, don't you worry. I grabbed mine on the way here while waiting for you."

Within minutes the hallways turned to the front automatic doors. I could see the trees, the setting sun in the horizon, my heart beating wildly in excitement to be out of this building and be back into the world in which I desperately belonged to.

Once outside, Ru parked me right in front of her car.

"Hang on, let me clear the passenger side for you."

I weakly got up, holding onto the wheelchair. Inhaling a breath of fresh Louisiana air. The humidity still hung in the air, but only slightly as it was now the very end of August. September was only days away. I got into the car once Ru was ready, she waited till I was in the passenger seat properly and buckled in before she closed the door and got over into the driver's side.

As soon as she was settled and turned on the engine, we headed towards our favorite coffee place – Starbucks.

"You gonna have another one?" I teased.

She smirked, "It's *STARBUCKS*. Obviously."

I laughed, coughing again slightly. "You sound like me. Lyon is now going to have to deal with two coffee addicts."

She nodded with a laugh as she focused on the way out of the hospital, onto the main road towards the coffee shop. I rolled down the window to get more fresh air.

"How is he? Lyon?" I asked finally.

I was dying to know how he was holding up.

"He's okay. Worried for you. I called him to tell him I was picking you up, so instead of coming late at night, we figured I'd get you early and he could set up your apartment and everything.

He's so sweet. I think he missed being in your space. Just around you, really."

My face softened, a small smile creeping on my lips, "As I told the nurse last night, he's the best. I love him so much."

As we approached Starbucks, she nodded eyes on the road, "That man loves you like nobody I've ever seen. I mean, he came back for you. He never let you go. He never gave up. He went through his own Hell and back for you, for your relationship. I can tell he's a keeper."

I smiled again. We got into the Starbucks line up and we ordered our coffees, she also got me a snack seeing as I didn't really eat at the hospital. We were then back on the road back to the French Quarter. My heart raced nervously and excitedly. I wanted to see Lyon, but this time our relationship would be different. Slower. At ease. Less stress and more stable.

"One thing though . . . you gotta be honest with him. He asked me some personal questions about what happened with your family. He wants to know all sides of you, and I think you owe him that." She gave me a serious but gentle look.

I sighed. "Yeah, you're right. I know he has a lot he wants to say too. Maybe that's why I'm so nervous. Yet, I am excited to be back in my own place again and to start over with him. Fresh energy. No more drama holding us back. Just us."

Ru gave me a smile as she looked over at me before turning down Basin Street towards my place. I saw the lush trees, the setting sun peeking through the magnolias and the smell of peonies and jasmine wafted through the window as we pulled up to my building. She got out and helped me out before holding me up so do the stairs – one thing I hated was no elevator. I couldn't wait to have my own house. Yet, most of the houses in New Orleans had many stairs. At least I could ask Lyon for some help if I needed, at least for times like these when I am incapable of such a feat.

"You got this." Ru said as we ascended. Once we got to my door, I barely had time to open it before Lyon almost whipped the door off its hinges in his excitement.

He moved to scoop me up into his arms hugging me to him. I giggled and snuggled into his shoulder. "Hi." He kissed my temple before lightly putting me on my feet.

"I'm so happy you're home." He said, my eyes catching his.

I felt myself melt and sigh lovingly. "Me too. And what a great welcome." I laughed taking his hand. Ru had the coffees in her hands now. I now just realized she held the coffees in a tray and helped me up the steps. She had great balance clearly. Something I did not possess, even at the best of times.

Lyon led me to the couch in the living room. Ru closed the door and locked it before coming over and placing the coffees on the coffee table. She put her purse on the armchair opposite to the couch before sitting down. Lyon pulled me into his lap, my head on his shoulder. His long arms enveloping me, long piano fingers clutching me close to his body. I closed my eyes, not being able to help how protected and loved I felt. I felt like Thumbelina cocooned in the clam shell, snuggled up tight and protected from the outside world. It was all thanks to Ru for getting him here, and to the girls who helped me escape. With that thought I popped my head back up, Lyon looking down at me adoringly, I could see the love shining in his eyes.

I smiled before speaking, "I forgot to ask. How's the girls? Raquel, Ali, and Beth?"

Ru looked between both of us. I had to shift in his lap in order to look at Ru better. "Well, they are safe. In the hotel Lyon and I put them in. But they need a place to stay, until they get on their feet. I don't know what we can do for them. They can't keep livin' in a hotel . . . " I nodded silently thinking, I didn't have enough space to have the girls here.

Lyon then spoke as if answering my thoughts, "Why don't they stay with my family? Just until they get settled. It's a big house, they clearly don't care that I'm a vampire. Maybe they could be housed there temporarily? Beth has an inheritance coming in, *non?*"

He turned his attention to Ru with the question. Ru nodded, "Yeah. Apparently, it's going to take some time before she receives it. The lawyers are still working with her." I saw Lyon nod and then he moved me off his lap gently before pacing the floor, his hands on his hips.

"Okay, what if they stayed with my family until she gets the inheritance, then she can go wherever she wants. Raquel and Ali could go with her, assuming that's okay with Beth."

I looked up at him with an adoring smile. He truly cared about my friends and that made me love him even more.

"I think that would be perfect. Why don't you have them come over here and we talk to them about all this? Then talk to your family and see what they're comfortable with. Besides, you and I need to work on some things here, and I need to get back to work when I can. It'll be a while before I even think about going to France."

He stopped moving and gave me a worried look, "Oh! I'm still coming, don't worry. I just mean . . . " I said with a blush. I didn't mean to make him worry.

He moved to crouch in front of me to take my hands, "We need to adjust, and you need to fully recover I know." He said as he caressed my face with his soft fingers.

"I just hope all this responsibility is not too much on you . . . " I bit my lip nervously. My heart starting to jump a little.

He gave a soft smile, "No, it's not. I decided while you were away . . . That I need to become the man I was meant to be." He looked over at Ru. Ru gasped. It was like they had their own conversation I wasn't aware of.

"What's going on you two?" I frowned scanning the both of them. There was something they both weren't telling me.

"We wanted to wait . . . . *I* wanted to wait till you were better to tell you." He moved to sit beside me, facing me towards him, hands in his lap. "Amelie, I'm a Prince."

I think I spaced out for a while before hearing Lyon's voice. I blinked many times before my vision cleared seeing his beautiful yet worrisome blue eyes.

"Uh, sorry. I think . . . I think I went into shock." My mind still felt hazy. "You're . . . a literal French Prince?!" I exclaimed, "Why didn't you ever tell me? I mean, I know you said you had a complicated family life, and that you were a rebel . . . but damn. This takes the cake!"

My anxiety was now spiking, question after question left my mouth without hesitation, "What do your parents think about us? I mean, I'm a commoner, a witch, I'm not even French! You said it yourself they have customs . . . "

Lyon laughed lightly and put his hands up to calm me down, placing them on my upper arms gently. "They absolutely love you. I spoke with my brother about you the whole time we were separated. My sister wants to be your sister. My mother is delighted to meet you. Besides, we're all in agreeance that we want things to change. Our societies will not be the same ever again. My father passed away many years ago. Vampire hunters or witches killed him, though it is still unclear as to who did it. My siblings, mother and I were very fortunate. I don't want that to happen again to witches or to vampires. The fact we do this to each other is unfathomable. It isn't fair. I want to be the man you can be proud of. I don't wish to run from myself or my duties any longer."

I cupped his beautiful face. "I am proud of you. Always. I never was not proud of you, no matter what you did or how you acted. I admit some of what happened hurt me. But that's what we need to sort through. Privately."

I gave Ru a knowing smile and she nodded in understanding. I turned back to him now. "But I am with you always, Lyon. You're the strongest man I know. Leo the Lion as I say."

A chuckle left me as he did the same.

"I definitely can see you as the best leader there is and I couldn't be *more* proud of you. I want to be by your side to support you. I too want the same things. Just next time, don't be afraid to tell me things." I reassured him. He leaned in to kiss me. After a moment I pulled away and my stomach growled.

"On that note, let's get you food." He said with a laugh. "Did you want me to order you something? Or I can cook for you."

Ru grinned seeing how happy we were. "Ru's staying for dinner too!" I professed.

Ru then got up and hugged us both, "Then let's order some Southern food, and sit on the rooftop garden? After dinner, I'll give you guys some privacy." She said.

I took her hand and gave it a squeeze, "Thank you. For everything."

She smiled squeezing my hand back before passing me my coffee before it got cold, and Lyon grabbed his phone to look up the best Southern food restaurants to order from.

A few hours had gone by, dinner was delicious and spending time with both of my favorite people was amazing to say the least. Now, I was sitting on the rooftop garden in my pajamas which consisted of track pants and a tank top, slippers on my feet. Lyon was beside me elegant as ever. We were sharing some wine while talking. Ru had taken the liberty to clean up and hang out in my living room while Lyon and I spoke in private.

"Hey." I said, taking his hand. He looked down at me calmly. I gave myself permission to open up energetically and I sensed that he was a little anxious. I was too.

"I want you to know that you are safe with me. Whatever we have to talk about is always sacred between us." I was preaching this to myself too. After everything I had been through it was hard to let myself be unguarded.

Lyon turned to face me more, crossing his legs on the couch. The twinkle lights that I had put up were illuminating his face so magickally. The hard edges of his face looking more refined and soft.

"I want to know about you more. I know you came from a messed up background. You didn't want to tell me before, will you tell me now?" His voice was so gentle and calm. It put me at ease. I shifted in my seat, my legs crossed as we held hands. I felt our hearts beating at the same time. Our energy moving as one. I took a deep breath as I looked down.

"Take your time." He said as he lifted my face to look at him better, "Don't hide from me." He whispered. I smiled slightly leaning into his hand.

"So, as a child my parents were often fighting. I never knew about what, but there always seemed to be negative energy I picked up on. My parents would hide it from me as best they could. Yet, I was always very sensitive and empathic. It was hard to not notice it. I always felt like I could sense spirits, energies, and often my dreams would come true. I would have visions of things. I tried telling my parents, but they didn't believe me. I was often alone. I grew up feeling very isolated and I only had my intuition to guide me . . . Looking back, I think they were trying to protect me, I think they held a lot of fear of what I could do, what power I possessed."

I stopped talking, my eyes feeling wet from the tears that ran down my face. I took another deep breath. "I knew that I wasn't entirely alone, but my friends just thought I was crazy and going through stress with my family dynamic . . . " I shook my head. Lyon stayed quiet and listened intently. "Anyway, flash forward to just before we met . . . I was dating someone who wasn't for me. We had been very close friends, and I thought we were somewhat soul mated . . . until of course I met you." I smiled at him then, "But at that time, I felt like they were the one. They knew my abilities. But I think in some way they tried to exploit them. They could read my mind, but I couldn't read theirs. It wasn't at all what I have with you. I often chased them because I so badly wanted to be loved. I didn't know what unconditional love was until you. I know that you and Katerina were . . . complicated . . . I know that it wasn't what you wanted. It just hurt Lyon . . . It hurt that you left me . . . You didn't tell me why, you just left. I just . . . I need to get this out . . . Because if we want this to work . . . We can't keep secrets ever again."

I sniffled and let go of his hands to wipe my face. I could see pure anguish and remorse on his face. "I don't want to guilt you or to blame you or shame you. I just needed to express how much I love you and how much that hurt me."

He nodded. "I know, Amelie. I am so sorry for that. For the bad choices I made. I regret it. However, I believe that if we didn't go through this, we wouldn't be here now. It does not excuse what I did. I was unnecessarily cruel – with the best intentions."

He sighed and hugged me close. "I love you very much, my darling. Please forgive me. I will not fail you again. I want to be better, and I want to choose this life with you."

I hugged him as if my life depended on it. It felt good to get this all out and to forgive. I pulled back and gave a watery smile, "I forgive you. I feel better now." I chuckled as I wiped my eyes again, he chuckled along with me too.

"I am sorry I was so guarded with you. I should have told you more about me. About my past. I just wanted to get away from it all. But I'd rather have no skeletons in the closet," I confessed.

He cupped my face and kissed my lips softly. "Good. One question though, despite your background with your family, you started practicing magick again. Why?"

I laughed lightly, "Well I think I always knew what I was. What I am. I wasn't going to let the past define me. Ru helped me too with that. We met six years ago, and she taught me all that I know."

Lyon grinned with a small laugh, "That's amazing! Actually, she wanted help to find out where she came from, her Creole roots. I promised her that after you and I reunited that I'd help her."

I gave him the biggest hug and kissed his cheek, "You are amazing, you know that? I think that's a fantastic idea. I want to help too!"

He laughed, holding me tight before I let him go. "Well, let's get you back to routine and settled and then we can help her. Besides, we need to wait for Beth and the other girls to vacate my home when it comes time to if Ru is going to move in."

I pondered this a moment before speaking. "What if . . . we get a home here in New Orleans? You, me and Ru can all live together?" This is what I wanted. A family with Lyon and Ru.

He thought for a moment. I waited on bated breath.

"Well, I don't see why not. It would be nice to have a home base for all of us, instead of being separated by distance all the time." He replied.

I pumped my fist in the air, "Yes!"

We both laughed and he hugged me again, pulling me into his lap, my legs around his waist.

"I love you." I said just above a whisper, like it was a secret I didn't want the rest of the world to know.

A chuckle was lingering on his lips before he responded, "I love you too."

We were finally making plans to live together. Ironically, we hadn't even had a reunion date yet, but that would come once I recovered.

"We'll take it one day at a time." He answered my thoughts again.

I scoffed, "Get out of my head, weirdo!"

He laughed remembering the first time I ever said that to him.

"Get used to it, *chérie*. Soon, that's all I'll be doing.' He joked. I slapped his shoulder playfully. "Ow! *Mon dieu*, what was that for?" He mocked hurt playfully.

I giggled and kissed his shoulder. "You'll be doing much more than reading my mind, sir." I flirted.

We just smiled at each other no more words were needed. I was happy to have the love of my life back, and to have a solid plan of what to do next. We just needed the girls to accept the offer we had for them.

A few nights later, after my reunion back home, Lyon and I had asked Ru if we could have the apartment to ourselves. We wanted alone time as a brand-new couple. The energy was different. Still the same love and passion, but there was no neediness or rushed actions. We could take our time and there was no need to worry about another person getting in the way. We both knew we had things to still work on as a couple, but it would take time. Tonight, on a deliciously crisp evening on a Saturday we sat on the rooftop garden again to spend time to look at the moon and bask in our loving energy.

Like a gentleman, Lyon made me a cheese plate, brought out two glasses of wine and a red wine bottle. I had a plaid blanket wrapped around my lap. Tonight, I wore leggings, black boots, and a plaid shirt to match the blanket. My hair was up in a high ponytail. Even for the very beginnings of September Mother Earth was getting ready for fall.

My heart leapt and my soul sang; I loved the fall. So did Lyon. My November Scorpio Prince. I inwardly sighed in contentment. I loved him so very much. I saw him watching me as he set every-thing down. The silver ornate rings on his fingers glistening in the moonlight as he sat the glassware down on the table.

"What?" He asked with a smirk as he sat beside me.

"Hmm? Oh nothing. Just admiring you. And thinking about how happy I am that we get to learn about each other more, that we can be vulnerable properly without fearing if something will take us away again. I never did properly thank you for saving me."

He delicately caressed my face with the back of his gorgeous hands the rings feeling cool to the touch.

He leaned into me and whispered, "You saved yourself, Amelie. Sure, I helped, and I had spent so long trying to find you. But you, *you* did that all on your own." He smiled a soft smile and kissed my lips tenderly.

I smiled into the kiss before pulling back to respond, "Yeah, you're right. But you can't discredit yourself either. You helped all of us. You protected us. *Thank you.*" I cupped his face now, my lips grazing his high cheek bones, my nose brushing against his before placing my lips against his generous mouth.

"I love you." I whispered then pulling away to look at him and grab my glass of wine to enjoy it.

I was so grateful to be able to enjoy this with him again. To enjoy life itself. I knew that complications would arise, but as long as we stayed in our own power and we stuck together, we could do it. We could overcome all obstacles. We enjoyed our time together for what felt like hours before Lyon took my hand and led me to my bedroom.

It was so nice to be in my own bed again after months in a cult house, and then a week in a hospital. He laid me down so gently, like I would break, his body standing at the foot of the bed. Our eyes locked on each other, and I couldn't help but smile at him. He stripped off his shirt, leaving it on the floor before leaning down to crawl above me. I sighed. He was everything and more. My hands reached up to touch his face, my thumbs tracing his lips, chin and jaw, then they entangled in his curly blond hair. I missed this. I missed *him* and his scent all over my body. I never wanted to let him go again. This time though, there was no jealousy, worry, chasing or doubt. Just love. He kissed me deeply, my eyes fluttering closed, his body against mine. And I think if I were to die, I'd die happy.

The leaves were finally starting to change on the trees. The days and nights were getting cooler, and Lyon and I had been planning everyone's living arrangements for a week. Along with my recovery. I now could breathe normally the smoke had cleared in my lungs and I was back on my feet. Ru helped with cleaning and organizing the shop.

It turned out I was almost getting evicted because I lost out on four months of rent for the office. Lyon decided to help me pay the back rent and told me to just save my money for the next month's rent. He was such a Prince – literally. He was offering his aid left, right, and center. I was not expecting this, but it was greatly appreciated.

On this sunny fall day, Ru came by to pick me up a Pumpkin Spice latte, since Pumpkin Spice season started. My favorite! I stood outside my apartment building as Ru pulled up and got out of the car to pass me my coffee.

"Hey girl! Cheers to another fall season together!" I toasted and took a sip of Heaven in a cup. I then hugged her, taking her arm in mine as we started to walk down the street. It was days like this I wanted to walk to enjoy the season.

New Orleans was often warm, luckily the fall was still gorgeous and cool. Though I didn't have to worry about snow in the wintertime which was great. I hated the snow in New York. I could smell the scent of fall everywhere. People were already starting to decorate shops with autumn decor.

As we walked, the sound of crunching leaves underneath my fall boots could be heard. Ru then looked towards me, "So, Beth is in agreeance to going to Lyon's family home temporarily. Ali and Raquel will also go with her. Ali is waiting for her own place right now, but until she gets something she'll stay there. Raquel doesn't want to go back to her family just yet, but she wants to stay in New Orleans in the long term – so Beth and her will find their own place once the inheritance goes through."

I nodded listening, taking a sip of coffee. "Okay, that's good. So, that leaves you."

We stopped on the sidewalk moving over as to not block passersby. I saw trees in all their ever-changing glory before looking back at Ru. Her face was a little concerned but waiting for me to continue.

"Lyon and I were thinking of getting ourselves a house here in New Orleans, and we'd like you to move in. Then we can help you get established and find out more about your roots here."

I had never seen Ru's face light up so much before this moment. She squealed in excitement. "Oh my God! Yes, that would be amazing! I just would need to figure out work . . . "

I laughed putting up my hand, "You can work with me!"

She hugged me tightly, "Thank you, thank you, thank you! Oh wow, I'm so excited! Girl, I can't wait! The three of us, we gotta celebrate! Once he's awake of course."

I laughed hugging her tightly before we started to walk down the street towards *our* shop now.

"New Orleans, look out, the Psychic Sisters are here."

We both laughed enjoying our time and company together. I knew that Lyon would be thrilled.

My phone dinged in my pocket. A message from him, right on time.

She agreed? - L
Yes, and she's so excited! - A
That's great! Welcome to the family. I'll see you both when the sun sets. - L

I snickered and pocketed my phone.

Ru gave me a questioning look, "What?"

I smiled, "Oh nothing, Lyon's happy you're joining us. He says, *'Welcome to the family'.*"

I knew that he'd go back to sleep but he clearly felt all the excitement about Ru saying yes to our offer. Tonight, we would celebrate as a family, and I would finally get my reunion first date with Lyon.

Later that night when Ru and I came back to my apartment, Lyon was already dressed and ready to go out and celebrate. He wore his famous red velvet coat with black jeans, boots and a cream-colored shirt. He looked absolutely divine. Ru and I quickly ran to my room to change. I kept my jeans on but decided to wear a more elegant deep red shirt to match Lyon.

"Hello, handsome." I said as I emerged from my room leaning on my tippy toes to kiss him. "You look beautiful."

Ru exited wearing a black gothic shirt with leggings while keeping her luxurious hair down, "Let's go celebrate! Also, you two are hot AF!"

We laughed at her compliment as we left the apartment, hailing a cab. We all decided to drink, and Lyon made sure to feed prior to going out. He was off of bagged blood now and was able to have small drinks from humans. I was proud of him, that he was trying his best and I knew that I could trust him.

Once we got to the bar, we ordered shots and cocktails. Ru held up her shot glass for a toast, "To this beautiful couple, I love you guys."

The three of us laughed and took our shots. I then remembered something and turned to Lyon, "Oh yeah, I forgot to ask. What's going on with your band? Since you're doing all these Princely things and living between France and New Orleans . . . Can you still have your band?"

He laughed lightly and took a sip of his Bourbon, "Well, I think before I become coronated as King, now that Maman has decided to step down, I should go on tour one last time. I did it to rebel against the system, and now, well I don't think having a rock band is very Princely, nor is it King-like. However, I do think that before I take on that responsibility in France that I should at least do it once more. I miss it. Besides, I made a whole set for you."

He winked and nudged me playfully. I couldn't help but lean in and kiss him. Ru was on board too, "Yeah, I told him he should go back on stage too."

He turned to Ru with his glass to clink it with hers, "Then it's settled. I'll start up The Devil and Desire for a goodbye tour and resign before becoming the King of France." We toasted to that. "And, to our reunion." I added. He kissed me sweetly before we drank to that too.

October came fast and I was still in awe of the fact we were planning our future together along with my best friend. When I was in the Coven, I knew he was the one thing keeping me tethered to reality. I had no way of being grounded by any other thing. His love, his energy, would envelope me like a warm hug on a cold day.

It was getting colder the air crisp as the fall was pushing through to winter. I sat on the rooftop garden, a pumpkin spice latte in my hands, a red wool coat wrapped around my body, and a black scarf to keep me warm. It was crazy to think that I was going to be spending Christmas with Lyon in New Orleans. A prospect that I didn't think was possible five months ago.

I leaned closer to the small fire pit we installed to warm me up, not like Lyon needed anything like that - but he liked it too.

I looked over at Lyon, my hands wrapped around my coffee to keep my hands warm. The moon shining brightly, the wind blowing in an eerie fall manner.

"Lyon?"

He was so quiet. I was not even sure what to ask him. Was he mad? Was he okay? What was going through his mind?

He turned to me; his blue eyes soft. He moved closer to me and held my hand. "I can read your thoughts, remember? I'm not mad at you, darling. I'm mad at myself that I couldn't protect you. That I was so stuck on myself, in my own life that I left you behind. I'm ashamed of that," He was still haunted by that even months later, "I wonder if the two of us – you and me, can change things."

I squeezed his hand before taking a sip of the deliciously warm coffee.

"I think we can." I smiled reassuringly. "We just have to be brave to face it. You came back, and we're starting over. A new beginning. And you're a badass Prince! Of course, I am nervous to become Queen, but I'd rather do it with you than any other person," I moved closer and cupped his face with my free hand, "I love you Lyon, more than anything on this earth. Nothing can stop me from loving you. Not the past and not the conflicting communities. You are my forever."

He smiled softly. "You mean that?"

I nodded, "Definitely."

He grinned and leaned in to kiss me. "Well, in that case . . ."

He moved to take something out of his pocket, my hand withdrew from him and held the coffee cup again with both hands.

My eyes then glanced down, and a little black box was in his well-kept hands. "Would you do me the honor of marrying me, Amelie?"

My eyes went wide, putting the coffee cup down. "Lyon! Are you serious?"

He nodded with a smile.

"Yes! Oh my God. Yes, of course I do!" I grinned, tucking my hair behind my ear. I held my hand out as he opened the box and placed the ring on my finger. "Forever, always." I whispered.

He grinned, "I guess you truly meant that," He teased.

"Of course I did!" I slapped him and he feigned mock hurt before giggling.

"Very good!" He grinned.

I giggled, "Yes!"

The ring was so beautiful it was simple, rose gold, Victorian. Traditional but it meant so much. I moved to cup his face fully and kiss him passionately. He grabbed my waist, holding me to him till I was straddling his lap.

Ru then came bursting out, "What's going on? I heard screaming - Uh oh! I-I'm sorry am I interrupting??" She was a little startled at my position on top of him. I laughed, "Ru, we have a wedding to plan!" I showed her the ring on my finger, and she dove towards the couch we were sitting on, "Oh my God! Okay, I got this! I'll set up the date, the location, and the venue . . . "

Lyon and I both giggled as Ru got so excited she was basically listing all the things to herself. I kissed him happily and we sat underneath the moon knowing that the next chapter would be difficult. Things wouldn't be easy, and a marriage would come with complications, but we were so happy to have each other back, none of it mattered. What mattered was that we had each other. We were like Dionysus and Ariadne. A mortal woman with an immortal man, destined to be together, forever.

Acknowledgements

I would like to say a huge thank you to everyone who has worked hard on this book with me, who supported me and who kept me going when I was knocked down. I want to say a special thank you to Anne Rice and all of her work on the Vampire Chronicles – you have been such a support and inspiration in my writing, of the world of vampires, and with how strong you were in life to keep going even when people told you no. You inspire me to keep going! RIP Anne <3

And to all my friends and family who supported me on the best days, on the toughest days, and who get to celebrate the magick of life, love and friendship with me and who get to explore this amazing world with the characters who mean the most to me.

Above all, thank you God for giving me this gift of writing and the courage to keep believing in miracles.

From the bottom of my heart,
Thank you!

ABOUT THE AUTHOR

Isabella Presley is studying English Literature at Concordia University. A former actor, she now channels her creative energy into writing. She grew up in libraries and bookstores, inspiring her love of vampire fiction and gothic romance. Isabella can often be found enjoying a coffee at a local café with friends. She lives in Montreal.

Printed in the USA
CPSIA information can be obtained
at www.ICGtesting.com
LVHW092014231024
794642LV00028B/71